Restless Night

Insomniac Duet - Book One

PERSEPHONE AUTUMN

BETWEEN WORDS PUBLISHING LLC

Books by Persephone Autumn

Bay Area Duet Series

Click Duet

Through the Lens

Time Exposure

Inked Duet

Fine Line

Love Buzz

Insomniac Duet

Restless Night

A Love So Bright

Artist Duet

Blank Canvas (Fall 2022)

Abstract Passion (Fall 2022)

Devotion Series

Distorted Devotion

Undying Devotion

Beloved Devotion

Darkest Devotion

Standalone Romance Novels

Depths Awakened

Sweet Tooth

Transcendental

Poetry Collections

Ink Veins

Broken Metronome

Standalone Horror Novels

By Dawn (published under P. Autumn)

For all the people who picked on me when I was younger because I was weird.

I'm still weird, but at least I kick ass.

PROLOGUE

PEYTON

Past…

ANOTHER DAY, another round of bullshit. High school…
it goes one of two ways.

You are either popular—the queen bee with a swarm
of followers. Every girl wants to be you. Wants your
boyfriend. Dresses and talks like you. Is at your beck and
call without question. And you are artificial as fuck.

Or two—my current life status—you walk around
with a "kick me" sign stuck to your back. Girls point and
laugh and say fucked-up shit. They write your name on
bathroom stall walls with the word "trash" or "loser" or
"slut" beneath it. They gather their posse and gang up on
you. Start rumors and throw shit in your direction. Toss
out every possible degrading word with your name to
boost their own esteem and make others laugh and point.

How I landed in category two is beyond me. But here we are, another day in hell.

I exit the bus and spot them as I step off. As if they waited for me to arrive in the big tangerine beast. Just to antagonize me. To start their day with a fresh load of assholism.

Do mean bitches have nothing better to do with their lives?

"Mandy, did you hear the school slut banged the baseball team last night?"

That would be Mercedes, Queen Bitch.

"Ew." And that would be Mandy, the girl parked so far up Mercedes's ass, she no longer sees light. "But what else do sluts do?"

They laugh and start following me as I pass them without so much as a glance. As pretentious and mighty as they believe they are, one would think they have more in life to do than follow "trash" like me around campus. But whatever.

I walk through campus and head for my locker. They continue their not-so quiet artifice. And I continue to ignore them as best I can. After dealing with their bullshit for the last four months, I learned to tune them out. On occasion, anyway.

I spin the dial on my locker as they prattle on. Voices loud as they encourage others to join in on their hate fest. Only one other does. Meredith. Now my day is complete. Triple M is here and in their full glory.

While I swap my books and folders in my locker, I

laugh at my own wayward thoughts. *Triple M. Damn, those are big tits. Slut tits. Who's the slut now?*

"What's so funny, loser?"

Shit. Did I laugh out loud? Oh well. No backpedaling now.

I spin around to face the blonde trio. Hair, makeup and clothes pristine and wrinkle free. Unlike me. My blonde locks currently wear a thick layer of black dye. My makeup equally dark and thick around my eyes. And my ensemble... you guessed it. Black. Let's just say the current phase of life revolves around the saying *black is life*.

Courage bubbles in my chest as my nails dig crescents into my palms. Sick and tired of these bitches, I am ready to blow my top. Go full-on banshee and punch the smiles off their cakey faces. But not now. Maybe just a dose to appease my dark heart.

Just a dose.

"You," I say with a laugh. "You're what's funny." Confidence builds and I run with it. "If you're not careful, someone might think you're in love with me. Obsessed. I mean, god, you seek me out. Follow me like a lost pet. Talk about me all day. Like you have nothing else you'd rather be doing." God, this feels good. Talking shit to her face. Calling her out in front of others. Should I kick it up a notch? Add to her embarrassment? *Do it!* "Hey, everyone," I shout and several eyes glance our way. "Mercedes is in love with me."

Her face turns stop sign red. If possible, steam would shoot from her ears. Her arms stiffen, hands fist at her sides and she literally stomps a foot. I bite my cheek to resist laughing at her charade, as it will definitely worsen the situation.

She shoves a finger in my face, centimeters from my glasses. "You'll pay for that. When you least expect it." She spins on her heel and storms down the hall with her followers up her ass.

At least she is gone for the time being. Shouldn't see her or the other two until sixth period. Thank fuck.

Classes start and end as the day ticks by uneventful. And soon, the bell rings and a sea of bodies ambles toward the cafeteria. I hoist my messenger bag up my shoulder and follow the masses.

A strange square chunk of mystery casserole, a banana and water bottle on my tray, I weave through the tables in search of an available seat. Parked in the corner, I poke at the food and remind myself—again—that I need to bring food tomorrow.

The buzz in the room quiets an octave when a group enters the cafeteria. Micah Reed and half the district-winning track team. They saunter past several tables, all eyes on them, and sit at their usual spot. Chatter resumes and people pick at their mystery lunch.

But I keep an eye on Micah through my raven locks.

The first time I paid any attention to Micah Reed was a week into the school year. Parked under a tree, I read *Wuthering Heights* for English Honors. Micah and several others on the track team jogged out of the gym in tank tops and short shorts in the school colors, with bright running shoes on their feet. I followed them as they went toward the paved oval track surrounding the school football field. Watched as they stretched and bounced on their toes before they took off running.

I dog-eared my page and observed Micah with fascination. His long, lithe frame glided over the pavement like the gazelles on nature documentaries. Blond hair a bird's nest from the breeze. Cheeks red as he huffed and circled the track.

He never saw me under that tree. No one did. No one ever sees me. And I am okay with not being seen. Okay with being the odd girl that makes others gawk. The loner who sits in the corner and keeps to herself. The quiet girl who admires a guy from a distance.

The next time I peek up, Mercedes stands beside Micah in the cafeteria. She smiles and laughs and flips her hair, all but begging for attention.

"Fake bitch," I mutter to myself.

As if she hears the words leave my lips, her eyes scan the room and land on me. She notices the one time my eyes dart between her and Micah, and I hate the action immediately. Because a slow, wicked grin plumps her cheeks.

Fuck.

She combs her fingers through Micah's short locks. He peers up at her with a *what the hell are you doing* look on his face. But what she says next wipes the look off his face.

"I had a good time the other night," she says to Micah loud enough for half the cafeteria to hear. Especially me.

"Sorry I'm not as easy as the school slut, though." Her lips protrude in a fake pout, but her eyes scream pure evil.

Not that I have expressed my baby crush on Micah, but she saw it the second I let my eyes drift to him. And I royally fucked myself.

Micah shakes his head and doesn't feed into her comment. This pisses Mercedes off.

"Didn't you hear?" she asks, as if her lies are common knowledge.

"Hear what?" he says with boredom in his voice. And he doesn't meet her gaze.

"Little Miss Slut" —she points her polished dagger directly at me— "had an orgy with the baseball team."

My face lights on fire as every set of eyes in the cafeteria turns my way. *I fucking hate her. Hate. Her.*

But the way Micah looks at me flips my stomach upside down. Has the mystery casserole ready to reappear.

The first time Micah Reed notices me, really sees me, and he stares me down as if I am an easy lay. A conquest to mark on his bedpost and brag over with his jock buddies. His eyes narrow as he rises from the table. For a split second, I think he may walk off and ignore the bullshit Mercedes dishes out.

But I am dead wrong.

"Hey, pretty slut." Eyes searing my skin, Micah fists his dick through the denim and licks his lips. "The track team is always game."

The silence of moments ago vanishes as the entire cafeteria bursts into laughter. Fingers point my direction as eyes spill tears from laughing so hard.

Whooshing floods my ears as the laughter fades and the room swallows me whole. Pressure compresses my rib cage and squashes the tiny, erratic beating organ in the center. The small bites of casserole in my stomach threaten to make an appearance.

God, I want to stab something. Or someone.

And just like that, I am done.

Can't. Do. This. Anymore.

I shoot up from the table, scream at the top of my lungs and throw my tray toward Mercedes. And before I act on my irrational thoughts, I scoop up my messenger bag and run. Run from the cafeteria. Run from every person in this piece of shit school. Run from a life I didn't ask for and don't deserve.

Fuck this place. Fuck Mercedes. And fuck Micah Reed.

ONE

MICAH

Present...

Music blares in my ears and vibrates my bones as I walk through Roar.

Hot, sweaty bodies rub against each other in time with the music. Hands grope and lips tease and hips grind. Alcohol drains from glasses faster than refills can keep up. And clothes get looser. As do inhibitions.

I weave through the crowd, brush arms with several women, and toss out my flirtatious smile. Some smile in return. Others reach out and graze an arm or my chest. And I let them. It comes with the territory when you manage a night club. Can't work in a place like Roar without being groped or hit on at least once a night.

I love and hate the attention in equal measure.

Love it because I have easy access to women. Love it because most of the women that come to Roar are hot as fuck. I have a different woman between the sheets each week. None complain when we go separate ways. And none beg for another round. They know the hookup is a one-time deal. No names, no numbers exchanged. Just sex.

Which is part of the reason I hate it. Hate my official manwhore status. A badge I wear often because of my cheating ex, Rochelle.

I hate that I let her tear me down. That she still holds power over my thoughts and life. That her actions still sway my decisions.

After walking in on her, I should be free. Free of her and the bullshit. Small things I didn't notice until after she was caught in the act. I had been her pawn. A middleman in her game to get an even younger guy. Cougar isn't an appropriate term for Rochelle. More like super cougar. Jaguar. Maybe she likes it when he calls her mommy.

A shiver rolls up my spine and I shake away all thoughts of Rochelle. I may be down to try new shit in the bedroom, but that isn't one of them.

"Hey, man," I shout as I approach Dan, one of the bouncers. "All good?"

Dan, a man twice my muscle mass, gives a thumbs-up. "Yeah, boss. Busy tonight." He scans the crowd with a straight, serious face. All business once he punches his time card, Dan is one of our best bouncers.

Outside of work, Dan is all smiles and laughter. But I appreciate his professionalism inside the Roar walls. Never know what someone will do after too much alcohol.

I pat his shoulder. "Let me know if you need anything." He nods and I move on.

Several times a night, I weave through the club. Check on each staff member. Make sure everything is on the up-and-up. And I always end each round at the bar. Where Peyton pours drinks like a bartender from *Cocktail*.

Peyton Alexander. The bane of my existence. Pure, undiluted, sexy-as-sin torture.

She glides around her end of the bar. Flirts with males and females alike. Bats her lashes and pushes up her breasts to enhance her cleavage. Licks her lips and leans in close.

I fucking hate her. Hate that she flirts with every goddamn person who sets foot in Roar. Every person but me.

Most of all, I hate that this eats at my psyche. Keeps me up at night while I fist my cock between the sheets.

I step behind the bar—where I hang when not doing rounds on the floor or managerial tasks in the office—and unleash my undesirable jealousy.

"Peyton," I shout. And I know she hears me because her spine straightens. Her fingers coil, then flatten out.

She glares past Adam, another bartender, and curls her lip a beat. "Yeah, boss," she shouts back, voice saccharine.

"Quit fucking flirting and pour drinks," I bark out. Adam cringes beside me as he pours a beer from the tap.

Peyton lifts her middle finger to her forehead and mock salutes me. "You got it, *Micky*."

"Bitch," I mutter.

She turns her back to me and goes back to flirting. *Goddamnit.*

Like every other night I work with Peyton, I regret the day I hired her. But one of the owners interviewed and loved her before I had a say in the matter. So now, I grit my teeth, make her life miserable, and trudge forward.

Peyton actually tends the bar better than the other employees. People gravitate toward her each night. Loiter at her end of the bar and wait patiently. Buy more drinks when she tosses them a bright smile and flirts without care. And her tips are proof the crowd loves her. She earns double, if not triple, what the others do in tips.

Her only downfall… she seems to hate me to the pits of hell. The *I want to gouge out your eyes* kind of hate. And I have no idea why.

Unable to witness her endless flirting any longer, I exit the bar and distract myself with another round. Engage in idle chitchat with the staff and patrons.

On the dance floor, I pass a curvaceous blonde. Her golden locks remind me of a certain feisty bartender across the room. So, I step closer and do a little flirting of my own. One song fades into another as she grinds her ass against my dick and wraps her hands around the back of my head to keep me close.

I'm not going anywhere.

Ani and Sean, the club owners, don't mind if the staff join the scene. In fact, they encourage it so long as the partying doesn't interfere with business. Drinks are acceptable, but we don't go past tipsy. Grinding patrons on the dance floor is fair game, but we don't make anyone uncomfortable or assume it will go further. If it does go further, it happens outside these walls.

So, I dance with the woman who grabs and rubs me like she would fuck me in the middle of the room. I kiss down her neck and fist her hips. When the song transitions into the next, I step back. She spins and pouts and it is adorable as fuck.

I bring my lips to her ear. "Gotta work, sorry. Stick around till close?" She nods. "Wait for me. We can have fun after." I back away and she smiles.

The next few hours go by as per usual. Alcohol flows freely, intoxicating the patrons as much as the music. Every now and again, I look down at the other end of the bar and watch Peyton. Inconspicuously stare at her as her eyes glitter under the lights. As she bites her lower lip and half smiles. As she throws her arms in the air and dances behind the bar and several people wolf whistle.

During those hours, my dick strains against my zipper. Aches for an ounce of her attention. To have those glittery eyes shift their focus my way. Her plump lips around my cock. Her curves bouncing above me in a dark room on cool sheets.

But that will never happen.

The blonde from the dance floor wiggles her way between people at the bar. After serving a drink, I saunter her way and she smiles at my approach. I catch Peyton in my periphery and note her not-so-subtle staring at our interaction.

Good.

"Should be done soon. Still good with waiting?"

She licks her lips and I hear Peyton groan. "Yeah. Got nowhere else to be."

And just to irritate Peyton further, I pinch the blonde's chin between my thumb and finger, then crush my lips to hers. The kiss quick and angry and meaningless and all for show. I give two fucks about this woman. Actually, only one fuck.

"Hey, *Micky*," Peyton shouts. Her nickname for me makes my blood pressure rise. She says it just to piss me off. And I let it, but don't flaunt that fact.

"Yeah, bar wench," I throw back with a cocked brow.

She bristles and my insides sing. "Shouldn't you be, I don't know, managing something." Her words meant to be a stab. To throw my own words in my face when I tell her to quit flirting.

But unlike her, I take her bait and roll with it.

I point to the blonde. "That's what I'm doing." Peyton furrows her brows. "Managing my hookup." Her eyes go wide at my bluntness. The fact that I own my manwhore status shocks her. "Should try it sometime."

She glances at the blonde, then back at me. Bass rattles the air around us while I wait for her comeback. Our banter turns me on and fuels the hungry beast inside.

"Nah," she shrugs and taps her chest. "Not one-night stand material." She turns her eyes on the blonde. "I have standards when it comes to who lies in my bed." Her eyes shift back to mine. "Sluts aren't my thing."

Internally, I laugh. But I mask it and come to the blonde's defense—kind of—who shoots daggers at Peyton.

"But sluts are so much fun," I tease. The blonde turns her attention to me. Her jaw drops, but closes when I suck my lower lip in my mouth. "Don't like fun, wench?"

God, I'm hard as fuck right now.

"Oh, I love fun." Peyton saunters closer, but keeps a good five feet between us. "Never been a fan of venereal diseases, though."

I don't hold back my laughter this time. In fact, I double over and release the sexual tension between us. She may not recognize it as such, but what the hell else would it be?

The blonde mutters, "Bitch."

Peyton faces the blonde, leans on the bar and cocks a brow. She shakes her head with light laughter. "I'm the bitch?" Peyton pushes off the bar and takes a step back. "Maybe I am." She shrugs. "But I'd rather be a bitch than spread my legs for every guy who gives me attention."

Heat crawls up the blonde's neck and blooms on her cheeks. I should be worried, but this whole situation amuses me too much to care.

The blonde shifts her attention from Peyton to me. "I'll wait at a table." She points in a general direction behind her.

"Be done soon." I pinch her chin again and crush her lips. "Don't worry about her."

The blonde melts in my hand. "She's just jealous." Then she turns and wanders to an empty table.

Peyton and I return to our typical uncomfortable, disgruntled silence. I pour a few more drinks before last call gets announced. The crowd thins and the first set of overhead lights kicks on. I grab and clean drained glasses. Then wipe down the empty sections of bar top.

When the next set of lights flicker on, ninety percent of the club is vacant.

I toss my towel in the bleach mix. Closing out the registers, I take the tills and tip jars to the office. Once the tills are reset and the cash balances, I stash the cash in the safe and lock up the office.

In the club, the blonde scrolls over her phone screen while Peyton throws her a murderous glare. Peyton has yet to see me walk out, so I hang back a moment and observe. How she washes glasses with aggression. How she wipes down the bar like she needs to remove the varnish.

Interesting. Is she actually jealous? Her actions indicate a flare of jealousy.

So, I use this to my advantage.

I step out from the hall and pass the end of the bar. Peyton locks on to me as I stroll over to the blonde. Her eyes burn my skin—not with hatred, though. They burn with bitterness and maybe a hint of lust. The fire trails over my skin and I stow it away.

I will need it in an hour.

"Ready?" I ask, approaching the blonde.

She peers up from her phone and smiles. In the light, she still flaunts pretty features. Not *take my breath away* gorgeous, but pretty enough to look at while I fuck her brains out. And when I flip her on her hands and knees, I will picture a different blonde.

"Yeah." She locks her phone and stows it in her back pocket. Her eyes shoot over my shoulder and narrow before coming back. "Let's get out of here." She slides off the stool. "Mine or yours?"

"Yours," I say as I wrap an arm around her shoulders.

No one comes back to my house. Ever.

"Perfect."

We head for the exit, but I halt us a moment and glance over my shoulder. "Peyton," I bark out and she glances up from the bar with a bored expression. "Bar better not look like shit in the morning."

Her jaw muscles tighten and shift. Scarlet pricks her cheeks. "Has it ever?" she bites.

I don't answer her question and opt to bark another order. "Don't leave until everything's spotless."

The blonde and I head for the door, but I don't miss Peyton's grumbled *asshole* as we walk out. The ammunition I needed to get through the next couple of hours.

TWO
PEYTON

"Morning, sunshine." Reese kisses my hair as he stumbles past the breakfast bar to the Keurig.

"Morning, bum." He swats me away over his shoulder and I laugh. "Late night?"

He sets his cup under the drip, inserts a pod and presses the button. Then he twists to face me. "Surprised you didn't hear." I widen my eyes as a chuckle spills from his lips. Not that Reese's shenanigans are anything new. "You either sleep like the dead or you came in much later than me."

"Probably the latter." I lift my own mug to my lips and sip the creamy brew. "Manager Asshole was in rare form the other night."

Reese adds sugar and hazelnut creamer to the mug, then gulps his morning elixir and sighs. He stands opposite me, hip leaning on the kitchen island, brow cocked in question.

"Sounds juicy. Tell me more while I make breakfast."

Before I get in a word of protest, Reese turns his back to me and grabs pans from the cabinet. I love when he makes breakfast. Everything he cooks tastes ten times better. Even scrambled eggs. Plus, it gives me more time to sip my coffee.

"He just raked my nerves more than usual."

Reese peeks over his shoulder with a devious smile. "Most people call that flirting, sunshine. You should fuck him already."

I shudder and he laughs. "Well, I sure as shit am not flirting with Micah Reed." The idea of purposely flirting with Micah makes my skin crawl. "Nor do I want to fuck him." I ignore the shiver that rolls up my spine. "He's just as much an asshole now as he was back in high school."

Reese grabs eggs, milk and cheese from the fridge. Then a bag of hash browns and sausage patties from the freezer. He cracks half the carton of eggs, adds milk and whips them longer than I ever do. Probably the secret behind why his scrambled eggs are so damn fluffy. I just don't have the patience.

He pours the mix into the pan and adds two handfuls of cheese. In two other pans, he starts the hash browns and sausage. I stare after him in fascination. Not that I can't cook. I just prefer to make simpler foods that only take one pan. Or the microwave. Less dishes equals less cleanup.

"Still think he doesn't know who you are?" Reese sips his coffee, then tends to the pans.

Does Micah know *who* I am? All signs and interaction with him lead me to believe he has no clue.

One—the first time he laid eyes on me, I was in my all-things-black, loner-girl phase. Black hair, black clothes, black makeup. If it was black, I probably owned it.

Don't get me wrong, I still love black. But the dark shade no longer rules my life. Sometime in the last decade, yellow took precedence. I don't plaster it everywhere like I did black as a teen, but I have splashes of it here and there.

Two—Micah looks at me differently now. In high school, he jumped on the Triple M hate train without learning a thing about me. Back then, he looked at me like gum stuck to his shoe. He said shitty things because he was a popular jock and it was funny to pick on the loner girl.

But now… his eyes hold intrigue when they look my direction.

He must think I don't notice his traveling eyes or the frequency of his stares. But I don't miss a single glance. Don't miss the spark of lust in lapis-blue eyes. Or how they drag over my curves when I face away from him.

I have always noticed Micah Reed.

His angular jaw and lean frame. His slight reservation unless he wants to impress someone. Or the truth his eyes tell, but lips can't manage. I once believed Micah was a good guy. Someone who would stand up for others when they need it most. But that rule seems to only apply to family, close friends and impressionable people.

Here is my opinion. Micah Reed can suck my dick. If I had one.

"He has no idea," I answer confidently.

Reese dishes scrambled eggs on to three plates, then adds a hefty portion of hash browns and sausage. He sets the mountainous plate on the bar, then hands me a fork. "His loss, sunshine. Think he'll figure it out?"

I shrug. "If he does, it'll be too late."

He picks up the two other plates and levels me with his gaze. "You say that now, but…"

"But nothing," I say around a forkful of food.

"Alright." He starts for his bedroom. "Just prepare yourself for the day he puts two and two together. May not be anytime soon, but it'll happen."

I point my fork at him. "Go feed whoever's in your room and leave me be."

He strolls down the hall, chuckling. "Love you, sunshine."

"Yeah, yeah. Love you, too."

"Is this right?"

Ms. Jenkins peers down at the yarn and hooks in my hand. Scrutinizes my crochet skills with crinkles at the corners of her eyes and lips.

She pats my hand. "Such a fast learner, dear. You'll make a hat or scarf in no time."

"Let's not get carried away. Plus, when would I wear a scarf? The one day a year it gets cold?"

She laughs, then lifts a hand to her mouth as it transitions to a strangled cough. Decades of smoking evident in the harsh, nonstop hack. If the doctor allowed it, she would still smoke today. But being attached to an oxygen tank and smoking doesn't mix well. So, she quit. Now, she almost always has a toothpick in her mouth.

"No, dear. You take a trip when it's cold up north and use it then. Thought you were smart enough to figure as much out."

Ms. Jenkins was once a world traveler. On my days at the assisted living facility, she takes me on journeys with her stories. Adventures I dream about taking one day. My bucket list grew miles longer when I learned of all the places she'd visited.

Hiking mountains and valleys and sand dunes. Camping under the stars in the middle of nowhere without a care in the world. Witnessing the aurora borealis. Seeing the pyramids in Egypt. Visiting the Inca citadel in Machu Picchu. Wandering the hanami—aka the cherry blossom festival—in Japan.

I envy her younger, fearless years. Packing a bag and exploring the globe on a whim. One day, I want to travel the way she did. Just get up and go. When? No telling, but I made it a goal.

"Never seen snow," I admit.

"What?" She stares at me in mock horror.

I laugh and raise my right hand. "Swear." She shakes her head. "Where would you recommend? For a first timer."

"You kids." We both laugh. In her eyes, I am still a kid. Not like we bring up age, but I haven't technically been a "kid" for fourteen years. "Where's your sense of adventure?"

My sense of adventure is on the back burner. Who has time or money to travel? Most people my age work more than one job just to live. Me included. I work at Roar four nights a week. And although I earn enough from Roar to pay the bills, I still work two days a week at Gulfside Assisted Living.

The small paycheck from the ALF helps pad my savings and save for rainy days. But adding to my savings isn't the sole reason I work here.

Before Gulfside, I spent several days a week with my grandma. We chatted mostly, but other memories were also made. Baking bread and cookies and pies. Tending to her small garden in the backyard. Sipping tea and coffee on her back porch while bird-watching. Organizing old photographs and adding them to albums. Short walks in the park.

Time with Grandma Isabel warmed my heart. She was a selfless woman. Did whatever she could, within her means, to help others. Always had a shoulder to lean on and offered sound advice freely. I remember her gentle spirit, and that she didn't take shit from anyone.

When she contracted pneumonia, we all thought she would pull through. Her fighter spirit had survived much worse. But her older immune system couldn't fight off the pneumonia. Not after all the years she smoked. Her lungs gave up the fight before her spirit.

I promised her I would give back in her memory. Help others, even if that meant contributing my time or learning to crochet baby hats. Plus, it lessens the void of her loss when I visit the residents of Gulfside. When I sit with Ms. Jenkins and talk about living life to its fullest.

"It's there, I promise. Just have some other obligations to tend to first."

She sets her hooks down and narrows her eyes. "I hope those obligations don't involve a man."

This makes me laugh harder than it should. "No, ma'am."

"Good. Women don't need a man to stand tall." She looks me square in the eye. "If my Stephen was still here, he'd tell you just as much too. We loved fiercely. But he never smothered my light. He helped me shine brighter." She lays her hand on mine. "That's what a real partner does. Helps make you a better version of yourself."

One day, I pray to have a love as fierce as the one she shared with her late husband.

"Enough of that," she says. "Let's finish. Then, you can wheel me to the dining room for lunch."

Over the next hour, I crochet two rows of a baby hat. After I wheel Ms. Jenkins to the dining hall, I hug her goodbye and promise to see her tomorrow.

Exiting Gulfside, I text Aunt Leanne to tell her I am on my way. Every Monday, we meet for a late lunch after I finish my shift at Gulfside.

I have always had a close relationship with Aunt Leanne. She feels more like a second mom than an aunt. When Dad passed ten years ago, I made a point to spend more time with family. To never take time or the future for granted. You never know what will happen from one day to the next.

On Monday, I spend time with Aunt Leanne.

Two songs and a radio commercial later, I park in front of our usual café. We hop out, exchange hugs, and wander inside. After we order, we chitchat and catch up on what we have missed in the past week.

She asks about Ms. Jenkins and how my crocheting is coming along. Asks if Mom and Harold are well—although she checks in with Mom every other week. And then she broaches the subject of Roar. She always skirts around the Micah topic, but she doesn't fool me. I see her secret need to ask intrusive questions and know all the dirty details.

Aunt Leanne, bless her soul, is a gossip queen. The unflattering trait has evolved over the years, but she still knows everyone's business. After our conversations, she forms her own opinions on why Micah is an asshole. I choose to ignore those opinions.

"So…" She drags the two-letter word out to ten. "How's nightlife going? Meet anyone interesting?" I also tend to believe Aunt Leanne lives vicariously through me.

She states life wasn't as interesting in her late twenties to early thirties. I beg to differ.

"Good. And yes, I meet interesting people every night I work."

I play coy. Every time she asks, I dance circles around the answer. The way her eyes narrow as I tease her makes me laugh. She never lets me off the hook, though.

She tosses her best death glare across the table, but gets disrupted when our server delivers our food. She stabs at her salad with faux aggression, then points at me with her full fork.

"Why are you avoiding the answer? Did something happen? You better tell me."

I bite into the sandwich and chew slowly to give myself more time before answering. The slower I chew, the thinner her eyes get. When the bite is soup in my mouth, I swallow and mentally prep for the onslaught of questions. Questions I don't want to answer.

"Nothing new happened. Not really." *Shit.* Why the hell did I add the last part? Might as well have handed her the gas canister while I held the match.

"Elaborate," she commands, her fork pointed my way again.

"Put that thing down. You'll take an eye out."

"Quit avoiding."

I sigh. Aunt Leanne knows bits and pieces about Micah. She remembers people bullied me in high school but doesn't know Micah was among them. All she knows of him now are the tidbits I share from time at work. His asshole tendencies, but also the way I spot him checking me out.

She has her own hypotheses on all things Micah Reed. And after today, no doubt she will add even more.

I rehash the events from two nights ago. Reiterate his order barking. Bring up the blonde and how he acted around her with me nearby. Like his goal was to make me jealous. How we went tit for tat. I give the whole rundown. And when I finish, her shit-eating grin irks my nerves.

After a moment of pause, she asks, "You want honesty?"

Yes. No. We never lie to each other, but occasionally keep opinions to ourselves. I want honesty, but don't want another person to say Micah is flirting. I have been on the receiving end of flirting many times. What Micah and I do is not flirting. Our back-and-forth exchanges are more about getting under each other's skin. And it doesn't take much effort.

I know my motivation. But what prompts Micah?

"Always." Even if I don't want to hear it.

"He likes you." She sips her drink. "More than likes you."

I shake my head. "How? This isn't elementary school. Adults don't pretend to hate someone because they have a crush on them."

"Says who?"

"Society."

She rolls her eyes and shakes her head. "So, because society says something, it makes it true. Really, Peyton?"

I hate when she gets semi-philosophical. I also hate when she makes a valid point when I thought otherwise. Ugh.

"Okay, fine. Say he acts like an asshole—"

"Peyton," she scolds me like a juvenile.

"Say he acts like a *jerk* because he likes me. Should I really pursue a relationship with someone with such childish behavior? Why not just come out and ask me on a date?" I pause to sip my water. "Not that I'd say yes."

"Oh, my dear sweet Peyton." She reaches across the table and pats my hand similar to how Ms. Jenkins does. "Because men don't always know how to use their voice. It's easier for them to act the fool than express how they feel."

I tip my head back, stare at the ceiling tiles, and let my vision blur. "Argh. This is so annoying."

"Yet another reason why I stay single. I prefer friendships. Less drama and scrutinization."

With this, she leaves the topic alone and we finish our lunch. Our conversation shifts to something that doesn't spike my blood pressure. She tells me about a new candle shipment they received at work. Practically sells me each scent. But she loves the small, independently owned shop. They sell a variety of knickknacks and stay busy near the beach.

Finished with lunch, we pay the bill, slide out of the booth and head toward our cars. We stop at the back of mine, exchange hugs and promise to see each other the same time next week. I unlock the car and toss my purse onto the passenger seat.

"Peyton?"

I spin back to face her. "Yeah?"

"Not everything is black and white. Be sure to look for the hints of gray and occasional splashes of color."

Skirting around her thoughts, Aunt Leanne just told me to consider the possibility that Micah may have feelings for me. Not the I-hate-everything-about-you feelings he so boldly displays. But perhaps the exact opposite.

Even if he does, I don't see the point. Micah may not remember me from fourteen plus years ago, but I sure as hell remember him. Remember the hurt he put me through and the web of lies he spun. The harsh words on his lips and how he painted me the fool among our peers.

Micah Reed is an asshole and a manwhore. No point seeing him as anything except that. He treats me like trash whenever possible. And dips his dick in anyone with a hole. No thanks, I will pass.

But I appease my aunt for the time being. Toss out a smile and tell her what she wants to hear. "Will do. Love you."

"Love you, too. See you next week."

Next week… Hopefully, I won't have anything new to share about Micah Reed. Not him ogling me behind the bar. Not him flaunting his promiscuity in my face. Not him barking at me to crawl under my skin. Nothing. Only him leaving me the hell alone.

THREE

MICAH

I LOVE DAYS LIKE THIS. Days when I kick back with my best friend and enjoy the outdoors. Hanging with Gavin equals time at the beach. The sun heats our skin while the sand sticks to it. Coconut and brine float in the air. And bodies fill every possible open space between the seagrasses and surf.

Just like old times. When life was less complicated and stressful.

I need more days like today.

Gavin said we should hit the beach. And wherever Gavin goes, so does Cora. Who called and invited Shelly —which is no big shake. Definitely like old times.

When Gavin flew back to the Bay Area last year for work, I knew shit would go down with him and Cora. With how they left things when his parents moved him to California, I expected shit to blow up. But sometimes, life works out when two people are meant to be together.

Maybe I will get lucky one day and find *the one*.

Gavin and Cora just click. They did from the very beginning. The ease of their relationship annoyed me. Hell, it still annoys me. Because I never found a parallel bond with a woman. Never shared a connection so deep, I felt lost without my other half.

My envy knows no bounds. And now that they are married, envy is too small a term for what I feel regarding their relationship. It isn't fair to begrudge my friend for finding love and happiness.

At one point, I thought Rochelle was *the one*. The woman I would ring shop for and get her name branded over my heart. The woman to make me say *I do*, invite friends over for game nights, and grow old and gray with in rockers on the porch.

Unfortunately, I saw Rochelle with blinders on.

Rochelle sought me out. Approached me. Brought up the conversation of a more serious relationship first. And I fell for each crumb she tossed at my feet. I never suspected a woman of her maturity level would treat me with such juvenile tendencies. Would stoop to such low-level actions. In my bed, no less.

All thanks to Rochelle, I now have an issue seeing women as anything other than a means to an end. Sexual gratification. A temporary fix to what ails me. A warm place to stick my dick when the loneliness peaks.

And I fucking hate it.

I don't want to see women as objects. I don't want people to look at my sister like she is good for one act and disposable otherwise. But after trusting a woman with my heart, I fear putting it out there so freely again. Fear the vulnerability of fully exposing myself. Fear another woman crushing my heart when she tires of me and moves on.

I glance at Gavin, my best friend of nearly twenty years, and notice how he eyes Cora. His observation isn't territorial. He has her heart, and she has his. No, his fixed gaze is more a fear of what he will miss if he looks away.

That is the type of love I want. Where you don't take your eyes off one another because you can't bear to miss a moment.

While Cora and Shelly swim, I opt to ask the questions I don't want the girls to razz me over.

"So," I say, and Gavin breaks contact with Cora to face me. "How's married life? Tired of each other yet?"

Gavin tips his head back and chuckles. "I will never tire of her, bro. Never." He pauses to look at his wife briefly. "But things are different than before."

Hmm, color me intrigued. "How so?"

He purses his lips and takes a deep breath. "Guess the best way to describe it is we're the same as before, but also new."

Now, I laugh. "Yeah, that explains nothing, my cryptic friend."

"Sorry." He shrugs. "When Cora and I first met, we lived in a fantasy world. Yes, we were madly in love. Although teenage love is intense and all-consuming, you're blind to what happens after high school. College, moving out, the weird phase of wanting to experience life on your own." He pauses and shakes his head. "We skipped all that. And tons of relationships don't survive those years post high school."

"So, you think you and Cora would've split after high school?"

He stares out at the water and watches Cora as she laughs with Shelly before returning his gaze. "No, I don't think so. But we wouldn't appreciate each other the way we do now. Thirteen years apart really fucked with both of us. We never forgot each other. But we remembered each other differently. I missed her, but the years of resentment I held for my parents painted the memories differently. Cora had no one to hate but me. And even then, she only hated me on the surface."

Yeah, I definitely envy my best friend. None of the girls from school were "forever" material. They all thought their shit didn't stink. They were either too consumed with themselves or had ugly personalities.

"How did that translate into how things are now?"

"Neither of us wanted a serious relationship with anyone but each other. Sure, our reunion wasn't pretty. But we had a lot of pain to hash out. And I deserved to feel every ounce of her pain. I fucked up, man. I left her when I said I never would. Instead of finding a solution, I took the easy way out." He presses his hand to her name tattooed on his chest. "Her pain is my pain, bro. Plain and simple. And I'll never intentionally cause her pain again."

God, I want to talk to Gavin about my own shitty love

life. Or lack thereof. Neither of us is an expert. No one is an expert when it comes to love. But maybe he can steer me in the right direction with advice.

Great as it is to experience life and all it has to offer; variety isn't always what it is cracked up to be.

Part of me longs for the comfort that comes with being in a monogamous relationship. Getting to know someone on a deeper level. Seeing the world through their eyes. Evolving with the same person. I don't envision children or gray hair at this stage—I am not that far ahead.

But I do see the same person at my side, day after day. Waking up with the same woman in my arms. Wrapping my arms around her and hugging her close. Kissing her ear, her neck, her shoulder. Loving her—not just physically, but in all aspects of life.

At thirty-two, though, I feel like time doesn't weigh in my favor. And I have no clue how to remedy the situation.

"Can I ask you something?"

Gavin pushes his glasses down the bridge of his nose and gives an inquisitive stare. I see the line of questions form, but he won't ask them. "Always, man. What's up?"

"If you and Cora hadn't reconnected, do you think you would've made a life with someone else?"

Without hesitation, he answers, "No. I tried relationships in California. Never stuck. I compared every woman to Cora. Which only made me want her more." He looks out at the water. "She's all I've ever wanted. Everyone else just filled time and provided a temporary distraction."

I nod. "There's someone…"

Without looking, I know his eyes are on me. "The blonde behind the bar?"

My eyes snap to him. "How?" It's the only word my lips form. Because how the hell does he know I meant Peyton? Have I mentioned her to him?

As of recent, my head has been a fucking mess. Whatever.

"The sexual tension between you two can be felt miles away. The bickering and constant eye contact. I only caught a glimpse, but sure as shit felt it. What's her story?"

Fuck, I wish I knew her story. The not knowing is half the problem. Peyton is elusive. An unsolved crime with a six-inch-thick file folder of stats. Only they are written in a foreign language.

"Wish I knew, bro." I shake my head. "For whatever reason, she's hated me since day one. And I did nothing to offend her."

Gavin laughs at this. Laughs so hard he bends at the waist as tears stream down his cheeks. *Dickhead*. I give him his moment to laugh at my expense. Let him get it out of his system.

"Gonna tell me what's so fucking funny?" I prompt.

"Mr. Hot Shit can't get a girl." He laughs again, but it doesn't linger as long. "You have always been a *lady's man*. You always got the girl with your smile and a one-liner. Insert new girl, one you actually *want*, and she won't give you the time of day. She actually throws shit back in your face." He winces. "Hate to say it, brother. Sounds like karma is working her mojo on you."

Ugh. Why the hell did I ask? Should have known Gavin would give me shit.

But I hate to admit… he has a point.

Over the last sixteen-plus years, I have been an asshole. Not just with women, but in general. I always saw myself higher and mightier than the guy next to me. Is this my punishment? To look, to want, to dream about, but not to touch. To never have the chance to show I can be a good guy.

I have no clue how to come back from that. How to make up for all the shit in my past. For all the one-night stands. For picturing one woman while I stared down at another. For wanting to belt out another woman's name when I orgasm.

Yeah, I am a goddamn prick. Is redemption even possible at this point? Or should I just give up and leave things how they are? Would be easier.

"Quit thinking so fucking hard over there." I peer over at Gavin, who drills holes in my temple. "You like her, man?"

"Yeah, but I don't know if it's because she fights me at every turn, or if it's actual attraction."

"Forbidden fruit always tastes better," he admits.

"Truth."

"But there's something to be said about having a favorite fruit. The one that never lets you down. Always tastes the same and makes you happy."

I chuckle. "This fruit analogy is getting dirty, bro."

He smacks my chest. "Shut up and listen a minute." I swat his hand away and feign pain. "You need to sit down and really think about this. Think about her. Whip out pen and paper. Write down what you're attracted to, the parts that make you want more. Then make a list of all the things that make you insane."

I stare at him, incredulous. "Gavin. Brother. Are you seriously telling me to make a pro/con list of this woman?"

He shrugs as if it is that simple. "More or less. You got any better solutions?"

If I had a better solution, would I be asking for help? After Rochelle, women are a haze of mixed signals and lost translations. The more time passed, the less I tried figuring it all out.

Keeping things short and sweet makes life a hell of a lot easier. It also keeps me from getting my heart broken again.

"No, obviously I don't."

I stare out at the horizon and let my focus relax. Can I do this? Write a pros and cons list on Peyton? The idea of writing down what I love and loathe about this woman makes me itchy. But what other option is there?

Any time Peyton is near, I gravitate toward her. Something about her is so familiar and bewitching. But I can't figure out how to scratch the surface. Get past the anger she harbors. Anger I don't quite understand. Anger she unleashed when Ani and Sean left the room and we were alone for the first time.

That rage stems from somewhere deep. A niggling voice in the back of my head tells me I am the root cause of it all. But how?

I met Peyton only a year ago. Right? I search my memory bank; search the long list of women I have been with over the years. But no hits pop up on my radar. Peyton is definitely someone I would remember.

But the boulder beneath my diaphragm begs to differ. And I have no clue where to go from here.

FOUR

PEYTON

I PARK in the employee lot behind Roar and survey the other parked cars. Most everyone is already here. Including Micah.

Great.

I really should talk to Ani about switching some of my days. Micah and Gina, the other manager, draft the staff schedule, but I would love at least one shift without Micah in the picture. A reprieve from his constant stares and assholism. If I talk to Ani, though, she will blather until my ears bleed and probe me harder than an alien abduction.

So, that is a no go.

Guess I just suck it up like a good cookie. Doesn't mean I should make his life easy, though.

Walking through the back door, I stash my purse in the employee lounge, clock in, then head to the bar. No sign of Micah yet. Good. If I'm lucky, he is in the storage room or doing paperwork in the office.

Without the worry of bumping into Micah, I get to work on my prep. I cut citrus and fill the bar condiment boxes. Stash the extras in the fridge beneath the counter. Next, I replenish the napkin stacks, drink umbrellas, and straws. Finally, I double-check the glassware is clean, wipe the counters down again, and scan the liquor bottles and keg levels.

Recently, Wednesday and Thursday nights have grown in popularity. After work gatherings hosted by local businesses or special events with larger parties keep the drinks flowing and the music booming. Fewer bodies and chatter, but still a busy night. My favorite weekday perk; the bar also closes hours earlier. And the tips are still great. Different populous, different mindset, different tipping standards. Of course, Friday and Saturday always bring in the masses and flood the tip jar. But I love the weekday vibe.

Tonight—and any other Wednesday without scheduled events—is Woman Crush Wednesday. Cliché, I know. Basically, it's ladies' night with an updated name. On ladies' night, we serve fruity drinks at half price.

Half price drinks equals lots of ladies soothing their workday with colorful, alcoholic beverages. Lots of ladies drinking and de-stressing equals hefty tips. Works in my favor.

The overhead lights flip off and the colorful lights come on. Music pumps out of the speakers. Not the same music we play on the weekend, but still upbeat and catchy. Moments later, Micah appears from the back and unlocks the front door.

He seems different today.

I shake off the thought as a flock of women storm the bar. Time to whip up some magic.

Five thousand nine hundred and a bazillion fruity drinks later and I am officially beat. One more hour until the door locks. Hallelujah. Then, I can clean up, drive home, and sleep until noon.

Micah joins me and Adam behind the bar. He fills drink orders, cleans glasses and restocks the napkins and fruit. He moves behind the bar as if this is his job, not managing the rest of us. Oddly, he doesn't look my way. Not once. Considering we never go one shift without snapping at each other, I question what parallel universe we landed in. Because silent-and-closed-off Micah is just… weird.

Maybe something happened with his family or a close friend. I peek down the bar, give him a brief once-over, and hope he doesn't notice.

He doesn't look sad or angry. No downturned lips or eyes. No slumped shoulders and hunched back. He just looks… blah. Meh. Like his emotions took a hiatus.

Does it make me a dick if I want to stir the pot? Provoke him a little for my own pleasure. Probably. But work isn't the same if Micah and I aren't going at it like alley cats. And his boring side makes the night drag out.

"Hey, *Micky*," I shout over the music. His spine stiffens and I know I hit the mark. Sweet relief.

He rolls his eyes and turns to face me. "What is it?"

His words have no punch to them. Although I hear the annoyance in his tone, the usual sting is missing. Part of me wants to drop it. Give up and call it a wash. But the feisty side of me says *hell no*. I like feisty me more.

"Your cat die or something? You get your period today? Take a break, I got this handled."

The muscles in his jaw tighten as he grinds his teeth. Inch by inch, his face stains red. His nostrils flare. But he takes slow, measured breaths and lets his frustration or anger with me pass.

Challenge accepted.

"Best watch what you say to me. Seeing as I'm your boss."

Ooh, he wants to play the boss card now. Game on. "Actually, you aren't technically my boss. Ani and Sean are my bosses. You just do everyone else's job plus paperwork and count money."

This pisses him off. The red resurfaces, and he turns his back to me briefly.

What's the matter? Does little Micah not know how to keep his feelings in check? Poor little baby.

He faces me again and steps forward until we are a foot apart. This close, I see the heat from his cheeks has trailed down his neck and onto his upper chest. Smell the woodsy amber scent of his cologne. Hear how hard he grinds his molars and resists speaking, the words dangling on the tip of his tongue.

But I want to coax every word from his lips. Want to hear the hatred and anger. The desire and lust.

I am no idiot. Micah Reed may hide parts of himself from others, but I have known him a long time. Longer than he has known me. For years, I watched Micah from a distance. Saw who he was when everyone was looking. But I also saw who he was when he thought no one was nearby.

Micah is an asshole and a manwhore. Nothing changes that truth. History cannot be erased. It is what it is.

But he is also a big brother and protector. A loner, when his posse isn't around. Although he humiliated me in high school, I still crushed on him. Still followed him when no one paid attention. Still got a glimpse of the guy behind the facade.

My stalker ways faded when Micah graduated and I still had a year left. Senior year was the best year of high school. No more Triple M and no more Micah Reed. The lack of harassment was a nice reprieve. But I hated that I missed seeing Micah every day. I hated that I wondered what he was doing out in the world.

"Maybe you should read the employee handbook again, *wench*." There he is, even if his tone still feels squishier than normal.

"Is this the Micah Rules Roar handbook? Because Ani never gave me a manual to do my job. She knows me better than that."

The few women left at the bar side-eye each other and throw smirks at our back-and-forth. *That will be ten dollars for your evening entertainment, ladies.*

If steam could waft from his scalp, it would be now.

"What is your problem?" he blurts out. He throws a cleaning towel in the sink and steps closer. So close his breath tickles my cheek. The sensation triggers a tingle at the base of my spine. "Why is it your mission to piss me off?" His hissed words only loud enough for me to hear.

Beside us, the women at the bar ooh and ahh. But I don't focus on them. I can't. Not with Micah close enough to press his lips to my skin. To my lips or my neck.

A light sheen of sweat slicks my skin. I resist the urge to step back. To let him win. I got this. Micah Reed doesn't hold power over me. Not anymore.

"I love how easy it is," I tell him. "And because I need to."

He cocks a brow at this. "You need to?"

Too close. He is still way too close. I need to step back. Need clean, cool air. Need to see something other than his supple round lips and beard stubble. Stubble that prob-ably feels so good between —

Shut. Up. Peyton. Do not go there. Do not think of Micah Reed and sex simultaneously. Just. No.

"Someone needs to put you in your place," I croak out. Great. Nothing like sounding less confident when I need to come across bolder.

"And where exactly is my place, Peyton?"

He called me Peyton. Not bar wench or wench.

Peyton. That doesn't happen often. It never happens when we stand this close to each other. Hell, we never stand this close. Ever.

"You don't know?" I tease.

His head shakes subtly. "Enlighten me."

The angry part of me wants to yell, "In the pits of hell." But I don't need to scare off the small number of people that visit on Wednesday nights.

I don't want to lie to him, but throwing down my whole hand makes me vulnerable. Micah Reed doesn't own those rights. He doesn't get to choose when I open myself up. Only I get to decide. Me.

So, I take the easy way out. Toss out a statement that still applies, but doesn't reach the heart of the matter. That he hurt me. He may not remember, but one day he will. And he needs to feel what I felt when it all hits him.

"With all the other assholes and manwhores." I step back and smirk. "No doubt there's a special place in hell for all of you. Don't you think?" I take another step back and twirl the length of my hair.

He winces. I expect him to lash out. To step back into my space and give as good as I deliver. But he doesn't.

Instead, he takes a step back. Then another. And without another word, he retreats and heads for the office.

The women at the bar watch his retreat, then snicker among themselves. I cash them out and they leave me a heftier than normal tip. Does bickering with Micah in front of customers equal better tips? If so, I need to turn that shit all the way up.

Once all the customers leave, I start my nightly cleaning routine. Micah has yet to return from wherever he went. He may not help clean up, but he needs to run sales numbers and take the tills to the office. Which means avoiding me until we leave is impossible.

The tables have been cleared of glasses and wiped down. The condiment boxes refilled and stowed in the fridge. Glasses cleaned and napkins restocked. When I start cleaning the floor, Micah reappears.

Not irritated. Not angry. But maybe a little defeated.

Did I cross the line? Was I too harsh? Banter and frustration are nothing new with Micah. But tonight feels different. Micah *seems* different. And I have no idea why.

Do I cave and apologize? No. Nope. Not happening. If I apologize, he wins. Not that the constant tension and barking at each other is a game. For me, it is all too real.

I have been on the receiving end of his shit and the people he associates—associated—with. I know what it is like to go home and cry until I pass out. Know what it is like to just want friends, not even a boyfriend, and have that squashed like a bug.

Micah Reed may not be the sole reason for my pain, but he holds a significant piece of the pie.

"Why?" I startle at his voice. His proximity. When did he step so close?

I swallow down the sudden lump in my throat. "Why what?" I choke out.

"Why do you hate me so much? Give me a real answer. Not some bullshit reason."

He wants the truth? How convenient. How fortunate.

Well guess what, Micah Reed? You need to work for the truth.

I face him head-on and shake my head. My gaze locks with his and all the words on my tongue swirl like alphabet soup.

Have I seen his eyes this close before? Seen how they shimmer under the brighter light. Earlier, I thought his eyes were lapis blue; a rich, dark blue. Now, with his proximity, I really see the resemblance. And the hints of gold. Like stars in the night sky.

Focus, Peyton. Now is not the time to get lost. Especially in his addictive irises.

"Always want things the easy way, huh?"

His brows pinch at the middle. His eyes dart between mine and try to read all the words left unsaid. But I don't wear my emotions on my sleeve. Not anymore. Now, I cover them in armor.

"I don't know what that means."

Of course, he doesn't. Why would he? Instead of sitting down and thinking, he just wants the answer handed to him. Sorry, Micah. No such luck.

"It means, if you want the answer, you'll have to work for it. Dig deep. Real deep. The answers are there. You're just looking in the wrong places."

Before he asks me another question, I back away and head for the storage room. I fetch the dustpan, but don't leave immediately. Instead, I grab hold of the shelf, bend at the waist, and heave for air.

Did I really do that? Did I tell Micah to go hunt for the truth? To search his past—our past—to find answers?

Damnit.

This isn't how it is supposed to go. I should keep up the back-and-forth quips. Not hand over the key to everything.

What if he unlocks the door? What if he remembers me from years ago? Remembers who I am, what he did and the cruel words he said. Will he look at me with fresh hate? Pity me, perhaps? Stir the pot and try to shove me down? Again.

No. Hell no.

You know… I hope he unlocks our history. Hope he remembers who I am and all the shitty things he did. Maybe, if I'm lucky, he will man up and apologize. Grovel. Beg for my forgiveness.

That would be a sight.

But I see the flip side of the coin. If it all comes crashing back, I picture him playing it off or acting ignorant to save face. Because that is who he is. Micah Reed. Asshole extraordinaire.

HOLY. Fucking. Hell.

Hot water sprays down my spine, but the temperature isn't what heats my skin. The scalding spray is the excuse my mind created so I could bury the guilt. The guilt that ensues as I grip my thick, angry cock in my palm and tug with too much aggression. Stroke and squeeze with eyes pinched tightly as I slap my free hand on the tile.

No matter how long I stroke myself, no matter how firm or soft my technique, satisfaction never comes.

My cock doesn't want my hand. What it needs is a feisty blonde who I can silence with my dick.

Fuck.

I finish jacking off, feeling no relief in the end, then wash up double time.

Peyton wants me to think. She wants me to dig deep to find the answers. Well, I did plenty of that last night while

I had lain awake in bed, staring at a cobweb on the ceiling for hours. I scavenged the corners of my mind and came up blank. Not a goddamn explanation. Hell, a hint would be helpful at this point.

The way she spoke… as if I *know* her. Or I did, once upon a time.

But I would remember Peyton. Her sexy as hell curves. Champagne locks and addictive eyes. Her unparalleled spunk and vicious banter. No chance I would forget any of those qualities.

Question is, if I *did* know her, was she not who she is now? Quite possible. If so, then yeah, I have no idea who Peyton is—or was—and rewinding time, week by week, is the only way to find answers.

That takes a lot of time and effort. Neither of which I will expend today.

Today, I suit up and prepare for battle. Give Peyton a taste of what she is missing. Give her a taste of what I have to offer.

"Game on, hellcat."

Stepping out of the shower, I towel off. I add product to my hair and comb my fingers through to give it that just-fucked look. The look women seem to ogle and beg to touch. Sliding open the closet, I yank a navy button-down and charcoal slacks off the hangers. After I zip up my pants and latch the last button, I add a splash of cologne, then slip on socks and dress shoes.

One last glance in the mirror—because looks need to kill tonight—and I smile at my reflection.

Before leaving for work, I cook a quick dinner, packaging half of it to eat during break later.

The drive from Clearwater to Tampa isn't clogged this time of day. Driving over the causeway allows me time to clear my head and take in the scenery. Sunny, blue skies with the occasional cotton-puff clouds. Salty breeze off the Bay. The occasional boom of music as I pass beachgoers. And the obvious jubilance of people as they enjoy the weather. The energy here invigorates me.

I park behind Roar forty minutes later. No one else has arrived yet. I don't expect to bump into staff for at least another hour.

In the office, I go through my normal routine before the crew trickles in. Reset the register tills. Count and verify the cash from the previous night. Log the sales numbers. Prepare the bank deposit for Ani or Sean. And do a once-over of the interior while the space is empty.

Ani enters the office just as I seal the deposit bag. "Hey, Micah."

I peer up from the computer and lean back in the chair. "Ani," I say with a nod. "How are you?"

Since tension has been slowly building between Peyton and me, I hesitate on what's safe conversation with Ani. Peyton and Ani have an obvious relationship outside of Roar, but I'm not sure what it entails. Ani hired Peyton without input from Sean, Gina, or me. One thing I have learned working for Ani and Sean, if Ani makes such a snap decision, she has her reasons. Which she keeps to herself.

"Good, good. Sean and I have been drumming up new ideas for the slower nights. If you have suggestions, shoot us an email. Business hasn't been bad, but I'd love it to be better."

Slow nights tend to be Monday through Thursday for Roar. Typical with most bars, clubs, and restaurants. When we changed Wednesday to ladies' night—aka Woman Crush Wednesday, Roar style—our profits doubled the first month. Tonight, Roar does Throw Back Thursday. Hours of '80s and '90s music and half-priced beer on tap. This draws more of a male crowd. Thursday sales… they tripled the first month.

Monday and Tuesday are my days off unless Gina goes on vacation. Monday and Tuesday at Roar are worse than sweaty balls stuck to your thigh. I suspect those are the days Ani wants to improve. Can't say I blame her.

"Sure thing. I'll think on it and shoot you guys an email later tonight or tomorrow."

Ani takes the deposit bag from the desk and stows it in her duffel-sized purse. "How're things otherwise? Any staff issues I need to be aware of?"

A layer of sweat builds in my armpits. Is she searching? Either that or I am reading into her words too much. *Paranoid much, Reed?* Bound to happen when you have a one-track mind.

"Not off the top of my head," I tell her. "We may need to hire more staff if you're plotting new ideas."

She taps a finger to her lip. "Good point. Let's see

what we come up with and we'll go from there." Ani starts for the door. *Thank god.* I never sweat in front of my boss, but today is an exception. Just as I breathe again, she spins to face me. "Hope you and Peyton are getting along."

Whiplash. Where did that come from? And why the hell is it important?

Tread lightly, Reed. "We get on fine."

She nods as her eyes look away from me, thoughtful. "So, she's doing well?"

Why does this conversation make my stomach twist? I don't recall past conversations where Ani seemed so invested in my compatibility with Peyton.

"Yeah. The crowd loves her. Hasn't messed up orders. People are genuinely happy to see her." I want to ask Ani why all the questions, but I remain tight lipped. No need to open another door.

"Glad to hear." She turns away from me and twists the doorknob. "Have a great night, Micah." Then Ani disappears, leaving me in a state of nauseated confusion, like I just exited the county fair roller coaster.

What was that all about?

Yes, Ani and Sean vet employees to make sure everyone meets specific criteria. Hardworking, ambitious, friendly, ethical. But they also aim to hire people who will fit in with our little family. Ani asking questions about Peyton is… odd. Especially since she hired her without anyone's input.

So, why the questions?

Who the hell knows. I also don't have time to ponder her reasons. Staff will be here soon and shit needs to get done before the doors open.

I finish reports and place supply orders. After I wrap up calls to businesses interested in hosting at Roar, I exit the office. The main floor smells of lemon bleach and artificial pine. The usually dark or dimly lit room is *shield your eyes* bright as the janitorial staff deep cleans every surface.

"Hey, Ma," I say and smile at the woman older than my mother. "How are you?"

Linda stops cleaning to wrap me in a hug. Hugs from Linda are like toasty blankets while watching windy beach sunsets. All you want to do is hold on and keep her close. No doubt her kids and grandchildren love her hugs too. Roar dubbed Linda and Norm—her husband and co-cleaner—Ma and Pop of our little family. They have worked here since the beginning and always lend an ear or strong opinion.

Linda releases me and holds me at arm's length. "Looking sharp today." I don't miss the twinkle in her eye. "Hot date after work?" She waggles her brows.

I laugh and shake my head. "If I'm a good boy," I tell her and smirk.

A hand slaps my chest. "Need to find you a nice girl. One that'll make ya want more from life."

What if I don't want a *nice* girl? What if I want a fiery, rip-the-clothes-from-my-body girl? One that begs me to spank her and cries when I don't. One that loves when I grip her throat. How about one of those girls?

"If you find her" — I pat Linda's shoulder — "be sure to send her my way."

Linda looks past me and smiles. "Will do, honey." The gleam in her eye doesn't go unnoticed. But she gets back to work before I question it.

When I spin to see what caught Linda's attention, I spot Peyton. Hope it was sheer coincidence she was here when Linda stared this way, all googly eyed.

Behind the bar, Peyton has her back to the main floor and I steal the moment to check her out.

A sleeveless black shirt hugs her like a second skin. Hair up in a high ponytail with soft curls sweeping her upper back. I lick my lips as my eyes trail the sun-kissed skin along her neck and arms. The way she glides from one end of the bar to the other, reaches high and bends low… I adjust myself and take a deep breath.

She spins to prep the front side of the bar, peers up, and rolls her eyes when she catches me looking. Funny enough, my dick gets harder. Like it loves this side of her. The spirited fighter banging their gloves together in the corner of the ring. Always ready to go.

Well, guess what? Me, too, hellcat.

I stroll toward the bar, crank my neck left, then right, and prepare to have a little fun with Peyton. She pretends not to watch, but fails. Time and again, I witnessed her scurry down the bar to someone with their hand up, just in the cusp of her periphery. So, her subtle *I don't see you* bullshit won't work. Not with me.

As I approach, she keeps her eyes downcast on the limes. She cuts them with such slow precision, I picture her screaming inside her own head. The thought makes me want to laugh, but I bite back the urge. Her stubborn determination to ignore me provokes me further.

Peyton and me... there is no love. Maybe shades of like, but definitely no love. The fire between us stirs a tolerate-hate relationship. And I live for the whirling pleasure in my chest each time I antagonize her.

"Cut those limes any smaller and they'll just be peels."

Her hand freezes mid-slice as she lifts her gaze. Eyes narrow as they meet mine; a slight snarl on her lip. "How about you let me do my job and you" —she waves the knife inches from my face— "go do whatever it is you do."

I prop my forearms on the bar and lean in, the knife dangerously close to my eye. But I don't flinch or back down. "This *is* what I do."

"What? Annoy the hell out of people." She lowers the knife and massacres the limes more. "'Cause it's working," she mumbles.

The corner of my lips kick up as I bite the inside of my cheek to not laugh. "No, wench. My job is to make sure you do yours." She rolls her eyes. "Probably why Ani was asking about you today."

That gets her attention.

She sets the knife on the cutting board and peers up at me as curiosity tugs at her brow. "She asked about me?"

Her voice squeaks at the end. Wonder why Ani asking about her makes her nervous?

"Mmhm. Standard stuff. How you're doing in your role. If the customers like you. If there's been any issues." I cock a brow. "And if you get along with the staff. Me included."

She swallows and her tension piques my interest.

"What did you tell her?" She tucks fallen strands of hair behind her ears, then shoves her hands in her back pockets.

I want to toy with her. Drag out the silence to inflame her uneasiness. After all the times she gave me shit, after all the times she threw daggers at me, I want her to feel a hint of discomfort before I answer.

This is me and Peyton. We go head-to-head. Give as good as we get. Purposely piss each other off and bask in the other's misery. Dangle bait and tempt the beast. I love and hate the way we bicker like juveniles. Her enthusiasm and irritation—which I'm not certain is real—fuel me on.

Do my snappy retorts give her ammunition too?

Her hands slip from her pockets, ball into fists, and rest on her hips. *Tap, tap, tap.* A foot taps the floor in sync with her head bobs. Lips pursed, eyes narrowed, Peyton is at the end of her lit fuse. And I love the surge of power it delivers.

She opens her mouth to speak, but I hold up a hand and stop her. A huff from her lips makes mine tip up.

"That you're a pain in my ass," I say with my best poker face.

Her jaw drop is priceless. "What the fuck, Micah?" *Micah, not Micky.* She scans the club as if Ani will jump out and berate her.

I let her panic to the count of ten, then put her out of her misery. "Peyton, calm down." Her dilated pupils land on me and suck me into a black hole. "I didn't actually say that to her. I may be a dick, but I would never do that without coaching you first."

Left, then right, her shoulders loosen. Her chest deflates faster than a balloon. And her eyes smooth out at the corners as her lips lose the paleness of tension.

"Why are you such an asshole?"

With a shrug, I say, "Natural talent, I suppose."

"Don't know why I believe a word that comes out of your mouth. Been nothing but bullshit since day one."

Since day one? What the hell is she talking about?

The day Ani introduced Peyton to the staff, I was all smiles. How could I not be? A gorgeous new woman to distract me while I worked. Ani must have thought the world of her to hire her on the spot. On her first night at Roar, as Ani introduced her to everyone, Peyton's eyes lit up, she smiled and said a kind *hello* to everyone. Except me. When Ani introduced me, Peyton remained straight faced and gave a lackluster wave. No verbal greeting. No smile or kindness.

Initially, I thought her disrespectful. But after a year, her behavior seems rooted in something incomprehensible. The worst part... she won't fucking tell me what about me bothers her.

"Since day one?" Peyton throws me a smug half smile. "Funny. The only hostility I recall on that first day was all you. Which I still don't get, but whatever." Before she counters me, I turn on my heel and go back to the office. "Don't need this bullshit," I mumble on the way.

The next hour, I scour mindless ideas online for Ani and Sean for the slower business days. Most of it is a crapshoot. Man Crush Monday would be a lame addition, but I won't veto it until something better pops up. Monday and Tuesday just aren't days most people want to go out. Attracting them won't be easy. But I have confidence that between the four of us—Ani, Sean, me, and Gina—we will find something better.

A knock at the door distracts the numbness of scrolling search engine results. "Come in."

The door swings open and Peyton fills the frame. Earlier, I didn't glimpse her fully behind the bar. But now, I see her crown to heel. The skintight black V-neck flashes her ample cleavage. Pants equally skintight hug her curvy hips and show off her muscular legs. Pulled altogether with heeled boots.

I fight the desire to lick my lips or adjust myself in her presence. That would give her the upper hand. Give her something to wave in my face and tease me with endlessly. Strong women are a turn-on. But the foreplay is so much better.

Clack, clack, clack. Her heels clap the concrete floor as she steps closer to the desk. Inches away, she stops, leans forward and plants her palms close enough to touch.

Don't look at her tits. Don't look at her tits.

I swallow as subtly as possible. "Something I can help you with?"

A slow grin lifts the corners of her mouth. Like she knows I struggle with her proximity. "Mmhm." But she doesn't elaborate. It pisses me off and makes me hard at the same time.

"Well…"

"You don't know?" My brows cinch together. "Guess you aren't all-knowing." *Poker face. Keep your poker face.* "Ted needs you," she says after a minute of silence.

Ted needs me? She came in here, went all temptress on me, for that?

Ted, another bouncer, works Monday to Thursday, so he isn't bored at home. All in all, Ted is a nice guy. But if he *needs to talk* to me about another one of his fishing trips, I may keel over and die a slow, boring death. I get it, the man is lonely. Just because we have the same genitalia, doesn't mean I like and do all the same activities. Sometimes, men want to swim or read, go bowling or play putt-putt. Organized and unorganized, sports aren't my jam.

"Did he say what for?"

Her eyes drift down the column of buttons on my shirt as she shakes her head. When her eyes meet mine, I detect a hint of mischief in their violet hue. "Nope." She pops the P.

The chair stutters back as I stand. And fuck my life as my eyes drop and zero in on her cleavage. *Damnit all to hell.*

I check my watch at note we have ten minutes until open. "Come on." With a hand, I gesture toward the door. "Get back to the bar and I'll go see what Ted needs."

Peyton saunters down the hall in front of me as I lock the office. A rumble rises in my chest as I witness the sway of her hips after getting an eyeful of her cleavage. Mix it with her fierce attitude and I want to fuck someone against the wall, here and now.

As I head toward Ted, Peyton goes behind the bar. When I reach him, he seems bewildered at my showing up.

"Need something, boss?"

At least some of the staff respect my position. "Peyton said you needed me for something."

Ted looks past me at what I assume is Peyton. Eyes back on me, he shakes his head. "No, I'm good. But since you're here…"

For the next nine minutes, Ted talks my ear off about his day. Fishing near the causeway. His buddies that he wants to introduce me to—he swears we will be buds in no time. All the fish they caught today. He offers to bring me some of the smoked fish tomorrow night after he cooks them. I humbly accept his generosity. May not like to bait hooked poles and catch fish, but I do eat them.

When the doors unlock, I walk behind the bar and prepare to help Peyton and Adam. After the initial rush, I sidle up next to her and smile at her sharp intake of breath.

"That was cute."

She side-eyes me. "Don't know what you're talking about." Her game face is strong tonight.

I point toward the main door. "Telling me Ted needed something. Cute."

She gives a one-shoulder shrug. "Thought that's what he said. Maybe he didn't say, 'I need Micah'. Maybe it was, 'I feed us dinner'. As in the fish he caught." Her nonchalance irritates and turns me on.

So, I turn the tables on her.

I step closer to her. Slip into her personal bubble. Invade her space. She shoots me a look of warning, but I ignore it. Instead, I push on. Breathe in her minty coconut scent and step within inches of her.

"You can admit it."

She turns to face me, her nose a breath from grazing mine, eyes narrowed. "I'll play along." A pause. "Admit what?"

My chest expands and contracts as quick as hers. Neither of us steps away. Both of us equally stubborn and unwilling to own it.

I inch impossibly closer. Kissing her would be easy. So fucking easy. "That you wanted me out here. That you wanted my attention."

Eyes locked in a silent battle of wills, now is the first time I spot small gray flecks in her vivid violet irises. Like a dusting of stars in a nebula. The contrast commands my attention. Invites me in like an old witch in the woods with cookies. I don't want to look away. Can't look away.

Then, in my periphery, her tongue darts out and wets

her lips. Without second thought, my eyes drop to bear witness. Soon as her tongue disappears, her lips kick up in a wicked curve.

"Hmm…" My eyes meet hers again. "Maybe I did. Maybe not." Her shoulders lift, then drop. "Even if I did, I'd never admit it." Without shame, her eyes drop to the bulge in my pants. Her smile in response makes me sweat. "But you admit it without a word spoken."

Before I bite back, she turns on her heel and goes to the end of the bar. Where customers stand idle and tap the bar top to the beat of the music. *When the hell did the door open?*

Passing Adam, I bolt to the bathroom with a limp in my step. In the privacy of a stall, I undo my pants, whip out my dick, and jerk myself to relieve the ache.

Argh!

Why the hell does this woman rake my nerves so much? *Thrust, pump.* What spurs her on? What did I do to her? *Thrust, pump, pump.* And why can't I stop thinking about her? *Pump, thrust, pump.*

I groan as my load splashes into the bowl. And then the bathroom door swings open. I freeze and don't make a sound. Well, any other sound than my semen splashing in the toilet. At least it sounds like normal bathroom business.

After I clean myself up, I straighten my shirt and pants, then exit the stall. I open my mouth to extend a friendly greeting to whoever came in. But I slam my mouth shut before a single word leaves my lips.

"You alright?"

My arm flies up, my forefinger pointing to the door. "What are you doing in here?" I belt out. "Get out!"

Peyton crosses her arms under her breasts, pushing them up in the process. I hate that I don't want to look away, but force my eyes to hers.

Her face shifts from professional poker player to pouty schoolgirl in point five seconds. And *fuck* if it doesn't wake my body back up.

"Is poor baby Micah okay?" she asks in a mocking baby voice while looking down at my crotch.

Gah! Why is she so frustratingly sexy? I should be irritated with her. The way she taunts and teases me. The way she shamelessly checks me out, yet acts as if I turn her off.

But I see the way her nipples pebble beneath her top. The way she steps closer and her breath comes in quicker bursts. Deny all she wants, but Peyton craves me too. And as bad as I ache to give it to her, I refuse. I refuse to be the one who caves first. Who gives in to the obvious chemistry and tension between us. Nope, my feet will stay firmly planted in place.

"Maybe you should come closer and inspect him yourself?" I cock my brow in challenge.

For a beat, she just stares at me wide eyed. The cogs in her mind spin over and over as she searches for a snappy response. A laugh bubbles up my chest and I bite my cheek to stave off my amusement.

When the pieces click into place in her mind, she

grinds her teeth. "A little much, don't you think? Ani might not like hearing management is sexually harassing employees."

Banter with Peyton is similar to walking through a minefield. Always on alert, mindful of where you step and ears focused for any little sound. And now it would appear I stepped on a land mine. Can I defuse the situation?

"You're joking, right?" I shake my head and chuckle.

She slaps her hands to her hips and narrows her eyes. "Do I look like I'm joking?"

Time to test the water. "Go on, call her. I'd love to hear what you tell her." Her knuckles whiten as her shirt stretches at her hips. *"Hey Ani, I lipped off to Micah. Then followed him into the men's room and asked him about his dick. But then he made a sexually suggestive comment to me and my feelings got hurt,"* I whine out in an attempt to mock her. Her face grows redder by the second. "I'll stand next to the phone when you call. That way I can explain the real situation when you're done bitching."

Head tipped back, Peyton screams at the ceiling. Splotchy redness coats her throat and chest. I stand frozen in place, unsure what to do.

"You're such an asshole." She pauses, her eyes sweep down and up my body, then her lip curls. "Never thought I'd be this disgusted by you. Guess things never change, do they?" Then she storms out of the bathroom and leaves me stunned.

What the fuck was that?

Jesus, this woman frustrates the hell out of me. If

someone threw hundreds of mixed signals into a blender and pressed liquefy, that might come close to what swirls in my head right now. Maybe.

I wash my hands and do a quick appearance check in the mirror while drying them. If Peyton wants to play hardball… game on. After all the bullshit surrounding my breakup with Rochelle, I refuse to bow or break for another woman. Ever.

Hours of '80s and '90s music drone on. At least the deejay plays enough variety we don't hear the same song until three or four weeks later. I go about the night as per usual. Helping behind the bar. Schmoozing the customers. Sparking conversations with pretty blondes. For the most part, the slower days draw an older crowd. Monday through Thursday has more of the thirty-plus crowd. The weekend is more the twentysomethings. I enjoy both.

Two hours in and I can't stop talking with a woman at the bar. Intelligent, gorgeous, and flirty as hell. From what I learned thus far, she works in corporate accounting and recently broke up with her boyfriend.

"He was too clingy," she says with an eye roll. "I'm forty, for crying out loud. Not fourteen."

My type of woman. "Some men don't understand the need for independence. I get it, though."

We chat and flirt and make plans for when the bar closes. Her maturity turns me on and is a nice change from the childish, younger women. I love a woman who knows what she wants and goes after it. A woman who stands tall and proud and self-sufficient. All qualities I deem sexy.

Down the bar, Peyton does her best to not look my way. She flirts and laughs and talks with several men. And as focused as I am on the woman in front of me, my eyes and ears drift to the other end of the bar every other minute.

Don't let her dominate your thoughts, Reed. No woman owns you.

The crowd thins as the evening comes to a close. I follow my usual routine and start cleaning and closing out the registers. When all but the blonde leave, I speed up the closing process.

"In a hurry for disease transmission," Peyton barks, loud enough for the blonde to hear. I clench my jaw and ignore her. But she doesn't give up. "Baby Micah feeling better? Know he had issues earlier."

Done. So fucking done.

I stomp over to her and immediately step into her space. "What's the matter, hellcat? Jealous?" Note, this is the first time I call her hellcat to her face. Usually, I reserve that nickname for when it's just me, my fist, and my cock.

She scoffs. "Please. Jealous?" A finger jabs her sternum. "Why would I be jealous?" I don't miss the slight crack in her voice.

I take a step back and wave a hand up and down my body. "Because you hate how much you want me. You hate that you love when I piss you off."

"Cut the music," Peyton calls out as she slashes her fingers in front of her throat. The music dies a second later. "You think I *want* you? After all the bullshit you've put me through." Word by word, her voice escalates. "News flash, asshole. The world doesn't revolve around you." Her eyes zero in on the blonde, who looks slightly alarmed. "You're aware he fucks two plus different women a week, right? Might want to save yourself now."

The blonde slaps me with her glare. Before I offer an answer, she shoulders her purse and walks toward the door.

Every cell in my body explodes with rage. She doesn't want me? But she doesn't want me with anyone else either? Did someone pick me up by the ankles, flip me upside down, and shake me? Because I have no clue what the fuck is going on.

Back in her space, I jab my finger in her face. "What's your problem, Peyton?"

"You," she screams. "You are my fucking problem."

My feet stumble back two steps. "Why?" I want to yell, but my traitorous voice is feeble and small.

"Because you ruin everything you touch." She pauses and shakes her head with glassy eyes. "Because you ruin lives and don't care enough to remember."

I narrow my eyes and *really* look at her. "What... I don't know what you're talking about."

She huffs and shoves past me. Feet pounding against the concrete floor as she heads toward the back. I follow with no clue what is happening. She retrieves her purse from the locker and shoulders it.

Before I ask where she is going, she knocks her shoulder with mine and exits.

"I hate you," she screams.

What the actual fuck just happened?

"Asshole," I scream as I slam the car door and bang my fists against the steering wheel. "Why? Why do I let him get to me like this?"

Question of the century. Too bad no one answers it.

I start the car, but don't leave right away. My eyes drift shut and I work to recenter myself. After a few deep breaths, my blood pressure lowers and my body sags with slight relief.

Every now and again, I question my sanity. Question why I keep working at Roar when Micah drives me mad. Question why I put up with his shit four days a week. Then I remind myself of the endgame. The discussion Ani and I had about the future. A future I refuse to let Micah Reed steal from me.

Digging through my purse, I locate my phone and send Ani a quick text.

Peyton: Heads-up. I left before close.
Ani: Anything I should be concerned about?
Peyton: Oh, ya know. Micah just being Micah.
Ani: He said you were getting along. Want me to talk to him?
Peyton: No and no. But I'll let you know if I change my mind.
Ani: Hey! Do me a favor. Think up ideas for Mondays and Tuesdays for the bar and text them to me.
Peyton: On it. Miss your face.

After my phone connects to the car audio, I crank the music, roll down the windows, and drive home. The loud lyrics, thumping bass, and wind on my cheeks slowly wipe away the anger Micah brought to the surface. And before long, my mood is ten times better as I park next to Reese's car.

Every light in the apartment appears to be on as I unlock the door and walk in. I pray Reese doesn't have a houseguest tonight. Not that I mind the company. My silent plea is answered when the door swings open and I spy Reese on the couch with a platter of tacos.

His eyes land on me as his lips freeze around the taco. "Home early," he mumbles.

Reese is exactly what I need. A soothing presence with the occasional laugh. An ear to listen as I gripe about life and words to give advice as I navigate what to do next.

"Any more of those?" I point to the taco.

He takes a bite and chews a few times. "In the kitchen."

I toss my purse on the floor, dash to the kitchen, and inhale the taco-scented deliciousness. I stuff the tacos full, add refried beans and cheese to the plate, then park myself next to Reese on the couch.

"Whatcha watching?"

"*The Haunting of Bly Manor*. Want me to start it over? Started it just before you walked in."

I shake my head. "Just tell me what I missed."

The next hour passes with the slow demolition of tacos as we can't look away from the screen. When the episode ends, I hope Reese wants to watch the next. But he presses pause and stares at me without a word. The air thickens and I have the sudden urge to cower. To shrink in the corner like a scolded child.

"You gonna tell me? Or do I have to pull it out of you?"

This is what happens when someone has known you as long as we have. Almost twenty years of friendship equals knowing someone better than you know yourself. And Reese reads every emotion I have better than anyone.

"Another day at the office, dear," I joke and he rolls his eyes. "Micah was in rare form tonight. And…" I pause, tip my head back and stare at the imperfections in the ceiling. "And I blew up." I level my head and meet his gaze. "I left work early. Ani knows, so at least I'm covered there."

Reese collects our plates and wanders to the kitchen without a word. Water splashes against plates and pans and utensils. Then the dishwasher kicks on. A moment later, Reese walks back in with two pints of ice cream and spoons. A man after my own heart.

Neither of us speaks as we dig into the creamy confections. Mint chocolate chip for me and cookies 'n cream for Reese. If one thing remains the same, it's our favorite ice cream flavors. Sure, we eat other flavors. But why not just enjoy the one you love?

"Sorry you have to deal with him," Reese says around his spoon.

I nod, swallow my bite, and twist to face him on the couch. "The worst part of it all… he doesn't remember."

Reese goes wide eyed. "Any of it? How is that even possible?"

My shoulders lift to my ears. "Your guess is as good as mine. I get how people forget from early childhood. But teen years are different. You make conscious decisions then. You *choose* to be nice or cruel."

"True. Maybe something happened to his brain." Reese laughs and I can't help but join in.

"No doubt." I sigh, stare down at the ice cream as I scrape the spoon over the surface. "I may not look the exact same, but how does he not know who I am?" The handful of times he's been in my face recently, how does he not *see* me? The goth chick he teased and bullied for three years.

The screen saver on the television flickers off and we continue eating our ice cream. Just as I scoop a heaping spoonful, Reese steals my pint and takes it back to the kitchen. "Hey!" I protest around the melting minty cream.

He returns to the living room, plops down on the couch and grabs hold of my biceps. "I have an idea." His warm, tawny-brown eyes sparkle as his lips kick up in a devilish smile.

"Don't know what you have in mind, but I'm suddenly scared."

The deep chortle I have come to love echoes from Reese's chest. "No need to be scared, sunshine. You'll like it."

"Says you. Bad enough I have to deal with Micah's annoying ass at work. I don't need anyone else adding to the problem or baiting him."

Reese gasps as he slaps a hand to his chest. "When have I ever made things worse?" He cocks a brow. When I don't answer, he continues. "Exactly, I haven't. Trust me, please."

Do I want to put Micah in his place? Hell yes, I do. But I also don't want to cringe every time I walk inside Roar. I love my actual job. Reese stirring the pot could cause future problems.

"Fine," I say with heavy exaggeration. "What do you have in mind?"

For the next thirty minutes, Reese spills his plan. During the first minutes, I wince. A lot. My forehead sore and tense from pinching. A slight headache forms beneath my brows. And my eyes beg to close for the night. Like a good friend, though, I sit and listen to every word.

"Sound like a plan?"

Actually, his plan does sound fun. Reese was never on the receiving end of Micah's bullshit, but he heard all the gossip. In high school, rumors and artifice pass faster than STDs. Although none of the shit was said about him, it impacted him as if it was his name and "slut" written on the walls. Ironic how the tide shifts.

"Yeah." I lean over and hug him hard. "Thanks for always being here for me. You're the best friend a girl could have."

We rise from the couch and head for our respective rooms. "Don't go getting all soft on me now. Need you in tough-bitch mode tomorrow night."

I salute him. "Yes, sir." His laugh is the last thing I hear before he shoves me in my room and shuts the door. "Good night," I yell into the darkness.

"Go to sleep, sunshine," he says before his door clicks shut.

The energy inside Roar buzzes more than usual. But the buzz is nothing compared to the adrenaline in my veins. Not sure if it's the crowd or the fact Reese will be here soon.

The spring break crowds fizzled out over the last two weeks. Now we get a slight lull until late May. The lighter traffic is a nice reprieve. Just means I have to work harder for the extra tips.

For the most part, Micah has distanced himself from me tonight. But it won't last long. When nine o'clock hits, the crowd always triples. Should really talk to Ani about getting an additional bartender for Friday and Saturday, even if just for a few hours.

Beer flows freely from the taps. Colorful fruity drinks get adorned with pierced cherries and citrus on plastic swords. And cash tips fill the jars behind the bar.

Just as I deliver a drink, I spy Reese at the end of the bar. I thank the man who tips me and move down the line to Reese.

I lift the flap at the end of the bar and step out to hug Reese. His arms wrap around me like the summer sun and I sigh, relieved he's here. Since the summer between seventh and eighth grade, Reese has always been my person. The one I could go to with anything and every-thing. We don't hide the truth from each other. And our shared truths are full spectrum. Nothing left out.

"Glad you made it," I mutter against his chest.

"I'd never let—"

"Peyton," Micah barks and I stiffen. I keep my eyes on Reese and steady my urge to scream. "You planning to work tonight? Or make out with the customers?"

Several sets of eyes home in on me and my face heats. *Fucking asshole.*

"You go," Reese says. "The night is still young." A

sinister smile stretches his lips and tips up the corners of his eyes.

I spin around, step behind the bar, and bark back at Micah. "What? You the only one allowed to get handsy with customers?" I hold my hands up in surrender and push out my lips. "Sorry, *Micky*. Didn't know the rules were lopsided."

"Just get to fucking work," he bites out, then storms to the opposite end of the bar.

Over the next hour, I make and pour countless drinks. A rainbow of colors flash and dance over exposed skin and gyrating bodies. Bass vibrates my bones and treble sings in my bloodstream. I get in my groove, dancing behind the bar as I fill orders. Every fifteen minutes, I chat and fake flirt with Reese. It reminds me of when we turned twenty-one and we would use each other to fend off undesirable hookups.

When a club favorite song comes on, half of the Roar crowd loses it and heads for the dance floor. With the bar quieter a minute, I hang out at the end with Reese.

"You bored yet?" I tease.

He throws his head back and laughs harder than necessary. All part of the game. "Nah, sunshine. Been scoping out the eye candy. Eye fucking a few."

I shake my head and chuckle. "And how will this" —I gesture between the two of us— "work if you leave with someone else?"

Reese leans across the bar and curls a finger at me. I

lift up on the bar and meet him in the middle, our lips a breath apart.

Reese and I, we will never be anything other than best friends. We tried more once and it felt wrong. So, we went back to how we have always been. Besties.

But that is not to say we won't kiss on the lips for extenuating circumstances. Circumstances such as this. A kiss between us is just that—a kiss. Nothing sexual, just two sets of lips pressing together. Like acting, and only when necessary.

"He can't keep his eyes off you," he says, only loud enough for me to hear. "And if I want to hook up tonight, I'll just tell whoever that I'm here to help make some dipshit jealous for my friend. Don't worry about me."

Reese closes the space between us and kisses me. He and I both know it is all for show. And I think we put on one hell of a show.

Question is, does Micah fall for the facade? If so, does it piss him off? That's the question I need answered.

SEVEN

MICAH

WHO THE FUCK is this guy? Who is this motherfucker with his lips on Peyton?

And why does seeing her kiss another guy make my vision red?

I grip the bar, knuckles white as pain shoots up my forearm. A spear lances me in the chest. Spreads fire through my middle. But I take hold of the pain and squeeze it tight in my palm. Shape it into a weapon. Hot and heavy swirls of green in my fist.

Call me a hypocrite, I don't give a fuck. But Peyton won't be sucking face with some prick. Not in front of me, anyway. Yes, I own my whorish ways. Yes, society doesn't degrade manwhores the same as women. Only so much I can do about that. And yes, my inner supreme asshole is about to make an appearance.

Whether it is jealousy or the fact she won't cave to my advances or that I can't figure out why she hates me so much, the charade has gone on long enough. Doesn't matter if I have flirted with the same woman all night. I won't condone Peyton and some fuckboy.

"Peyton," I yell down the bar. She continues to kiss mister tall, dark and possessive, ignoring me. But I am not having it. "Peyton," I yell louder. "Time to quit playing with your fuck toy and do your job."

Several sets of eyes land on me and I bite my inside cheek. Adam sidles up to my right. "Boss, might want to go over and talk to her," he suggests with a quiet hiss. Adam means well and I don't want to dole my skewed emotions out on him.

I shoulder slap him in thanks and nod. "Sorry for the outburst." Kaylynn, working the far end of the bar, forces a smile my way. Scrubbing a hand over my face, I give her a sad smile and mouth *sorry*.

My eyes shoot down to the end where Peyton lingers. Thank god she no longer has her tongue shoved down some guy's throat. Though, every other second, she makes eyes at him. Smiles so big I swear her face may split in two. Has she smiled this much before? Can't think of a time when she glowed like this.

Has she smiled at *me* before? I sift through night after night. Replay shift after shift. Not a single night flashes through my mind where Peyton smiled. Not at me, anyway.

Sure, she smiles and laughs and teases other men in the bar. But never once has she done that with me as the recipient. With me, she spits vitriol and abhorrence and repulsion.

More than once, Peyton has suggested I dig deep for answers. Indicated we share history during some point in our lives. I have yet to peg down when we met or when I knew her. It has me second-guessing her and the possibility she has me confused with someone else.

The spear beneath my ribs thrusts deeper. Tightens as it twists and digs. Burns as I consider the prospect of what I may have done to Peyton in the past. Something wretched enough to warrant her immediate hate.

But how can I apologize for missing moments? How can I redeem myself when I don't know what I have done?

I stop three stools down from Peyton and fill a drink order. Then I swallow my pride. Something I haven't done in years.

"Peyton…" I say, loud enough to be heard, but softer than usual.

Eyes focused on the drink she pours, she ignores my call. But I don't budge. After she serves and thanks the customer, she spins to face me and plants her hands on her hips.

"What, Micah? What is it you need that can't wait?" She waves a hand down the bar. "You have eyes. And I have work to do."

Why can we never have civil conversations? Just now, I planned to apologize. But her bitterness dissolves the apology on my tongue like acid.

"You're right. Wanted to offer an olive branch, but nah." Her eyes widen and I wonder if she regrets not hearing what I had to say. Oh well. "Get back to work. And quit fucking around."

I turn my back to her. "The day you apologize, the day you offer me kindness…" My feet are tree roots anchored to the earth below. I don't look back, but can't move until she finishes speaking. "That day will mark history." Now I peer over my shoulder and furrow my brow. "The day Micah Reed says something nice about me. That's a day I'll never forget."

What am I missing? Wish I fucking knew. Unfortunately, now is not the time to relive the last thirty-two years of my life.

Peyton goes back to work and I exit the bar to do rounds in the club.

I walk the perimeter of Roar. Check in with the servers and bouncers as per usual. Hang out by the door with Ted and catch up on his life. He and his wife recently welcomed their second child. When there is a lull in the line, he takes his phone from his pocket and shows me pictures.

"Here she is," Ted all but squeals with delight. "Baby Rose."

Image after image, he scrolls through with a heart-stopping smile. Pictures of a pink bundle in a bassinet. Pictures of their three-year-old son, Theo, holding his baby sister with pure awe on his face. Ted with baby Rose. His wife cradling her. And so many family photos.

Ted stares down at the screen as if nothing but those three people exist. And part of me wonders what that feeling is like. Aside from Shelly, my parents and extended family are all I know. But familial love doesn't compare to love that smacks you in the chest and doesn't let go. Love so powerful, you lose all sense of morality. You don't know which way is up or down—and it doesn't matter.

Once upon a time, I loved Rochelle. The sentiment never passed either of our lips—thank god—but the emotion settled comfortably in my chest. My thoughts sparsely drifted to the image of wedding bells, but I wanted more with her than a notarized document bonding us. I wanted to experience life and the world beside her. Unfortunate for me, she just wanted a younger fuckboy.

"She's beautiful, Ted." I lay a hand on his shoulder and squeeze. "You did good. Congrats to you and yours."

I continue my leisure rounds and park myself in a corner. One song after another plays as I people watch. When I glance across the club and spot Peyton laughing with the guy again, I groan.

What irritates me most with Peyton is the not know-ing. The invisible truth that hangs in the atmosphere between us. That she won't help me find the missing puzzle piece and snap it in place.

People dislike each other all the time. But her anger with me is rooted deep. Stuck in place and unwilling to budge.

I push off the wall and weave through the crowd. Before I make it to the bar, a hand wraps around my arm and stops me. I turn to see a slightly younger, pretty brunette. Her smile lifts some of my weighted thoughts.

"Want to dance?" she shouts as her other hand grabs the opposite arm.

The distraction she could provide has me agreeing without hesitation. Music swims around us as she swings her hips left and right. Ass pressed against my groin, hands over her head. I grab her hips and tug her impossibly closer. Close my eyes. Get lost in the rhythm, her body plastered to mine. Her head tips to the side and I press my lips to the spot beneath her ear.

Fingers comb through the back of my hair and fist the strands. With a slight shift, she lifts her lips to mine. My hands glide across her body, fingers splayed on her belly. A moan rumbles from her mouth and vibrates my chest.

In the middle of the dance floor, I mouth fuck this woman. Taste sweet strawberries on her tongue. Inhale the floral scent on her skin. Graze her heated skin as she spins to face me and I slide a hand up her back until I fist the hair at her nape.

I love and loathe everything about this woman.

No doubt, she is beautiful. I love her bravery and extroversion. How she takes what she wants and doesn't shy away from it. How she owns who she is and flaunts her charm. Her boldness turns me on more than anything.

But... she isn't my type.

It is no secret, I love blondes. Don't get me wrong, there is room for every woman in my world. But the women I find most attractive all look the same. They all look like Peyton.

Fuck my life for realizing this while I kiss another woman.

I break the kiss and hate myself for my wayward thoughts. "I have to work." She tilts her head with narrowed eyes. "Club manager."

She pushes out her lower lip and makes weepy eyes. Damn, she is cute. I resist the urge to lean in and suck her lip.

"We were having so much fun," she says.

Yes, we were. "And we can have more fun later, if you want. But it'll have to wait until after close."

Leaning in, she presses a chaste kiss to my lips. "I'm good with that."

I take a step back and run my hands down her arms until I reach her hands. Another step back. "Catch me later. Either behind the bar or wandering the club."

She winks and I walk off. The brunette may not be my first choice, but I will never turn down a beautiful woman who pursues me.

As I near the bar, I spot Peyton talking with the guy again. All smiles and laughter. It pisses me the hell off. Time to cut the rope. She may know him, but I don't give a fuck.

When Peyton sees me, her spine stiffens and she steps away from the guy. Perfect.

I insert myself between the guy and the customer at

the bar beside him. "Hey, man." Slowly, he faces me. "You know Peyton?"

The smug bastard smirks. "Yeah, we go way back." He doesn't elaborate and I grind my molars.

"*Great,*" I mumble with a layer of cynicism. "Then I'm sure she's told you how busy this place gets." He cocks a brow, but doesn't respond otherwise. "And that she needs to focus on paying customers."

He lifts a tumbler of Jack to his lips and sips it. "Yep. Last I checked, I paid for this drink. So…"

Who the hell is this guy? My fingers curl into fists at my sides. In and out, I breathe deep and remind myself of where I am and the position I hold. The last thing I need is to lose my shit over a woman who mind-fucks me four days a week. The last thing I need is to lose my job over defending said woman who royally hates me.

"So… as one of the managers, I ask you to not hoard my staff when she has a job to do."

He glances down the bar where Peyton pours and blends drinks faster than Adam and Kaylynn combined. "Seems like she has everything under control, boss man." He sips his drink behind a smug grin.

Don't know who this fucker is, but he grates my last nerve each time his lips part. "Yes, unless she's over here talking with you. So, do me a favor, *friend*. Let her do what she's getting paid to do. Her job."

I push off the bar and turn to walk away. But his words stop me. "Oh, I'll let her do her job. Now… and later tonight." I grind my molars, but don't face him. "Cheers, boss man."

For the next hour, I occupy my mind with paperwork in the office. Yes, coming in here is a pussy move. But if I didn't step away and calm down, things would get ugly. Real quick. If I dive headfirst into a different task, the distraction will help extinguish the fire in my blood.

Calm and collected, I head back out to the club. I make my rounds and settle in behind the bar between Adam and Kaylynn. One song blends into another and the drinks flow easily. Peyton and I keep our distance, but she never leaves my sight. Neither does her *friend* at the end of the bar.

As closing time nears, the crowd thins. The brunette from the dance floor sips a strawberry daiquiri twenty feet from the bar. Adam and Kaylynn start the bar closing cleanup while Peyton preps to leave. Friday and Saturday nights, the three of them rotate who stays past close. And tonight, Peyton leaves early.

Finished with her tasks, she lifts the bar flap and heads down the hall to get her things. Before I walk after her, she reappears and loops her arms with *him*. I stare after them as they head for the exit.

My eyes still on them, everything turns red when *he* peers over his shoulder, meets my gaze and winks with a smug smirk on his lips.

And then, they vanish. A chill blankets me as I question if Peyton actually does know him. Or did she just leave with a strange man? A man who seemed all too eager.

The protector in me wants to run outside and chase after them. To tell Peyton not to leave with some random guy who claims to know her. But I don't. Can't. Instead, I stay put and finish my routine tasks.

When I leave, it is with a brunette on my arm. A woman I don't want to spend time with, but will, in order to distract myself from the woman I want but can't have.

EIGHT
PEYTON

BEST NIGHT AT WORK. Ever.

Reese and I walk out of Roar in a fit of laughter and clenching our stomachs. Every minute behind the bar with Micah tonight was nothing short of perfection. I bit my tongue so often it went numb. He fired round after round at me, but I restrained more than normal to get a rise out of him.

Each time I seemed unaffected by his words, his jaw flexed and face reddened. His response was quite intriguing.

Micah spends more time barking versus biting. Spends more time whoring himself around the club than caring about me or the staff. Tonight was different. Micah flashed a new side of himself. An anomalistic side.

The possessive, semi-protective side of Micah Reed made an appearance. And it has me seeing him in a new light. A light similar to the early days, before he jumped on the Triple M train and ruined my teen life.

Reese and I reach my car and I unlock it. "Food?" he asks as he unhooks my arm from his.

"Definitely."

We agree to meet at our favorite twenty-four-hour diner near home. Once I crank the engine, Reese jogs over to his car and gets in. Within minutes, we drive over the bridge, crossing the Bay and wind through Clearwater.

The diner is busy as always. Bright lights shine down on worn booths and paper placemats with crossword puzzles, word searches, and hangman. A coffee mug full of crayons sits next to a napkin dispenser, salt and pepper shakers, sweetener packets, and a half-used bottle of ketchup on the table. Fresh brewed coffee scents the air with a hint of bacon grease and toasted bread. Mumbled chatter, the clinking of cutlery, and the cook calling finished orders echo throughout the dining area. The hostess, an older woman with a messy updo and a pencil behind her ear, hands us laminated menus.

"Andy will be over in a minute." Then she resumes her position near the front door, rolling cutlery in paper napkins.

Don't know why either of us reads over the menu, we always order the same thing. But we read the long list of greasy goodness anyway. When Andy arrives, Reese orders the western omelet with home fries and I get the two pancake breakfast with an egg, crispy bacon and hash browns. Decaf coffee for both of us. Andy takes our menus and waltzes off with exaggerated enthusiasm.

"He has it bad for you," Reese says after the coffee carafe and mugs are left at the table.

I fill my mug and ignore the fact Reese refers to Micah. Grab a packet of raw sugar from the caddy, shake it, tear it open and add it to the coffee. Peel back the lid on two creamer pods and dump them in the mug. Stir with more noise than necessary, all while staring at the decaffeinated beverage and not Reese.

I lift the mug to my lips and blow on the surface. "What makes you think that?" The coffee sears my tongue but tastes like heaven.

Reese fixes his coffee how he likes, then stares at me as if to say, *"You're joking, right?"* He doesn't, though. "Let's count them off, shall we?"

I roll my eyes so hard it causes ocular muscle pain. With a wave of my hand, I say, "If it makes you happy, enlighten me."

For a moment, he leaves me hanging. Sips his coffee and holds my gaze with a hint of mischief. I white knuckle my mug and this makes him laugh.

"Fine," he huffs out. "One, the man can't keep his eyes off you. Literally. Every time I looked his way, his eyes were on you or us."

"That doesn't mean anything." Micah stares at anything with boobs.

"Maybe not to you, but guys don't look—not like he was—unless there is definite interest." I shake my head and gesture for him to continue. "Two, the way he tries to steer you from men. It's quite telling. Possessive."

"You mean when he barks orders? That's just because he's an asshole."

Reese sets his mug down and shakes with laughter. "No, my dear, sweet best friend. He barks at you, and only you, when you give other men attention. It's his way of making you stop and telling the guy to back off."

Why can't men just be straightforward? Although I would still despise Micah, maybe the intensity of said hatred would be less if he were honest. Honesty says a lot about character. And when it comes to Micah, honesty may tip the scales in his favor. Slightly.

"Whatever you say. Still think it's because he's an asshole."

Reese reaches across the table and lays his hand over mine. "Not denying that. But you should accept the fact he has a thing for you. Even if it makes your skin crawl, it doesn't make it less true."

I open my mouth to argue, but the server interrupts as he sets plates between us. My mouth waters and stomach grumbles. All thoughts of work and Micah and his possible infatuation with me go out the window as I dig in.

I stab the last bit of pancake, swipe it through the last of the yolk and bacon grease, then shove it in my mouth. *So freaking good.* Tonight, I will sleep solid. I swallow down the last of my coffee and we settle the bill.

"See you back home," I tell Reese as we each get in our cars.

The drive home takes less than ten minutes. And some of the conversation with Reese at the diner rolls back in. I don't know how to feel about any of it, so I shove it away for another time.

Reese parks in his space as I hop out of my car. Thankfully, neither of us has to be up early. Late nights/early mornings aren't new to either of us, but Reese aims to be in bed—not sleeping—before midnight. I regularly tease him about his *old man status*.

Inside, we hug and go opposite directions at the end of the hall.

"Night, sunshine."

"Night, Reese. Thanks again for tonight."

He bops me on the nose. "That's what best guy friends are for."

I go about my nighttime routine and soon switch my bedside lamp off. As the light fades to darkness, my mind flips on and runs ramped up.

Reese's words from the diner repeat in my head. *"The man can't keep his eyes off you. Literally."*

Does Micah look at me *that* often? Not possible. Reese only noticed Micah looking because he was keeping an eye out for such things.

"The way he tries to steer you from men. It's quite telling. Possessive."

Is Micah really trying to keep me away from other men? Does he actually believe he has a claim on me? Ha! Not a fat chance in hell, Micah Reed.

What I don't understand is why Micah would feel

possessive. On day one at Roar, I radiated nothing but abhorrence when we were introduced. He felt it, too. Mom always said hate is a strong word. I use the term sparingly and only associate it with a handful of people. Since age fourteen, I have hated Micah Reed. He was cold and callous and hurt others to make himself look good.

Question is… is it time to grow up? Is it time to let go of teenage pain and trauma? Is it time to give someone I have loathed more than a decade a fresh start?

Maybe.

I don't want to live life with hate in my heart. Don't want to be someone who focuses solely on all the negative aspects. If I let go of the past so easily, does it make me weak?

Part of me says yes. By giving in, all the hurtful words, constant teasing and bullying… it feels as if I accept them. That Micah and those bitches all get a free pass. I may be the bigger person by extending forgiveness, but I don't want to be a doormat.

The other part of me says no and states, in order to grow and evolve into a better version of myself, I must make peace with my past. To make peace, I have to battle my inner demons. The voices of doubt that tell me to build a wall around my heart, to keep people like teenage Micah Reed out. People who know nothing about me, yet hand out opinions like Halloween candy. People who know nothing about my life, yet they mock and judge and lie about me.

I am not that girl anymore. That fragile teenage girl

who only wanted to be accepted for who she was. Now, I stand tall. Strong—physically and mentally.

Perhaps it is time to expand my strength to emotionally as well. Perhaps it is time to be the bigger person and give Micah Reed a chance. A chance he probably doesn't deserve, but maybe needs.

Tomorrow, I will offer up his second chance. How he handles it is up to him.

"You planning on handing out heart attacks tonight?"

I glance over my shoulder in the body-length mirror at Reese in my doorway. His eyes rake over the length of my body before he whistles. The reaction is exactly what I hoped for, and I laugh.

"One. Maybe." I spin to face him. "Think it'll work?"

In three long strides, Reese stops in front of me and grips my shoulders. "Yes. And if not, someone might need to visit an optometrist." He shakes his head. "Damn, sunshine. You don't play fair. Best have 911 on speed dial."

I step out of his touch and go to my dresser. Add a few spritzes of perfume to my wrists and at the base of my skull. Snap on my favorite leather bracelets. Swipe one last coat of clear gloss on my lips. I have never been the type to wear a lot of makeup, but I do like to accentuate the features I love about myself. So, my eyes and lips always get attention. Even if minimal.

After I fetch my four-inch-heel boots from the closet, I plop on the bed and finish getting ready.

Not sleeping the first three hours I had lain in bed last night, I devised a plan for work tonight. Let's just say I will test Reese's theory about Micah. And in order to do that, I have to be on my best behavior. I have to be the first one to hold up the surrender flag.

But there is no reason to not look like the smoking-hot temptress I am. Mom always said use what life has given you. She probably meant talent and skill, but I reserve the right to believe she silently included beauty too.

I shoulder my purse and head for the front door. Reese follows in my wake. "Never said I played fair. Do you blame me?"

The corners of his mouth droop slightly. "No, of course not. But it wouldn't be right if I didn't give you some shit before you left."

"True." I turn and hug him. "Thanks for everything."

His arms tighten around my middle. "What'd I do?"

I loosen my grip and kiss his cheek. "Nothing. Just being you. And that's exactly what I need. So, thank you. You really are the bestest best friend."

As the words leave my lips, Reese slaps my ass. Hard. "Get out of here, sunshine."

I rub my butt and jab a finger in his chest. "Damn, that stings."

"Good. Now go." He shoos me out the door. "And you better tell me everything in the morning."

Pivoting slightly, I lift a hand to my forehead in mock salute. "Yes, sir. I'll have my report on your desk at oh-three-hundred hours."

He shakes his head. "You're such a weirdo. Love you."

"Love you, too" I blow him a kiss before he shuts the door.

Now, on to the most challenging night at work. Hope my claws don't come out.

NINE

MICAH

HAVE I stepped into another dimension? Either that or I am seeing shit. I rub my eyes and blink a few times.

No fucking clue.

Glass bottles clang against loud music as they get tossed in bins. Sweat mixed with perfume and alcohol floats through the air. Colored lights dance down from the ceiling and bounce over exposed skin and gyrating bodies.

Roar is in full swing, as busy as any other Saturday night, yet I don't see or hear any of it.

Because Peyton fucking Alexander just smiled. At me. Smiled.

Has hell frozen over and I missed the memo?

"Can you hand me that jigger?" Her dainty finger points to the steel measuring device less than six inches from my hand. But I don't move. She waves a hand in front of my spaced-out eyes, a bright as sunshine smile on her face. "Hello? Earth to Micah. The jigger."

I shake my bewilderment away and hand it over. "Sorry."

She doesn't bitch or scowl. Nope. She simply laughs it off. "No worries. Thank you."

For a moment, I scan down the bar and throughout the club. Looking for something else out of place. A camera, maybe. Or people watching us as this whole turn of events takes place. I wait for the shoe to drop. For everyone to burst out laughing at my expense.

But everything looks… normal.

Then a knife stabs me between the shoulder blades as realization hits. A thought I don't *want* taking up residence in my mind, but would make sense, if true. Because, let's face it, Peyton is an attractive woman. An attractive woman who left here with a guy last night. A guy I have never seen at Roar but swears he's known her years.

Is Peyton happy because she hooked up with him?

My stomach churns and I turn my back on the bar. I grab the back counter and take shallow breaths with my eyes closed. Swallow down the bitterness on my tongue, the thick lump in my throat.

No woman, aside from family, has bent me out of shape. Has riled me up or tossed me to the wayside. But for some unknown reason, Peyton does. She spirals in like a tornado, tears my world up, then leaves me dazed in the aftermath.

Her combative side is one I enjoy, though. The unpredictability and sarcasm and tough as nails exterior. Where others may see her as a bitch, I see her as fierce. And damn if that doesn't make me want her more.

But this…

A hand rests on my shoulder and I glance to see the owner. Of course. Peyton.

"You okay?" Her violet irises scan my eyes, my cheeks, my lips with an edge of concern. "You look kind of pale." She hasn't taken her hand off me yet and I don't know if I should enjoy it or freak out.

"I'm fine," I croak out, then clear my throat. "Just need some water. Probably something from dinner." The lie rolls off my tongue with too much ease.

"Go sit in the back a minute. We'll be fine." Then her hand slides down between my shoulder blades and rubs small, gentle circles. I close my eyes and relish the touch until she removes her hand.

When I no longer feel the heat of her body near mine, I turn and exit the bar. I rush to the office, plop down in the chair, plant my elbows on the desk and my head in my hands. I take slow and steady breaths. In through my nose, out through my mouth.

What is going on? And why does this change in Peyton put me on edge?

Since the beginning, she has been nothing short of hostile toward me. Is it weird that her wrath is something I look forward to? After a year of working together, her malevolence is all I know.

Over the next hour, I occupy my mind with the staff

schedule. Stare at the empty boxes on the spreadsheet and will them to fill in. Then I remember Ani asked for fresh ideas for the slower days. I switch my focus and zone out as I search the web.

A soft knock, followed by the office door opening, snaps me out of my incessant scrolling. Page after page and I still haven't found worthwhile ideas to spruce up Mondays and Tuesdays.

I look up to see Peyton smiling near the door. As heart stopping as her smile is, seeing it so much in one night has me dizzy.

"Getting a little crazy out there. Might want to do your rounds and help Adam and Kaylynn after."

Any other night, she would bark at me for slacking off. She would have stormed in here without knocking, stepped up to the desk, slammed her hands down, and bitched at me for not doing my job. But not tonight. Tonight, she offers suggestions and uses polite tones.

"Yeah, sure. Thanks for letting me know."

"No problem." And then she leaves and closes the door behind her. Quietly.

I make my way back out into the club and do my rounds. After I touch base with the last staff member on the floor, I weave through the crowded dance floor.

Working anywhere with high capacity, you have to be okay with random people touching, bumping, or engaging with you. It comes with the territory, no matter which role you hold.

But as people dance beside me, rub up against me, reach out for and grope me, my tolerance level vanishes.

The world shrinks and blurs. People appear out of nowhere and steal my air. The music booms louder and thumps harder. Sweat breaks out across my skin and my breath won't come quick enough. My pulse whooshes behind my ears. The room spins and I wobble on my feet. I stumble out of the crowd and stagger sideways until I hit a wall. My stomach churns as I drop to the floor, shirt drenched.

And then she is there. Peyton. In my face. Holding my cheeks and yelling. But I don't hear her. She shakes me gently and yells again. This time, the faint tones of her voice break through the white noise.

"Put your head between your legs, Micah." My brow tugs together at her words. "It'll help you from passing out."

Oh. I nod and do as she says. Head between my knees, I close my eyes and breathe steadily. A chill hits my neck, but I don't move. It feels good. Settles the pang in my chest and stops the constant flow of sweat. Fingers comb through my hair and a wave of comfort washes over me.

I want to lift my head and see if Peyton is still here. If she is the one nursing and consoling me. Providing me with this unfamiliar comfort. Comfort I don't want to end.

"Micah?" Her voice is soft next to my ear. "Slowly sit up straight. You need some water."

I do as she says and she hands me a glass of cold

water. One sip at a time, I drink the cool liquid. She watches me like a mother would a sick child. I love and hate that I worried her, but am glad I didn't collapse.

"What did you eat for dinner? Maybe you got food poisoning."

Here comes my inner asshole. Yes, I lied to her earlier. Said maybe it was something from dinner. Which isn't possible. Because I haven't eaten. Not since yesterday.

"Uh, I may have fibbed about dinner earlier." Her brows creep down. "More like I haven't eaten since yesterday."

"Oh, Jesus." She shakes her head, rises from her haunches and offers her hand. "Come on."

"What? Where are you—"

"You need to eat something. Before you actually *do* pass out."

I wince but recover. "I have snacks in the office. Maybe we can grab something to eat after work. Together." The word vomit leaves my mouth before I stop it. No way to retract or turn back now.

Hour-long seconds drag out. Peyton stares at me with a novel of confusion written on her face. Confusion morphs into something akin to struggle. I hate that she has to put so much effort into the decision. And I have half a mind to rescind.

"Sure. How about Teddy's?" she proposes.

Teddy's is a modernized version of homestyle. Open twenty-four hours, they let you order anything from the menu any time of day. Best part, it is less than a mile from Roar.

"Sounds perfect."

She proffers her hand to help me stand and I take it without hesitation. Once upright, I hold steady a moment and get my bearings. Less dizzy, I put one foot in front of the other and inch my way down the hall toward the office.

"Eat something," she hollers down the hall as I open the door.

"On it, boss."

This grants me a smile just before she walks off. I swear I have seen more smiles from Peyton tonight than I have in the last year. Combined with the lack of food in my system, the constant smiles fuck with my head. And body.

On the tattered couch in the office, I lie back and eat one of the emergency packages of peanut butter crackers. When I reach the bottom of the package, the room looks less like a house of distorted mirrors and my hands tremble less. My stomach grumbles, suggesting the crackers better be the appetizer.

I close my eyes and throw an arm over them. The music from the club vibrates the walls and lulls me to sleep. A hand shakes my shoulder and whispers my name. I ignore the dream until it happens again, a little louder.

"Huh?" I lift my arm a bit and spot Peyton's chin and lips.

"Time to wake up, sleepyhead." Slowly, I sit up and she inches back. "If you're too tired, we can skip food."

I shake my head. "No, I'm good. Just give me a minute." Now is when I notice the silence. The lack of music or blended chatter. "What time is it?"

"Almost three."

Well, damn. Definitely needed the sleep, but I didn't mean to sleep the last three and a half hours. With tomorrow off, the additional sleep shouldn't throw my schedule off much.

"You ready to go?" I ask as I stand and stretch.

"Whenever you are." She points to the desk. "Brought the tills in."

"Thanks."

After I stow the money and lock the vault, we leave through the back. We head for our individual cars and I wait for her to put hers in drive before I take off.

In the seven minutes it takes us to drive from Roar to Teddy's, I question every reason why Peyton agreed to eat with me after work. Was it out of sympathy? Did she feel bad because I almost fainted in the club? The Peyton I have known the last year would have left me on the floor and hollered at someone else to call 911 while she stood behind the bar and watched.

But something is different about her. And, for the life of me, I have no clue what.

We step inside Teddy's and are promptly seated at a booth in the corner. Peyton smiles ear to ear as she scans the menu. Meanwhile, I stare at the laminated page and let my eyes lose focus.

I just don't get it. After all this time, why be nice now? What does she stand to gain? Is this a game?

Or has she turned over a new leaf?

My hope leans toward the latter. Because if this is just a game, the end may be severe.

TEN

PEYTON

WHY AM I HERE? Why did I agree to come here with him?

Obviously, I am an idiot. That's why.

I have been to Teddy's enough times to know what I want to eat. The best breakfast sandwich this side of the Bay. Egg, sausage, hash brown patty, and cheese slapped between two pancakes.

So. Freaking. Good.

But I dart my eyes over the menu as if I need time to figure it out. Meanwhile, I spot Micah in my periphery. Staring at me like a stoner. He doesn't open his mouth to speak, doesn't flinch or move his eyes to read the menu. He just stares straight ahead as if he's broken.

The wicked part of me wants to reach across the table and slap his cheek to wake him up. Instead, I sit here like a friend would and fake read the menu. I scan the egg breakfast plates so many times I have the entire section memorized. So, I move on to the sides.

Just as I read cheese grits for the fifth time, our server arrives with a pen pressed to her green guest check pad. From across the table, Micah eyes me with a silent request to order first. I bite my cheek to stop myself from laughing.

After I order my sandwich and juice, Micah orders enough food for two and a coffee. Wasn't kidding when he said he hadn't eaten since yesterday.

"So…" It feels awkward just sitting here. But I have no clue what to talk about with him. Not like we have ever been friendly.

"So…" he repeats, but continues. "Sorry about earlier."

About to tell him he doesn't need to apologize, I get interrupted when the server drops off our drinks.

"Just don't do it again."

A corner of his mouth kicks up as he stares down at his mug and dumps several packets of sugar in the brew. "Didn't mean to. Nice to know you were concerned." He picks up his spoon, stirs the overly sweet caffeine and lifts his eyes to mine. "Nice to know you wouldn't leave me to die."

I roll my eyes with a headshake. "Things may not be great between us, but I'd never wish death on anyone. I'm a firm believer in karma."

"Lucky me," he teases.

We both go silent a moment. My hands sit firmly

between my butt and the booth while Micah has his clasped in front of him on the table. He fumbles with his lower lip like he wants to ask me something, but doesn't know how. His reluctance and uncertainty douse my blood with a thrill. Funny yet odd, I have never been this excited by someone feeling out of sorts.

He takes a sip of his coffee, then slowly sets the mug on the table, eyes fixed on the steam. "If you don't mind my asking…" His eyes lift to meet mine. The gold hints shimmer in the brighter light and it throws me off balance for a breath. "Why do you hate me so much?"

I stare back at him with pursed lips. It would be so easy to just tell Micah my reasons. To spill my truth and help him remember the past instead of learning the answers on his own. But I won't. After years of having to rebuild my confidence and strength, I vowed to never let anyone walk all over me again. Especially the man sitting across from me.

"The answer to that would take more time than we have tonight. And I'd have to answer that when *I'm* ready. Hope you figure it out before then."

He drops his hands to his sides and leans back into the booth. "See, that's what I don't get." I lift my brows in question. "More than once, you've insinuated we knew each other. Before you worked at Roar."

I lean back and match his position. Stare at him and study every line and twitch of his face. Look for indications of deception in his brow line, eyes, or lips. But all I see is honesty and perplexity.

"You really have no idea, do you?"

He leans forward and wraps his hands back around the mug. "No. So, will you please tell me?"

"Not tonight," I whisper before picking up my juice to drink. "Let's talk about something else. Anything else."

Anger still eats away at me for all the pain and embarrassment Micah and half the high school student body created. Yes, it happened several years ago. Yes, a therapist once told me I would never get past it if I don't let go. But damn, letting go of such cruelty inflicted on me is difficult. If only he remembered. If only he apologized.

Maybe then I could move past the imprisoned emotions. God, it would be nice to free those demons.

"What do you do when you're not at work?"

He wants to know about my life outside the bar. Learn more personal details. The question is vague enough to leave it open for any response. I doubt he wants to hear about my grocery trips and spring cleaning. He wants dirty details. Like if I have romantic interests with anyone. Especially after seeing me with Reese last night.

But he needs to work harder to earn that information.

"Mondays and Tuesdays, I work at an assisted living facility."

His head jerks back in surprise. "You do?" I tuck my lips and nod. "What do you do there?"

Does he really want to know? Or is this just some jab at polite conversation?

Micah Reed finding anything I do interesting seems far-fetched. But he also doesn't remember who I am. Not the younger me, anyway. Would he still be keen on knowing me if he did remember? A voice in the back of my head screams *no, you dumbass!* A different voice chimes in with *what if he has changed?*

Is it possible he has matured? That he actually cares about what women have to offer, other than what lies between their legs. I suppose all things are possible.

"Mostly crafts and games. I entertain and give them someone to talk to. Many don't have family in the area and they get lonely. Friendships within the ALF help, but it isn't the same."

"Wow." His lapis blue eyes hold mine and sparkle with amazement. "She's beautiful and kindhearted."

I don't know how to respond to his sentiment. The compliment throws me off balance and makes me question what I have thought of him over the years. I may have started out the night with a charade, but it has opened my eyes slightly. It has shown me a side of Micah Reed I didn't know existed. A softer side with gentle words.

"Well, my family would murder me in my sleep if I weren't. So…" I shrug, drop my gaze to the table and toy with the corner of the napkin.

He laughs. "Mine, too."

This grabs my attention. Makes me want to shake his shoulders and yell, "Well, they obviously don't know everything about you." But making a scene will open up a fat can of drama I don't want, so I keep my thoughts to myself.

Before the air around us shifts to awkward, uncomfortable silence, the server steps up to the table with our food. Soon as my plate hits the table, I reach for my sandwich and chow down. The server drops one large and three small plates in front of Micah. He dives fork first into the biscuits and gravy before the server asks if we want drink refills. We both give a thumbs-up.

Odd to think, but it feels like tonight has been pivotal between me and Micah. Like we have reached the center of our book and the story is shifting. Flowing more smoothly. The tension has eased slightly and made room for something else. What that something is, I have no clue.

Not sure if I want to know.

The server returns with a fresh glass of juice and refills Micah's coffee. After he steps away, Micah spears a sausage link on his plate, then points it at me.

"Don't think just because food arrived we're done talking." Why not? I want to ask, but bite my tongue. "What do you do for fun?"

I would be an idiot to ignore his obvious attraction for me, now that I'm paying closer attention. Can't exactly say Micah is hard on the eyes, either. Before he opened his mouth my freshman year, my black heart swooned over him. Hard. Then he crushed it with his words. Over and over again.

Now, though, he seems different. A bit more mature, if I discount our never-ending banter and his predilection for a new female every night of the week.

Are women what he does for fun? Fucks 'em and

leaves 'em? I don't picture him playing basketball with the guys or having a movie night with piles of junk food.

"What I do for fun would probably seem lame or old ladyish to you."

He eats the last of the sausage off his fork. "Humor me."

Micah Reed wants to know what I do for fun. Alright.

"Fun for me is curling up on the couch with a good book or movie. Maybe bingeing on my favorite ice cream and greasy takeout with a friend." I sip my juice. "Working where we do, I don't care about going out to party. What about you?" He tilts his head. "What is it you do for fun?"

Micah cuts into his French toast, dips the chunk in syrup, then brings it to his lips. For some idiotic reason, I follow the entire process with my eyes and salivate when he opens his mouth to eat it. I pray I don't look like all the other women who fawn over him.

Last thing I need is him getting the wrong idea.

But he watches me with obvious interest. Watches as I bring my own food to my lips and distract myself from whatever it is that is happening. Is this some weird version of food porn? People who get off watching other people eat. A sexual fetish. Like *"Hey girl, eat the toast next. Does it have butter? You like it all buttered up, don't you?"*

And now I have that stuck in my head. Fuck my life. Guess my dreams will be bizarre as hell tonight.

"A little bit of this. A little bit of that," he says after a sip of coffee that makes his face scrunch. He grabs two packets of sugar and adds them to the cup.

"Vague much?" I point to the coffee he now stirs. "I like sweet stuff, but I think you have sugar issues."

He waves me off. "Nah." Another sip and his eyes blissfully close. "And maybe I like to be mysterious." His brows waggle.

"Or… you don't want people to see the real you."

Across the table, he pushes scrambled eggs around his plate with a fork as a child would. Finding ways to avoid eye contact. Doing menial things to distract from the conversation at hand. Doing everything and anything to not own the truth.

"I let someone see the *real me*, as you call it."

What? That's it? Finally going to open up, then shut it down just as fast. Why am I not surprised?

"And?"

His brows pinch at the center as he forces out a breath. "And… she fucked a guy ten years my junior while she thought I was working. Except, I left work early that day. Thought it'd be nice to surprise her. When I walked in on them fucking, it was definitely a surprise."

The teenage girl inside me wants to jump up, poke my finger in his chest and yell, *"Ha! That's what you get."* Maturity clears her throat and wags her finger. Damn maturity.

"Sorry that happened to you," I tell him instead. "Can't say I know what that feels like."

"I don't picture guys stepping out on you," he mumbles, but I hear it clear as day.

True. No guy I dated has cheated on me. Two of my three serious relationships ended somewhat tragically. I believe all things happen for a reason, but I wish they could have happened differently. Death should never ever be the reason you lose love.

"So mysterious, Micah. Tell me what you do for fun." I work to pass the somber mood.

"Relentless, aren't you?"

I shrug. "A trait I've gotten good at over the years."

He plucks a grape from his plate and pops it in his mouth. "Hang with buddies, I guess. Friends of mine get together on Sundays and we just bullshit and catch up. When the weather's great, we hang at the beach. And the occasional gathering with the fam."

"Sounds nice. I lost some family and would give anything to spend time with them again."

Just like that, I bring us right back into sad territory. Not that my life is sad. I make the most of what I have. Spend time with Mom, Harold, and Trina—my stepfather and stepsister—when able. I see my aunt Leanne more often, though. She reminds me so much of Dad.

The server steps up to the table and surveys our empty plates. After stacking the plates on his arm, he lays the check facedown on the table. "They'll cash you out up front." Then he walks off.

I go for the check, but Micah beats me to it. "It was my idea to come here. I'll pay."

The notion unsettles me. Only because it makes tonight seem more like a *date* and not two coworkers grabbing a bite to eat after work. And this was not a date.

"That's nice of you, but I don't mind paying for myself."

He scoots to the edge of the booth and rises. "Look, you're independent. I get it. But it's okay to let people buy you a meal every now and then." He starts for the register near the door. "It's the least I can do after my episode earlier."

I don't want to fight with him. Not after we have spent the last hours cordial. "Fine." I cave. "But only if I get to tip the server."

"Deal."

While Micah pays, I toss a stack of bills on the table. I wave to the server and head for the exit, Micah on my heels. Feels like his eyes are on my ass, but I don't check.

He walks me to my car. The air thicker as we approach and I dig the fob from my purse with shaky hands. My throat drier than burned toast as I swallow. My teeth clack together as I press the unlock button.

This isn't a date. And we aren't technically friends. So why the hell am I so fidgety?

Tonight ends with us both getting in our cars and driving away. Alone.

There will be no affectionate exchanges. No kisses or promises to talk later. No "I had a nice time." or "Let's do this again."

None. Of. The. Above.

Yet, this still feels like the end of a date as Micah

opens my car door. As he looks into my eyes, equally as confused.

He steps closer, his arm lifting up. Is he going to hug me? No. Nope. Not happening.

I move to get in the car and he drops his arm. "Glad you got some food in you. Don't do that again."

His eyes drop to his feet, then meet mine again. "Yeah, sure," he says as he closes my door and I roll down the window. "Drive safe."

"You, too." The corners of his lips curve up slightly. "Night, Micah."

He steps back. "Night."

I leave Teddy's and make it home in record time. That is the beauty of driving the highway in the middle of the night.

After I brush my teeth and dress in pajamas, I snuggle under the blanket and shut my heavy eyes. My body relaxes one limb at a time. On the verge of sleep, I hear a fire truck siren nearby and it jolts me awake. Once it passes, I wiggle in place and try to settle my alert brain.

But my brain and I are obviously not on the same wavelength. Nope. Now, my brain wants to do a minute-by-minute replay of the whole evening. What it was like to have a cordial evening with my archnemesis. To smile and laugh and share a healthy conversation. To feel something, if only for a moment, other than hate for this man.

Good thing I don't work tomorrow. It's going to be a long night of overanalyzing.

Stupid brain.

I PARK behind Gavin's Range Rover, two houses down from Jonas and Autumn's place. Our Sunday get-togethers are the best tradition started with our group. Friends, family, and food—three of my favorite F's. My other favorite F wouldn't be appropriate in a group setting. Not my kink.

Feet from the front door, hickory hits my nose as rock music vibrates in my eardrums. I knock and Autumn yells from the other side. "It's open."

I twist the knob and step inside. In the open floor plan, I spy Autumn as she bustles around the kitchen. Takes buns out of packages, dumps cold sides into bowls, grabs condiments and toppings from the fridge. Her pace makes me dizzy.

I set down a bag with beer, tortilla chips, and salsa. "Anything you need help with?" Mom taught me and Shelly to always offer assistance, especially when we are guests. Long as Autumn doesn't need help cooking, I will pitch in.

My cooking skills are a running joke in the Reed family. When we were growing up, Mom wanted to make sure we were all—me, Shelly, and Dad—self-sufficient in the kitchen. That we knew how to make basic meals in case she wasn't able to. Let's just say I flunked from day one when I made gummy pasta with burned tomato sauce. Not my finest hour.

Can I cook now? If following microwave directions counts, then yes. If ordering takeout or dining out counts, then yes again. Basic breakfast foods and I are friends. But it works best for everyone if I stay away from stoves and ovens. Besides, every now and again, Mom stops by because she is "in the area"—she lives a solid twenty minutes from my house—and brings me a casserole dish of my childhood favorites.

Or nights like tonight. Everyone leaves with a container of leftovers. Autumn demands it. No matter what, I never starve or burn down the house.

"Could you dump the snack foods into the big bowls?" She points to a stack of large bowls at the end of the counter.

"On it."

Maybe Shelly told her not to let me near anything that requires heating. If so, I need to thank her later.

As I dump cheese puffs into a bowl, Jonas comes in from the backyard with Clementine on his heels. She is the cutest little girl ever. A spitting image of her mom, but with additional sass and a major bond with Spartan, Jonas's husky.

"Hey, man. Didn't realize you were here." He steps up to me and we backslap hug. "Gavin and Cora are out back with your sister and Erin."

"What? They left Autumn in here to do everything. Shelly is definitely getting a ration of shit."

Autumn shoves a large spoon in the coleslaw and spins to face me. "No, leave them be. I forced them outside."

"But you asked me to help?" I deadpan.

She shrugs. "I like to rotate through my helpers. What can I say?"

A knock at the door has Spartan running to the window and peeking through the blinds. His tail wags just as Jonas opens the door to Penny, Rex, Reznor, Tatyana, and Ashton. Everyone files in and exchanges hugs. The house is abuzz with chatter. Smiles and laughter float around the room easily.

But right now, I feel the odd man out.

Although I'm not the only person without a significant other here, it feels… wrong at my age to be so alone. The moment my thoughts veer down this path, Shelly comes out of nowhere and bumps my shoulder with hers.

"Hey, big brother. What's new?" I wrap my arms around her and lift her from the floor. She squeals and smacks my back. "Put me down, dumbass."

I set her back on her feet and she swats my chest. Hard. "Ow! What was that for?"

"Did you really need to pick me up?"

"Are you my sister?" She rolls her eyes. "Nothing too exciting."

She grabs my hand and leads me out the door to the backyard. "Too crowded in there." She plops down on the lounger and brings me with her. "Life may not be exciting, but surely there must be something you've done since we last spoke."

Gavin and Cora take a seat across from us. Hickory clouds billow from the smoker, thin out with the mild breeze, and scent the air. A Bluetooth speaker shuffle plays rock music near the house. The late April temperature's mild enough to not make you sweat outside this time of day.

Three sets of eyes on me feel like a packed concert crowd.

"Work is much the same. Maybe less chaotic."

"The blonde?" Gavin pipes up and I want to slap him.

"Yep." I grit my teeth.

"What blonde?" Shelly asks Gavin.

Great. Here goes the attention I do not want or need.

"The bartender he banters with. You remember her from our last outing?" Shelly rests a finger on her lips, deep in thought. Gavin trudges forward and I want to smack him upside the head. "The one getting Micah all hot and bothered."

Shelly taps her lips and looks to the heavens. "Must've been otherwise distracted. Tell me more, big brother. What's her name?"

If I don't open up now, Shelly will be on my ass all night. Annoying the hell out of me.

But what is there to say about Peyton? We work together. She drives me absolutely mad, in the best ways. Her body is stellar, and I bet she isn't all fire and claws. Although, I like those aspects of her.

Hanging out with my sister and friends and talking about a woman I work with seems… wrong. Inappropriate. It feels like hair salon gossip. But if I keep my mouth shut, she will spend the next few hours in my face. Then she will pay a visit to Roar. Ogle my every move as Peyton and I work behind the bar. That is the last thing I need.

"You are a pain in my ass," I say.

She sticks out her tongue. "And you wouldn't want me any other way."

I inhale a deep, methodical breath and speak on the exhale. "Her name is Peyton." Shelly jerks back as her brows pinch together. "What?"

"Peyton?" she asks and I nod. "Has to be a weird coincidence."

"What are you talking about?"

"In high school, there was a girl. Peyton. She was a year ahead of Cora—and me, if we'd gone to the same school. Anyway, I remember Cora saying she was super nice, but half the school bullied her. I heard all of the horror stories secondhand, but…"

A fist wraps around my stomach, squeezes and twists. Bile rises up, up, up in my throat.

No. No, no, no.

"Do you remember her last name?" I croak out.

Five seconds feels like five hours as Shelly looks to Cora, then back to me, tilts her head and stares. Written all over her face is *you seriously don't remember* and *how did you not recognize her*. I bite the inside of my cheek until tangy iron hits my tongue.

"Alexander," Cora answers.

I bolt up from my seat and dash around the corner of the house to vomit in the yard. But seeing as I haven't eaten in hours, making room for the feast here, I spend more time dry heaving than actually expelling stomach contents.

A gentle hand rests on my shoulder. Soft floral, citrus, and earthy notes hit my nose. Shelly. As only a sister would, she rubs small circles on my back and remains silent. When I stand up, she hands me a napkin and bottled water.

Without a word, she guides us back to where we sat. The moment I return, I expect everyone's eyes on me. But my friends don't embarrass me with daunting stares and endless questions. When I stepped off, and Shelly followed, they sparked new conversations.

Now that I have returned, though…

"So, I assume you don't remember her from school?" Shelly asks for clarification.

I shake my head before taking a sip of the water. The cool liquid soothes the residual burn in my throat. "No. How do I not remember? People don't change *that* dramatically from high school to early thirties. Do they?"

Shelly turns her attention to Gavin. "You said she's blonde?" Gavin nods as he lifts a beer to his lips. Shelly faces me again. "That's it."

Dear, sister. Please elaborate for the rest of us who cannot hear your thoughts. Sincerely, brother. "What's it?"

"Sorry." Shelly smiles, then taps her temple. "Cora, correct me if I'm wrong. In high school, Peyton wasn't blonde. She was a goth chick. Black hair, black clothes, black everything. It's why…"

The way she trails off sends a chill up my spine. I flashback to high school, some of the best and worst years of my youth. Frame by frame, I search old memories. Try to see Peyton with dark hair and clothes. But I didn't pay attention to girls like Peyton. At least not the type of girl she was then. My preferred type has always remained the same.

Looking through four years of memories will take longer than tonight. Maybe Cora and Shelly will do me a solid and jog my memory with more specifics.

"I hate it when you leave me hanging, Shell." She winces. "Just lay it out. I'm a man. It's why what?"

Shelly finds every means to procrastinate. One small sip of water after another. She eyes Cora, who shrugs and flaunts the *might as well* face. Argh! Any second, I am going to lose it if someone doesn't speak up.

"It's why she was bullied," Shelly says. That wasn't so hard now, was it? "By you."

Wait, what? "Come again." I glance around to my

closest friends. The ones I spent time with during those years. And they all nod at me.

When the hell did I bully Peyton? Pain scrapes my throat as I swallow. I chug half the water as I think harder. When the hell did I bully anyone? My hand fists my hair, tugging at the strands until pain shoots down my neck.

"It happened the year before we started high school," Cora chimes in. "Think she was a year behind you. But the rumors ran wild during my freshman year too. Girls wrote on bathroom tiles with Sharpie, *Peyton Alexander is a slut*. Never stayed on the tile long, but was up again within a day or two. Guys whispered, *Micah Reed called her a slut*, and with your popularity status, people believed. From what I heard, you called her names in the cafeteria in front of half the school."

The nightmare of that day rolls in like an evening thunderstorm—angry and violent. My friends and their lighthearted chatter disappear. A second-by-second replay of the day flashes through my memory.

Mercedes and her bitch friends were annoying the hell out of me that day. Coach had been pressing me to push harder on the track. And Mercedes found me at the perfect moment to verbally bash some unknown girl. Peyton.

All Mercedes ever wanted was to be seen and heard. My popularity on the track team attracted her. But there was nothing about her I deemed attractive. She was a bitch. Through and through.

That day, she pranced over to me and I wouldn't give her the time of day. So she riled me up. Told me the girl in the corner had been eye fucking me for days. Then she told me the girl had slept with half the baseball team and was slut-shaming the guys. In my hazing thoughts, I thought *this bitch isn't messing with any jocks at this school.*

So, I shut her down. Or at least that is what I thought I was doing.

Obviously, I had no moral compass. Instead of opening my mouth, I should have left well enough alone. I should have known Mercedes was a conniving bitch. But I was too wrapped up in myself. Worried some girl would try to ruin what was already toeing the line.

Leaning forward, I rest my elbows on my knees and my face in my hands. "Jesus," I mumble into my palms. "What was I thinking?"

Shelly rubs a hand up and down my back. The motion meant to soothe me. But hatred runs rampant inside me like a viral contagion. "Think of this as a second chance. A way to right your wrong."

"No wonder she hates me. I was so self-absorbed, I gave no fucks about her feelings. Or how my words messed up her life."

"Yes, you screwed up big time." I peek up at my sister and she shrugs. "If Mom and Dad knew, they'd be pissed. All those years of teaching us to put other's thoughts and feelings before our own."

I comb my fingers through my hair and sit up, eyes on

Shelly. Her eyes, just as blue and sparkly as mine, stare back at me with deep sympathy.

"How do I fix this, Shell?"

She takes my hands in hers and holds my gaze. "First, you apologize. Apologize like you never have before. And mean it." I nod and she continues. "Second, you beg for her forgiveness. Grovel if necessary. After what you did to her. After how she was treated during those pivotal years, she may not forgive you. That's her call. You can't just ask for forgiveness, either. Show her you want it."

"How do I do that?"

"Be the man I know you to be. The man Mom and Dad raised. Simple gestures and kind words. They go much further than most expect."

I take mental notes of the sound advice only a sister can provide. "I will."

"And lastly, don't do anything to hurt her. Ever again." I nod and she pokes my chest with a finger. "I mean it, Micah. You already hurt her once. Who knows what would happen if you did again."

When I don't respond, Shelly turns toward Cora and chats about the next bowling or karaoke night. Everyone around me carries on various conversations. Me? I stay in my own head and sort through the onslaught of memories and advice.

Little by little, I devise how I will fix this. Fix what I broke all those years ago. Fix the hatred Peyton harbors.

Because I like her too much to let her hate me any longer.

TWELVE

PEYTON

AFTER A FULL CRANK of the handle, the black-and-white ball rolls down the shoot. I pick it up, twirl it in my fingers, then peer up at the crowd of hopeful eyes.

"B4."

Whack, whack, whack. The slap of bingo markers fills the room, followed with the occasional groan or *yes* with a fist pump.

Ms. Jenkins looks up from her ten-card spread, gives me a thumbs-up and a wink. The woman to her left, Ms. Roberts, darts narrowed eyes to me, then Ms. Jenkins. They exchange words as I crank the handle for the next ball to drop. Ms. Jenkins waves a hand at her, then shakes her head.

"G53," I call the next number, then crank the handle again as the bingo markers create music. "125."

"Bingo!" Mr. Calhoun croaks from three tables back. He lifts his winning card and waves it above his head.

One of the nurses takes the card from him and brings it to me to verify his win. Once I confirm Mr. Calhoun's win, several people ball up their cards and grumble.

Metal chair legs screech against the linoleum in stilted beats as several players inch back and rise from their seats. Ms. Jenkins lets her reading glasses hang around her neck as she stuffs her lucky bingo markers in the seat of her walker. She wheels to the front table where I clean up the bingo cage and master board.

"Sticking around for lunch?" She tugs her pink cardigan closer to her midline.

"Wouldn't miss it. I'll meet you there."

I stare after Ms. Jenkins as she leaves the game room and notice her gait stutters more. Since I started at Gulfside, I have never not noticed her slow pace. But the hobble is new. Seeing her wear herself out to leave the room pinches my heart.

Once I have the game components boxed and stored, I walk over to one of the nurses still in the room.

"Hey, Jim."

"How are you, Peyton?"

I give him a weak smile. "Same old, same old." I shrug. "Hey, is Ms. Jenkins okay? She seems more frail today."

His eyes divert to the door then back to me, lips slightly downturned. The pinch from a moment ago intensifies and I press my palm heel to my chest.

"Last night, she pressed her panic button. When the nurse got to her room, they found her on the floor. She says it was a slip when she walked from the bathroom to her bed. But the nurse thinks she may have fallen out of the bed."

A hand slaps over my mouth. "Oh no!"

"Although she argued, they took her to X-ray. No broken bones. Just bruises—on her hip, arm, and ego."

Ms. Jenkins is a sweetheart. Willing to help anyone in need. Talk your ear off for hours and listen with equal skill. Teach you how to crochet or knit as if she invented the craft. Most importantly, she gives the best hugs. So full of warmth that has nothing to do with temperature. She may be up there in age, but she still has so much love to give.

"Just glad she is okay."

Not sure what I would do or how I would feel if I lost Ms. Jenkins. Seeing her smile and being wrapped in her arms each week provides me with so much love and happiness. A solace I once shared with my grandmother, Isabel. A peacefulness that shattered three years ago when she passed away.

I didn't start working at Gulfside to replace what I lost with my grandmother. But being here with Ms. Jenkins each week helps sew the fissures of my heart. The fault lines that opened when Nana passed. The ones that barely started to heal from losing Dad seven years earlier.

I shoot Aunt Leanne a quick text and tell her I'm eating at Gulfside today. She responds and says we will catch up next week.

Down the corridor from the game room, I hook a left and enter the dining hall. The beige painted walls hold several pictures from over the years. Of staff and residents. Special events and holidays and birthdays. Alongside the photographs are paintings and drawings from current and past residents. Plus, framed posters with beautiful scenery and positive sentiments. Long wooden tables are spread throughout the room, with four chairs on the long sides and one on each end. Each table decorated with a centerpiece for the season. Residents can walk to the counter and get food, cafeteria style. Or they can sit at the tables and have the staff bring food to them.

The setup is pleasant and welcoming and provides a level of independence and community.

At eleven fifteen, the lunch crowd has already packed the room. I shuffle to the end of the line and grab a plastic tray. After I select a sandwich, fruit and water, I pay and find Ms. Jenkins at her usual table.

We catch up for a bit while she enjoys her tomato soup and grilled cheese, and I have my turkey sandwich. She tells me how upset Ms. Roberts was during bingo. Swearing I only called numbers on Ms. Jenkins's cards. Which is laughable.

As lunch fills our bellies, I contemplate how to ask about her fall. Last thing I want to do is upset or embarrass her. But I need to know if she really is okay. Since the day we met, Ms. Jenkins has been nothing but forthcoming and honest with me. It is one of the reasons I love her so much. No beating around the bush.

"So…" She sets her spoon down and grants me her attention. "Jim tells me you had a fall."

Anyone who says eighty-seven-year-old women can't roll their eyes or show indignation needs to meet Ms. Jenkins. Her skills could trample teenagers, which is quite telling.

"He needs to mind his tongue."

I rest a hand on hers. "He only told me because I noticed your limp and I asked about it."

Her other hand pats, then covers mine with a layer of reassurance. "Don't you worry about me. A little fall won't keep me down."

Therein lies the problem. I do worry. If the last decade of my life has taught me anything, it is that time with people you love should never be taken for granted. Losing too many loved ones matured me in many ways. It also inhibited me in others.

People I love? I love them fiercely and let them know often. And I have learned to let smaller fights go when it comes to loved ones.

But losing them also hardened my heart. Made letting new people in that much harder. I loved hard in a few committed relationships, but life just kept throwing me one curveball after another. So, I threw in the towel. My heart couldn't take the endless cycle of pain anymore.

Now, I don't allow myself to travel down the road to love again. Not saying it will never happen. But when heartache knocks on your door over and over again, you find every possible way to not let it in. Turning my heart to ice has been the only method to work.

I appease Ms. Jenkins, but only because she is stubborn and will shut me down if I keep talking about it. "Alright. But if I hear this happens again, you're not allowed to argue about me caring."

"It won't, so the point is moot."

That's it. End of conversation. When Ms. Jenkins puts her foot down, it is best to just bite your tongue and let it go. Although, I plan to check in with the nurses more frequently and have them reach out if something else happens. I may only work here more as mental support, but I adore Ms. Jenkins—and several other residents at Gulfside. They're like a second family.

We finish our lunch in relative silence. After I take our trays to the bin, I help Ms. Jenkins to her feet and we wander from the dining hall, through the community room and exit the double doors that lead outside. I walk at her pace and never give her the impression she needs to hurry.

Today, Ms. Jenkins selects the wooden bench between two old oak trees. The canopy shades the seat, but allows the occasional sunrays to highlight your skin. Birds chirp from the branches as squirrels run from tree to tree in a game of tag. A gentle breeze tames the too warm spring temperatures—not that either of us mind the heat. Hints of jasmine and rose drift in the wind from the flower garden to our left and I let the perfume fill my lungs.

The facility also has a fruit and vegetable garden. Residents with green thumbs are welcome to tend to the plants but aren't required to keep them maintained. The facility has a groundskeeper that checks the plants weekly and tends to any needing attention.

As per usual, we sit the first few minutes in silence. Both of us soaking up the warmth and breathing easier.

"Peyton." Ms. Jenkins rests a hand on my forearm and brushes her thumb over the skin. Her touch is gentle. Soft. Kind. A reminder of my nana. "You worry about me too much." Her words are tender and quiet. "I have lived a full life. And as you get older, things change. Your perception of life, what matters… it all changes."

Why is she telling me this? Has a new health issue come up that I don't know about? I don't like that she talks about herself as if she doesn't have much time left. It unnerves me. Makes my stomach twist in knots. Robs me of breath.

With a slow twist of her body, she faces me head-on. The crinkles near the corners of her eyes and mouth turn up. "I love that you come to see me. That you want to spend time with a cuckoo old bat. But sweetheart, you need to live life too. You're so young. Have so many years ahead of you. Don't waste them visiting me."

I shake my head, unwilling to absorb her words or give them life. "No. You don't get to say that." The backs of my eyes sting. "Coming to see you matters to me."

"Why, Peyton? Not that I don't enjoy our time together. But why does seeing me matter?"

Because you make me smile. Because I love hearing your stories similar to those my nana told. Love how I experience a simpler happiness with you. And how life doesn't feel as messy and complicated when I get to talk with someone wiser.

"Seeing you makes me happy." My thoughts summarized in that singular line. It doesn't matter why. Spending time with this woman makes me happy. Provides some peace.

She pats my forearm, then leaves her hand to rest there. "Okay, Peyton."

The next half hour ticks by with the sun on our shins. We don't speak again until I walk her inside and leave for the day. She gives me a hug and says she will see me tomorrow. As I drive home, pain radiates beneath my rib cage. Pulsing and pounding and unrelenting.

Why did it feel like Ms. Jenkins was saying goodbye?

Reese laughs as Mom regales us with one of the weddings she catered over the weekend.

"Over the years, I have seen every kind of wedding. Or so I thought. But having livestock in the crowd and pictures... definitely new."

"Cows?" Reese asks and Mom nods. "Pigs and chickens?"

"Yep. The whole shebang. Cows, pigs, chickens, goats, horses. Ducks, too."

"Why?" Reese voices the question we all want answered.

Mom shrugs. "Said she grew up on a farm out west.

She moved to Florida two years back to be with her now-husband." My brows lift. "They met through a dating app," she clarifies. "When the couple started planning the wedding, she got the groom's approval for a country theme. But I don't think even he knew how country she meant."

Wow. Just wow.

After being less than cheerful once I left Gulfside, Mom's story definitely lifts my spirits. Not one hundred percent. But some is better than none.

Reese and I attempt to help her make dinner, as we have every other time we visit, and she shoos us away. Suppose that's what you get when your mother cooks and bakes and caters for a living.

Sweet T's isn't a big operation. Mom caters four to five events a week. Most of them office events or weddings with less than a hundred people. She appeals to the masses and is willing to explore all food and baking options with her clients. With two full-time employees working alongside her, they are a booming small business.

I may be biased, but her quiche, almond cake with layered fruit and whipped cream frosting, and macaroons are pure heaven. Being the daughter of a woman who loves the kitchen is never a bad thing. Unless you are concerned about your figure. Which I am not.

"Tracy, you have to take me to the next wedding," Reese tells Mom. "I need these stories firsthand."

She waves a hand at him. "They're not all this outlandish."

"Maybe not, but I love weddings. Don't you, Peyton?" Reese flashes me with sparkling irises.

What the hell is he talking about? Reese and I have never discussed anything wedding related unless chatting with Mom. And never once have I mentioned a love for weddings. Hell, I barely hold on to boyfriends.

"Not so much," I respond with narrowed laser eyes.

Mom adds roasted root vegetables to a serving bowl and the lemon-rosemary chicken to a platter. Without request, Reese takes them to the large cedar table in the dining room. Mom preps the last of the salad as I add a sliced baguette to a basket.

"You two sit. Be back in a sec."

Mom wanders down the hall and disappears from view. Off to get my stepfather, his daughter, and her girl-friend. Who never seem to participate in family time until absolutely necessary.

Don't get me wrong, Harold is a great guy. He loves my mom fiercely, which she needs and deserves after what happened with Dad. His job is safe and nine-to-five typical in the print shop he owns, Designs of the Times. But he is otherwise aloof. At least when I am here. Mom says Harold is simplistic and introverted. When it's just the two of them, he is more outspoken and affectionate.

As for my stepsister, Trina, she just does her own thing. Five years my senior, Trina Williamson struts around like she knows all. I long since gave up offering support or opinions. Since Mom and Harold first started dating three years ago, we have always been cordial with one another. But it isn't difficult to read her body language and determine she would rather not spend time with me or Mom.

As adult children, yes, it is weird to have our parents find new love. Especially when we both had parents we loved. Harold's first wife, Trina's mother, and he divorced when she was thirty. They had been married thirty-one years. But in the last year of their marriage, the misses went through a late midlife crisis. She wanted freedom and independence. With no way to recoup his marriage, Harold agreed to let the love of his life go.

Three years later, he met Mom.

She had a booth set up at the local Saturday market. So did Harold. Before the influx of traffic, Harold stopped at her booth and sampled some of her food. They kept in touch after that day. Harold initially said it was for business, but later told Mom he couldn't stop thinking about her.

Their story of finding love again melts my heart. Mom dealt with major depression after losing Dad. It is one thing to grow apart in a relationship. But when the person you love dies in a tragic, fatal accident, there is no easy way to overcome the pain. Harold helped steer Mom from the darkness. For that, I am eternally in debt to him.

"Hey, guys." Speak of the man. "Sorry I didn't come out sooner. Was finishing up with a new client."

If he can print it, Harold does it. Business cards, fliers, bookmarks, car wraps, trinkets, and more. Harold started his business decades ago. Once a one-man operation,

Designs of the Times has boomed over the last five years. Partly because Harold had nothing but time when he and his ex-wife separated. But also because Mom encouraged and supported him wholeheartedly.

"No worries. We were just catching up with Mom," I tell him.

Trina and her girlfriend, Sierra, walk in. No *hello* or *how's it going* or even eye contact. None of us dislike each other, but Trina isn't fond of her father remarrying. She and Mom get on fine. But Trina loves her own mother and has admitted as much to her father when she thought no one else was listening. Not that she wasn't especially quiet about it.

So, Trina tolerates me and Mom. Her problem, not mine.

After everyone fills their plates, idle chitchat circulates the table. Harold tells us about the new client he and Trina just acquired. Yes, Trina works with her father. It isn't odd they work together, but it surprises me she doesn't want more distance from her parent.

Reese mentions the influx of people at the restaurant and rec center. Mom blathers on about her upcoming week and the next wedding she will cater. Reese immediately jumps in and asks to attend and Mom shakes her head with a laugh.

Then the table goes silent. Too silent.

I glance up from my fork and knife, ready to bring the bite of chicken to my lips, but stop when I notice all eyes are on me.

"What?"

Mom gives a small smile. "I asked what was new with you. Anyone new in your life?"

Oh, lord. Here we go.

Since Mom and Harold fell in love, she has been adamant about finding someone for me. I love my mother's natural determination and desire for me to have the best in life. But her meddling in my love life is *not* something I want to deal with.

I spear the chicken harder than necessary and shove it between my lips. Chewing the bite until it turns soupy won't take long, but at least it gives me a moment to mentally prepare. Because this conversation won't finish with my answer.

"No, Mom."

She sips her wine, then sticks out her lower lip. "Aw, Peyton." I hate when she does that. Makes it sound like my choice to be alone is horrible. "Sweetheart, I know things ended on a sad note with James, but don't let that darken your heart."

James. My last boyfriend. The first guy I had truly loved since Chad—my first everything. James said he would always be there for me, through thick and thin. But when Nana passed, and I mourned, he didn't know how to be there for me during the darker days. Said he didn't know how to make me smile or love me anymore. He went to two joint therapy sessions with me, but couldn't seem to grasp why I didn't easily snap out of my sadness.

Bless his heart for trying, but we drifted apart after a

year and a half together. Deep down, we still had love for each other. We just weren't meant to be more than what we had.

And we were okay with that. Although we broke up two years ago, we still catch up from time to time. His current girlfriend understands our friendship and has zero jealousy when we talk. She is a true woman.

"Mom, James and I are still friends. Nothing about us *darkens* me or my heart."

"I just hate to see you so alone."

Why won't she let this go? I don't want to hurt her feelings, but the continual conversations about relationships make me feel as if she thinks life isn't worthy if you don't have someone at your side.

I take a deep breath and prepare for the calm storm that is Tracy Williamson.

"What if I want to be alone? Have you considered that?"

"Why would you want to be alone?" Her voice shakes slightly.

I stab at the lettuce and cucumber in my bowl. I don't want to fight, not with Mom. But she needs to understand that not every person *needs* another person to have happiness. It is possible to be happy and be single.

"Mom, there's nothing wrong with being single. I come and go as I please. I don't have to worry about upsetting someone if I don't come home immediately from work. I get time to feel comfortable in my own skin, without the pressure of pleasing someone else. The list goes on and on." She goes to speak and I hold up a hand to cut her off. "And before you say something like *what about love...* Mom, I've had love. Twice. One I lost and can never get back. And the other, well, it morphed into a different love. I have come to terms with both of those. But for now, I want time for me. If I get lucky enough to find love again, I will accept it with grace. I won't go hunting for it, though. When it's meant to be..."

"I just feel like you're missing out," Mom mumbles to her plate.

Mom is the second person to indicate as much to me today. Although Ms. Jenkins didn't necessarily mean love, she thought I was missing out on life by hanging out with elderly folks.

Everyone at the table falls silent. Not that Trina or Sierra have said much anyway. I didn't raise my voice at Mom, but this is the first time I have really laid it all out in front of others. Reese knows how I feel. He teases me about dating every once in a while, but he gets that I'm enjoying me time. Mom, on the other hand, doesn't seem to get why I want independence. Maybe because she loved belonging to someone. It made her whole.

But I want the ability to feel whole *without* someone. Once I achieve that, being with another person is a bonus.

The rest of dinner goes by with quieter, blander conversation. After we help Mom clean up, Reese and I exchange hugs with Mom and Harold and say our goodbyes.

Back at home, Reese and I change into comfy clothes

and he tells me to grab my Caboodles box of nail polish. The very same Caboodles I have had since high school. Once upon a time, it held only black polish, black mascara, black eyeliner, and shades of black shadow. Now, a rainbow of polish rests inside. Nothing else.

Reese plops down on the sofa with two bottles of beer and chips. After he tears the bag open and pops the top from the beers, he grabs my feet and starts rubbing them.

"Did Mama T upset you tonight?"

I shake my head and moan as he massages the ball of my foot. "No. Just wish she'd let me live life how I want."

"She means well."

"Yeah, I know. Her persistence frustrates me, I guess. It's like she doesn't understand that women don't *have* to be in a relationship to be happy."

"True." Reese switches to my other foot. "But all she knows is her own experiences. It's hard to speak of what you don't know or understand."

"I get that." Grabbing my bottle from the table, I take a sip. "But after countless conversations, you'd think she'd understand *my* stance on the matter. I love that she wants me to be happy. But she doesn't get that romantic relationships don't always equal happiness."

Reese grabs his beer from the table and extends it toward mine to clink necks. "Cheers to that." We both drink, then set our bottles down. "So... you went out with Micah the other night."

"Not now."

When I agreed to eat at Teddy's with Micah, I texted

Reese. All I got in return was a slew of emojis and obnoxious GIFs.

"Fine. But we will talk about it. I don't care what does or doesn't come of it, we will discuss Micah Reed."

"Fine," I agree with a huff. "For now, will you just paint my toenails."

"Only if you do mine." Reese drops his feet in my lap and wiggles his toes. "I'm feeling the sky blue." I grab said blue from the Caboodles along with the bottle for my toes. I toss it at Reese and he looks at the color. "Really?"

"Yep."

"You got it."

For the next hour, we decorate each other's toes. Reese's in a bright baby blue. Mine in a rich, bold red. The color I reserve for when I want something. Thing is, I don't exactly know what I want. Mom's and Ms. Jenkins's words continue to ring through my head.

Is it true? Am I missing out?

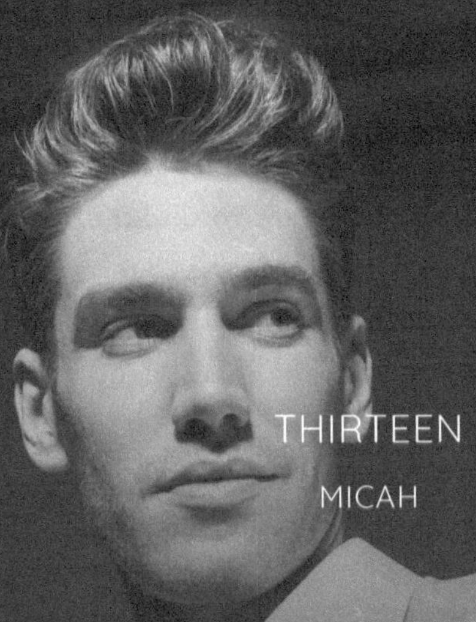

THIRTEEN

MICAH

PEYTON HASN'T BEEN the same since last Saturday. Can't pinpoint what is different, but something just seems *off*.

Wednesday and yesterday, we only spoke when absolutely necessary. Every time I peeked in her direction, she appeared lost. Somewhere besides Roar. Eyes staring off in the distance, but without focus. She chatted with patrons in the bar, but her conversations lacked their typical zeal. Her harrowing smiles seemed forced.

Between the early morning hours of Sunday, when we parted ways at Teddy's, and early Wednesday evening, something shifted in Peyton's world.

But my life and perspective had shifted too.

After the conversation at Jonas and Autumn's Sunday night, I didn't sleep for shit. Didn't get much sleep the two days following, either.

What I had done to Peyton all those years ago weighed heavily on my mind and heart. Made me twitchy and restless, night after night. I had lain awake in bed for hours and replayed all the horrible words I'd said to and about her. Each night, I counted the bubbles in the popcorn ceiling to distract myself or fall asleep from boredom. But it neither distracted nor induced boredom. To my amazement and pitifulness, the highest I counted was 412. The only reason I stopped… the wind kicked up outside, swept the tree branch near my window and the dancing shadow caught my attention.

Exhaustion is no comparison to how I feel. My cement-pillar legs drag with each step forward. My lead-beam arms and robotic hands move only because my mind wills them to. Thank goodness my lungs and heart do their job without directive.

Did our conversation Saturday upset her? Dredge up old memories?

I grit my teeth and hang my head, ashamed at the person I was to her years ago. Had my parents known how I behaved back then—especially to a girl—they would have had me booted from the track team and on house arrest for months.

The question now is… how do I fix this? How do I make up for the asshole juvenile I once was? Will she forgive me and my deplorable behavior? Or will she forever harbor hatred for me in her heart?

When a crowd favorite booms through the speakers, the horde of bodies shifts from the bar to the dance floor.

I inch closer to Peyton, her eyes downcast, and

focused on the glass she has cleaned three times. I knock her shoulder and she lifts her gaze and blinks.

"Everything alright? Seems like you're somewhere else tonight."

She smiles, but it doesn't reach her eyes. "Yes. No. I don't know."

"Want to talk about it?"

One shoulder shrugs as she sets the glass down. "Not now. Another time, maybe."

Seeing Peyton like this stirs the memories I recalled this past week. Although I was a royal prick to her, I did see her around school. I honestly don't recall any feelings for her—positive or negative. Back then, Peyton was just a random girl. Day after day, week after week, month after month, she remained the same. Decked head to toe in black. Baggy pants and a hoodie with the hood up. A black-and-white, checker-print backpack hooked on both shoulders. A folder, textbook, and mass market-sized book clutched close to her chest. Head up, but eyes on the ground.

Yes, Mercedes and her twat gang of besties got me to call Peyton a slut. But when I caught sight of her during my senior year, I wondered why those girls had it out for her. Were they jealous of her individuality? Did they envy she had male friends without having to put out? Was it her curves that had them calling her names and spreading lies? Or were they just bitches who refused to like people not similar to them?

Not that it matters now, but I think it was all of the

above. Plus, Peyton wasn't a follower. Still isn't. She does her own thing, in her own time.

Before she walks off, I wrap a hand around her forearm. Her eyes drop and stare at her arm a beat before she lifts her gaze. "Meet me at Teddy's after work," I say with an added softness in my voice. Hoping she doesn't hear it as a demand.

Her eyes dart between mine. Brows twitch imperceptibly. Glassiness highlights the gray flecks in her vibrant violet irises. She licks, then tucks her lips between her teeth.

Not sure why, but she looks on the verge of tears.

The chambers of my heart contract and expand faster. An ache climbs from beneath my ribs and up my throat, lodging itself at my Adam's apple and swelling. I swallow and it does nothing to taper the sensation. To quell the emotion stuck firmly in place.

The overwhelming urge to hug her weighs my limbs. To haul her into me and press her close to my chest. Wrap my arms around her waist, squeeze tight and slide a hand up her spine to her neck. To feel her breath and heat on my skin.

"I'll think about it," she says hoarsely.

I drop my hand and she drifts to the end of the bar. A smile dons her face, but the gesture is all for show. The feisty and vivacious woman that lights up the bar four nights a week is nowhere to be found. In her place is a woman with a difficult past and wounded heart.

Hopefully tonight, she will let me heal part of her wound.

Neck deep in logging invoices, I press the heels of my palms to my eyes. This is what happens when I lose focus. Shit piles up. Work doesn't get done and mounts up day by day.

Invoices don't necessarily take long to input. But my mind has been elsewhere this week. Focused on a woman I hope joins me later at the diner.

"Only a dozen more to go. Just get it done, Reed."

The stack thins as I key stats into the spreadsheet. Three invoices from the bottom, a knock at the door startles me out of my zone. Then it swings open. I finish keying in the line, then look up to see who entered.

Peyton stands just inside the door, the fingers of one hand picking at the nails on the other.

"What's up?" I swivel in the chair to face her head-on.

"Three things." I lift my brows. "Yes, I'll meet you at Teddy's later." A corner of my mouth kicks up, but falls flat as she winces. "Dan has an issue with someone's ID at the door. And Ted is trying to break up a fight near the bar."

"Shit." I bolt from my chair and race out the door with

Peyton on my heels. "Let Dan know I'll be at the door as soon as I'm done with Ted."

"On it."

The moment I round the end of the hall, chaos smacks me in the face. A crowd encircles Ted and two men. A woman hovers behind one of the men and I assume she is the reason the two men are throwing punches.

When I approach, Ted spots me with wide eyes. He has one man pinned in his grip, but the other won't calm down. I step between the two and get in the free man's face.

"Back the fuck up," I yell.

His bloodshot, glassy eyes wobble as he stares me down. He holds his ground; well, rocks a little. "Asshole touched my wife."

I step into him but don't make contact. Yet. "I said, back the fuck up."

The man peers over my shoulder with narrowed eyes. Jaw muscles taut. Shoulders to his ears. He jabs his finger in the direction of the other man. "I ever see your face again, you best run." He meets my gaze, takes a step back and nods. "I mean no disrespect. But no one touches my woman without permission or repercussions."

I lift both my hands to either side of my face. "I get it, man. But take the fight outside. Can't be having that shit in here." I peer over my shoulder at Ted and lift my chin. He escorts the other man to the door and I turn back to face the couple. "You're welcome to stay. But no fights."

He extends a hand and we shake before I walk to the

door to resolve issue two. Thankfully, this resolves much faster. Fake or forged IDs get spotted easily with all the UV lighting. The hardest part is convincing the person we know it is tampered with. The old days of laminated or non-hologram licenses are long gone. Fakes are easier to spot and confiscate.

"Your fakes may work at other bars and clubs, but not this one. Have a good night." I take the ID, grab the scissors we keep at the podium near the door, and cut the ID into jagged pieces. Then walk off as the punk curses me out.

Back in the office, I collapse in the chair behind the desk and run my fingers through my hair. I love my job, but sometimes it sucks.

I love the fast pace and upbeat energy that bleeds from the walls and floats in the air. The thump of the bass and pitch of the treble. The bright lights and dark corners. The smiles and bright eyes and exhilaration. I love it all. Hell, I even love the desk work. Filling orders and spreadsheets. Writing schedules and implementing procedures. Inventory is a beast, but I do it with a smile on my face.

But every once in a while, my job comes with a pile of bullshit.

The occasional bar fight over women or spilled drinks. Fake IDs and dealing with underage people trying to enter. Idiots harassing the staff or touching them inappropriately. Dealing with people who can't settle their tab.

Each instance is never pretty, but most resolve without bloodshed or police.

I focus back on the computer and the last of the invoices. *Almost done.* Just finish the last of the desk work and wrap the night up behind the bar. Get the brunt of the work done, then round out the work night with Peyton nearby.

With a deep breath, I pick up where I left off. Line by line, I input the last of the invoices and save the spreadsheet to the cloud. Once everything is filed away and I straighten up the desk, I roll back the chair and exit the office.

Smile on my face, an extra bounce in my step, I walk down the hall and out to the bar. Peyton glows like the sun. Her bright smile hasn't quite returned, but I hope to make it shine again later.

Peyton agreed to meet me at Teddy's. And tonight, I will man up and apologize for every time I hurt her in our formative years. I pray she accepts and allows me to make it up to her. However she deems worthy.

Peyton saying yes gives me hope. I hold on to that hope with every ounce of strength I own. Because hope is all I have right now.

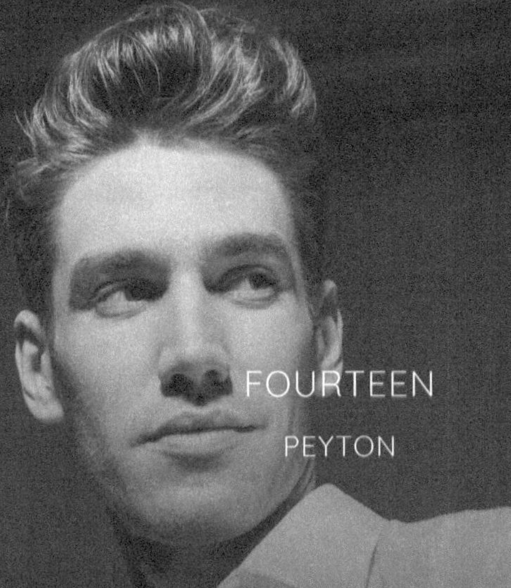

FOURTEEN

PEYTON

I REALLY WANTED to say no to Micah when he asked me to Teddy's after work. But the severity in his eyes wouldn't let the word slip between my lips. When I said I would think about it, I hoped my resolve would strengthen. That the word *no* would fall from my tongue with greater ease.

Alas, it did not.

Which leads to now. Me, parking my SUV and getting out to join Micah inside the bustling diner up the street.

We step inside and the hostess seats us right away. More than half the tables are occupied. Conversation and laughter erupt from all corners and the spaces between. The hostess seats us near a back corner. The two tables near us empty.

"Thanks for agreeing to meet me here again."

I nod and scan the menu. Although I always order the same thing, I feel a change of pace might be nice. Just as the server steps up and deposits water glasses on the table, I decide on the two egg breakfast with crispy bacon, home fries, and a biscuit. Micah orders the same as last time and we both ask for coffee.

The server takes our menus and wanders off to check on another table before going to the kitchen.

"So, why'd you ask me here?"

Micah fiddles with the edge of the paper placemat and avoids my gaze. His reluctance to speak or make eye contact has me curious and a little on edge. Since last weekend, Micah has been… different. Quieter. Hesitant whenever he gets within twenty feet.

This side of Micah piques my interest. What makes a man like Micah Reed soft?

"First and foremost," —he finally meets my eyes— "I want to apologize."

Is this *the apology*? An apology fifteen years overdue, but necessary. Is Micah Reed about to apologize for being one of the most epic assholes?

Slow down, Peyton. Best not to assume and get my hopes up. For all I know, the apology may have something to do with Roar.

"For?" I clutch the hem of my shirt beneath the table until my knuckles burn and nails bite my skin through the fabric.

His lips tilt up a fraction at the corners. The smile loaded with sympathy and regret.

This is it, isn't it? *The* moment. Would it be wrong to take out my phone, open the camera, switch it to video, and record this moment for posterity? Would he tell me to not act so childish? Tell me to take the moment seriously?

When you wait for a moment such as this for more than a decade, wanting to document it isn't strange. After living with self-doubt and being taunted for years, wanting to replay the moment one of the instigators apologizes is *not* wrong.

"I think you know what for." He tilts his head and holds my gaze with watery eyes.

"Humor me."

He yanks his hand from the paper placemat that now misses bits of the lower right corner. His hands drop to his sides. And by the way he shifts, I wonder if he now sits on his hands.

"Peyton, I was young and stupid. What I did to you… What those girls provoked me to do to you…" He drags his lips between his teeth and looks to the side for the count of three before meeting my gaze. His eyes red and veiny. "I'm sorry for the things I said to you and about you in high school. They weren't true. It was all a ruse to make a jealous, egotistical *girl* feel better about herself. It was wrong of me to say and I am truly sorry."

Frozen is the only rational term to explain my physical and mental state. Frozen.

Micah Reed just apologized. To me. Of his own volition. He admitted his words and actions were wrong and cruel and hateful. The bidding of a girl—a bully—who would do whatever it took to make those not in her circle feel worthless. But he owned the role he played in it all.

Nervous energy zips through my limbs and begs for me to jump off the seat. To garner the attention of everyone in the diner. To scream at the top of my lungs, *"Micah Reed apologized."* The words *I'm sorry* left his lips and hit my ears.

Weight lifts from my shoulders. My teenage self sags with a sigh in my mind. His apology doesn't wash away all the hurtful words and unkind acts he and his group of friends enacted. But his apology heals some of the old wounds that marred my heart long ago.

I hold his gaze as I stretch out my fingers. His normally bold blue eyes are dull and damp. Lips firmly tucked between his teeth as he fights his body's inclination to cry.

This apology is real. From the heart. Sincere and honest. Exactly what I waited all this time to hear.

"Thank you."

He sucks in a breath, then turns his head to the side. A hand meets the cheek not facing me and swipes. Then a tear rolls down the other cheek and I drop my eyes to the table. Grab my napkin-rolled silverware and unravel it. Toy with the tacky napkin band. Organize my silverware on the placemat—fork on the left, knife on the right, spoon at the top.

I give him this moment. Let him soak it up. Give him a chance to process the reality of what happened years ago, bask in the ownership he just took, and the apology only he could deliver. Couldn't have been easy. Owning the atrocities of your past never should be.

Once he collects himself, though, I have questions.

The server stops at the table, grabs each of our empty mugs in turn, and fills them with coffee. Then sets a thermal carafe on the table and walks off.

Micah tears open several packets of sugar and dumps them in his mug while I add one and some creamer. Our spoons clink the mugs in tandem with each other. Like synchronized swimmers, we both lift our mugs, blow on the steamy caffeine and sip the nectar of the gods. Although, I still don't understand how he tastes the coffee with that much sugar.

He sets his mug in the center of the placemat but doesn't remove his hands. Eyes on his thumbs as he paints them along the rim. Then he meets my gaze. His addictive lapis-blue eyes still a bit dull, but more beautiful. Raw. Real.

I swallow and try to quell the flurry rising and expanding in my chest.

"Now it makes sense."

"What?" I choke out.

"The instant hatred you had for me. It makes sense. I would've acted the same."

Arms at my sides, I lean forward and press my chest against the table, eyes locked with his. "How did you not know?"

"Who you were?" I nod and lean back. He lifts a shoulder, then drops it. "Guess I just forgot. Does that make me more of an asshole? Probably. But it's the truth.

With the exception of track and my closest friends, high school is just a blur."

Wish it was a blur for me. Wish there was some way to make all the horrible memories and name calling and stunts vanish. Hypnotherapy. A magic pill. Years of speaking with a therapist helped, but it never made the memories disappear.

But all things happen for a reason.

If it weren't for those girls bullying me and the guys following their lead, I wouldn't be who I am now. Without their hurtful words and acts, I may not have thick skin. I may not be as bold and outspoken. Who knows… I could have ended up as some doormat.

There are no pros to bullying. No justifiable reasons to be hateful. But I found strength and courage and ferocity because of my high school experience. Yes, there were definitely some low points, but I had Mom and Dad to help me keep my head high. To not let me drown in the trenches. And for that, I am a new woman.

"One day, I hope it disappears for me too."

His back stiffens and eyes go wide. "I didn't mean it like that," he rushes out.

"Yeah, I know." He sags against the seat. "What I mean is, I hope enough time passes that I don't let those memories own me anymore." I lift the mug to my lips and sip. "What made you remember?"

"Shelly." I scrunch my brows and tilt my head. "My sister," he clarifies. "She was two years behind me, one behind you. She went to a different school, but her best friend, and mine, attended ours. And friends talk."

"Ah."

"Shelly, my friends, and I get together often. Gavin, my best friend, asked how work with *the blonde* was." I perk up at this. "They were in Roar a while back and noticed us barking at each other." He laughs and I join.

"Our bickering is an art form."

"Indeed. Anyway, I guess neither Cora nor Shelly had paid attention or were focused on the dance floor that night. They never saw your face. But when I said your first name the other night, they probed me for answers."

"That must've hurt." I smirk at him.

"Ha ha." He turns up the corner of his mouth and makes a goofy face. "Then, they took me on a trip down memory lane." His eyes drift to the table, then back up. "If it makes you feel better, it made me sick. Literally."

"It doesn't. But I'm glad you weren't okay with it. Says a lot."

"Peyton, I—"

The server interrupts Micah to set plates on the table. Once the buffet is spread out, the server double-checks the carafe, then leaves.

"Peyton, I may not be the best guy out there. I have done plenty of stupid and horrible shit. Shit I'm not proud of. Haven't we all. But adult me is disgusted by teenage me."

I break the egg yolk, spear some home fries and dunk

them. Micah stares, fascination glittering his eyes as I bring the yolky potatoes to my lips.

"What?" I mumble around my food with zero care for manners.

"That's cute."

Cute? Eating food is cute? Or is he mocking how I eat now?

I grab a strip of bacon and crunch down on it. "Define cute."

He shakes his head with a laugh. "Don't know many other people who do that." He points his fork at my runny egg. "Break the over-easy yolk to dunk their potatoes."

"And toast," I interject.

His head tips back and he laughs before leveling with me again. "And toast." Inch by inch, he leans closer. Face over the center of the table. "Like me," he whispers.

I stop chewing. Stop breathing. My body frozen and eyes unblinking as I stare straight ahead. The gold flecks in his rich-blue eyes twinkle. Is he serious? Or just yanking my chain?

"Are you making fun of me?"

A shadow passes over the line of his jaw. His smile flattens out. But that damn twinkle is still there.

"No. Definitely not." The corners of his lips curve up. "Never again," he states with reverence.

The muscles in my jaw contract as I chew the remaining bacon. "Good." I point the last of the bacon strip at him. "Wouldn't want to hurt you." Then I shove the bacon in my mouth.

"Might like that," he mumbles and sits back.

I drop my focus to the table, pick up my toast and dunk the corner of the triangle in the yolk. Peeking through my lashes, I spy a look I have never seen on Micah Reed's face. A look I never thought him capable of portraying.

Less than three feet away, eyes on his plate, fingers toying with his fork, Micah Reed blushes. At this time of night, others may pass it off as a night of partying or too much alcohol. But the only thing he's had to drink tonight is Dr Pepper and coffee.

Since our food arrived, I noticed slight variations in Micah's posture. Less rigidity. His spine not as straight and arms not as stiff. The fidgeting has also tapered off. As if he carries a new level of comfort. With me.

Other hallmarks I notice… more softness. The ridge of his cheekbone and how it accentuates his masculinity. The plumpness of his lips and the way they transform when he looks me in the eye. Firmer edges. The angle of his jaw, the light dusting of stubble, and the straight line of his nose until just the end where it bends slightly left. A gentleness. The way his lashes splay and stick beneath his eyes when on the cusp of crying.

When was the last time I saw a man cry? Saw them spill their emotions for all to see. I don't recall.

Maybe when I was seven and fell from the tree in the backyard. When Dad rushed from the deck chair, cradled me gingerly in his arms, and asked if there was pain. Was he crying then? The memory is there, but I don't see his face as clearly as I once did. Not without photographs or home movies.

We finish eating in relative silence. But a new tension builds between me and Micah. A tension I never would have imagined possible with this man. A man who currently has one leg between mine while the other skirts the outside. He has yet to touch me, but I *feel* how close he is. All it would take is the slightest move from either of us and we'd make contact. And hell… my skin flames from the near touch.

The server clears our plates and leaves the check. And just like last time, Micah snatches it first. He throws me a boyish, flirty smile and I can't help but smile in return. Once he pays and I leave a tip on the table, we walk toward my car.

Near the hatch, I stop and face him, hands fidgeting with the hem of my shirt. Why does this suddenly feel like the end of a date? This isn't a date.

Keep telling yourself that, girl.

"Peyton…" Micah stares over my shoulder, but his eyes seem out of focus. Then he blinks and brings his gaze back to mine. "Hope you believed me earlier when I apologized. I meant it. I mean it."

I nod. "Thank you, Micah. And I do."

He takes a step closer. Close enough to touch me without effort. "And I hope you can forgive me. Don't expect you to right here and now. But one day. I'd like…"

His eyes drop to my lips and I lick them. He follows the movement but doesn't speak.

"What?" Bright eyes leap to mine. "What would you like?" My voice low and rumbly.

Hundreds of words and phrases flash in his eyes. Across his face. His lips part, he takes a breath then closes them. He does this again and again. Unspoken words on the tip of his tongue. Wanting. Waiting. Hopeful.

"It's been a long time since I've smiled and laughed this much." He nibbles his bottom lip, then swallows. "And I have zero expectations of anything." He shoves his hands in his pockets. "I'd like if we can be…"

If we can be what?

Why am I sweating so much? And in the most awkward places.

"If we can be…" I parrot his words and drag them out.

"Friends." Oh. Friends. Why was part of me hoping he would say something else? Jesus, he only just apologized. He notices my shift and jumps back in. "Unless you're not okay with that."

"No," I answer, too quick and rowdy. "Yes. Sorry." He laughs as I straighten out my thoughts. "Yes, we can be friends."

"Good." He takes another step closer. His eyes all I see now. And then he wraps his arms around me and presses me to his chest. "Really am sorry, Peyton."

My arms encircle his waist as I rest my chin on his shoulder. Do friends hug like this? Opposite-sex friends. Reese and I hug all the time. But Reese is more of a brother, someone I have been close with for decades, and someone I ask for advice. Micah is definitely not in the same spectrum as Reese.

His breath hot on my neck, I close my eyes. Then the breeze cools my cheeks and neck as Micah takes a step back.

"Drive safe, hellcat." Another step back and a wink. "See you tomorrow."

I lift a hand and wave. "Tomorrow."

In the car, I press the ignition, buckle my seat belt and stare out the windshield. The radio plays, but all I hear is white noise. The lights from the dash brighten the cab, but I zone out into the dark night.

Micah drives off and waves as he goes. I mimic the movement but don't focus. Not really.

Tonight, Micah Reed apologized. More than once. Then, just minutes ago, asked for my forgiveness. Said he wants to be friends. But his flirtatious behavior and his arms around me screamed much more than friendship. Those sweet smiles and warm touches and soft tones spoke volumes. Of what happens beyond friendship.

And that nickname. Hellcat. That is new. Well, he muttered it once before, but I don't think he meant for me to hear it.

Damn, am I confused. Thrown off. Flabbergasted.

"What the hell just happened?" The question of the hour. One I have no idea how to answer.

FIFTEEN

MICAH

WHAT THE HELL was I thinking? Hugging Peyton had not been part of the plan. Not by a long shot. But now that I had, I wanted to hug her again. And with more frequency.

God, she was so warm in my arms. So responsive. Her minty coconut smell, potent and intoxicating and addictive.

How long had I wanted to do that? Hold her in my arms. Inhale her fragrance. Be impossibly close to her. Can't recall a day since she started at Roar where Peyton hasn't crossed my mind. Her fiery spirit wouldn't let me forget.

But I wanted more. More than the borderline friendly hug we exchanged.

What I wouldn't give to trace the tip of my nose along the bridge of hers. Taste her plump lips and impassioned tongue. Feel her soft skin under my fingers, her hot breath on my neck. Her gasp at my ear. And those brilliant violet eyes… I want them on me. Everywhere.

"Hey, big brother."

I jolt on the barstool at the high-top table as Shelly rounds it and parks across the table. Judgment billows off her as she narrows her eyes.

"Hey," I choke out, then clear my throat.

"Everything alright?"

"Yeah. Of course," I answer too quickly. "Why?"

Eyes that match mine rake over my face. Study every crease, line, and twitch. Search for clues why I jumped at her presence—something I have never done. But my poker face is strong and she gives up sooner than expected.

She huffs, sets her purse down, and laces her fingers on the table between us. This is Shelly's way of telling me we aren't leaving this table until I speak the truth.

Great.

"Micah, I have known you my entire life." *Here we go.* I roll my eyes. "Which means I pick up on everything. *Everything.*" Her added emphasis makes me squirm in place.

I shift my gaze to the parking lot through the window. Get momentarily lost as the sunlight gleams on the row of cars. When I look back to my sister, her brows lift and lips purse.

"Can we at least order lunch first?"

"Fine."

She snatches a menu from the metal clip on the table

caddy. Not that she needs to read it. This bar and grill is a regular destination for our group. More during the evenings for karaoke, drinks, and laughter. But if I have more than half the menu memorized, she has the entire thing etched in stone. She, Cora, and Jonas ate here once or twice a week before Gavin moved back. Now, it's half that—which is still more often than my attendance.

A guy sporting a black polo with the bar logo sidles up to the table. He sets glasses of ice water in front of us. "Hey, Shelly."

The flush on my sister's cheeks poses new questions. "Hey, Tom."

He glances my way. "Micah." I give a polite smile and lift my chin. "What can I get you guys?"

Shelly and I place our orders. Tom scribbles them on his small notepad, tosses a stellar smile at Shelly, then walks off.

"What was that?" I gesture over my shoulder with a thumb.

With a slight shift to the left, she peers over my shoulder, then straightens. "Tom and I have gone on a couple of dates."

"Really?" I ask with humor in my tone.

She narrows her eyes and jabs the air with a finger in my direction. "Don't try to distract me from what's going on with you." I mentally sag but show no emotion. Both her forearms rest on the table as she leans closer. "What *is* happening, Micah?"

Sometimes, I wish I hated talking with my sister. Wish

we weren't as close as we are. Don't get me wrong, I love Shelly. Would walk through fire for her. But when the more intimate topics come up—my dating life and hers—we both tend to clam up. There are just certain topics and details siblings shouldn't discuss. Right?

No matter how much I dance around answering her, she won't let up. Like when we were kids and she followed me on her bike. I had told her I wanted to play with boys my age, not my little annoying sister. But she never backed down. She pedaled faster. Kept pace with me. Told me boys and girls can play together. And her refusal to play with only girls led to us bonding more each year. If two years didn't separate us, people would swear we connected like twins.

Unwrapping the straw, I jab it between the ice and take a sip of water. Desperate to swallow past the nervous clump in my throat. This is Shelly. My sister. The one person I can spill all my truths to. She may be judgmental a moment, but once she processes, that harsh criticism falls away.

"I apologized."

She tilts her head and regards me for three, two, one. A light kicks on in her thoughts as her eyes grow wide. "To Peyton?" I nod and take another drink from the glass. "How'd that go?"

"Better than expected."

When I don't expand, she lifts a brow. "Elaborate for me, big brother."

Conversations with Shelly will never be basic. Will

never be brief. We come from the same parents, were raised the exact same way, and will always want more details. To understand all the ins and outs in full description.

So, I lay it all out for Shelly. Tell her how I mulled over what to say all week. How I didn't say anything unnecessary to Peyton until last night. That I asked her to Teddy's after work—which piqued her interest and created a slight detour. A detour where I tell her we had gone there once already.

When I veer back to the original topic at hand, I explain how the apology went down. How I only remembered what happened all those years ago after talking with my sister and her friend. How my behavior made me physically ill.

"Shell, she accepted my apology with such grace. Made me feel worse."

Reaching across the table, her hands wrap around mine. "If you'd actually taken the time to know Peyton years ago, you would've learned then that she's pretty great. But everything happens for a reason. Cora said she kept to herself and had a small circle of friends. And that she was always with a tall guy with dark hair." I lift a brow and Shelly reads my curiosity. "Reese, I think. Her best friend. Anyway… my point is Peyton is kind and genuine. Your reaction is normal. That's called guilt, big brother. And feeling it, owning it, admitting it is a step in the right direction."

Is Reese the guy who occupied her attention in Roar last weekend?

The eight days since I watched Peyton smile and laugh with that guy feel more like months. Never-ending, nails-on-the-chalkboard months. I had never seen her so relaxed and carefree as I did that night. The way she leaned his direction. How easily she gave him the smile I wanted from her. Her comfort with another man made my skin crawl and blood pressure rise. Made my thoughts scatter like fall leaves on a windy day.

But if they were friends... well, that changes everything.

Did he come into Roar to intentionally provoke me? Was the idea hers or his? The answer makes all the difference. If it was his, I would venture to guess he was making a statement. Flaunting how incredible Peyton is and how easy it is to *not* have her. To say *see what I have and you don't, asshole.*

But... if it was Peyton's idea. That opens a whole new door.

If she asked her friend to fake flirt with her all night to piss me off, it says I cross her mind more than inside those four walls. That thought alone has my ego high above the powdery clouds.

Best not to get ahead of myself, though. Not without answers. Shelly is right. First, I need to absorb what my apology to Peyton means and where it leads us next.

"Have I told you lately how much I love you?"

She brings a finger to her lips and taps, eyes skyward

to the left. "Hmm." Tap, tap, tap. "I'm drawing a blank, big brother. Better tell me again."

"You're ridiculous." I ball up my straw wrapper and fling it at her. "But you know I love you."

Her mouth drops open as she picks up the offending paper projectile and launches it back at me. "Love you, too."

Just then, Tom reappears with burgers and fries. His eyes dart between us and he sets our plates down with too much ease. Soon as his hands are free, he shoves them in his back pockets and gives Shelly a sheepish smile.

"Anything else I can get you?" His voice shakes.

"I'm good." Shelly smiles at him, then looks to me. "Need anything, brother?" The word brother leaves her lips louder than the rest.

Does this guy think Shelly is on a date with me? By definition, this is a date. Between two siblings. Zero romanticism going on here. But the fact she needed to clarify who I was says this guy is not only insecure, but has no clue who I am to Shelly. Yes, he knew my name because I frequent the place. But his knowledge doesn't extend much further.

When his shoulders drop and eyes land on me, he appears less concerned. I may not be of romantic interest for my sister, but *who* I am should bother him. Shelly is my baby sister. Which makes me her overprotective, overbearing big brother. That should make him shake in his Nikes, not sigh in relief.

So, I pull an asshole move. Because that is what big brothers are for.

"Thought I asked for a side of barbeque." Tom's brows pinch in the middle and Shelly huffs.

Tom goes from at ease to freaked out in point five seconds. "Shoot. Sorry, man. I'll go grab that." He scurries off to the kitchen without another word.

The moment he's out of earshot, I laugh. Shelly throws a fry at my face and I dodge it. "Not funny, asshole." I laugh harder. "And you didn't ask for a side of anything. Why are you being a dick?"

I pick up the fry she hurled and toss it in my mouth. "Because that's what big brothers do."

Tom rematerializes and deposits a full dipping cup of barbeque sauce on the table. "Sorry again. Anything else?" I bite my tongue at his shortness of breath.

"We're good. Thanks, Tom," Shelly answers. The guy flashes her an award-winning smile then leaves us to our lunch.

"What's going on with you and him?"

Rather than answer me, she scoops up her burger and takes the biggest bite possible. She did this to avoid speaking for the next however many minutes, but I pick at my fries and wait for her to finish chewing. Once she swallows down the last of it, she takes a sip of water and pretends I'm not waiting on her answer.

"Shell?"

She shakes her head. "Ugh. Why can't you just move past this?"

"Because I'm your brother. Why do you want me to?" If that guy so much as laid a hand on her without permission, I will kick his ass.

"No reason." She sighs and hangs her head. "Tom is nice. Like I said, we've been on a couple dates." Picking up a fry from her plate, she swirls it in the ketchup over and over.

"But..." I drawl out the word. "Has he... done something you're uncomfortable with?"

Twin eyes bolt to mine. Her head shakes furiously. "No. No, Micah." She drops the fry and wipes her hands with the napkin. "He's actually been sweet. Never makes me feel pressured."

"Good. 'Cause I'd kick his ass."

"I don't know. It's just..." She trails off and I give her a moment to collect her thoughts. "Have you talked to Mom in the last week?"

I search my memory for the last time I spoke with either of our parents. Last I remember was a few weeks back. "No. Why?"

"Well, she called me a couple nights ago. Said she'd call you, too. Anyway, she wants to start regular family dinners. Like scheduled dinners once a month or every two weeks. I don't remember the specifics."

"Okay... is that a bad thing?"

Shelly speaks with and sees Mom and Dad more often than I do. But I don't see anything wrong with spending more time with them. Maybe I am missing something.

"Normally, I'd say no. But Mom started dropping hints."

"Dropping hints?"

"Shelly, your father and I aren't getting any younger." She mocks our mother's voice. *"Would love to have more Reeds to love."*

"What?" Not sure if Mom is insinuating what I think she is, but I sure as hell hope not.

"Yep." She pops the *p*. "Mom basically told me she wants grandbabies. Seeing as neither of us is in a relationship" —her eyes dart across the bar to where I assume Tom stands— "that's not happening anytime soon."

"Are you not in a relationship with Tom?" I whisper-ask, unsure of his presence.

A huff leaves her lips. "He's nice. Treats me well. And I can tell he wants more." She looks over my shoulder again. "But I don't."

"Then you need to end it. Don't drag it out. It'll just make it worse."

"Yeah, I know." She stares down at her plate and shoves a fry in her mouth. "After that talk with Mom, it got me thinking." She peers up and winces. "Please don't be weirded out."

I place a hand over my heart. "Promise I won't be."

Shelly takes a deep breath, places her palms flat on the table, and looks me in the eye. Her lips twitch every other second as her eyes dart between mine. I have never seen her like this. Concerned about sharing her feelings.

"Micah, I haven't…" She takes another deep breath as

I wait patiently for her to finish in her own time. "I haven't been with… anyone."

Setting down my burger, I tilt my head and study her expression. The way she bites her lip to stop the occasional twitch. How her eyes dance around the room every few seconds to be sure no one eavesdrops on our conversation. And how she keeps stretching out her fingers, then balls them again. Her actions have me on edge.

Is she still a virgin? Not that I ever want to imagine my baby sister with any man, but how? How is it possible my thirty-year-old sister is still a virgin?

"Ever?"

She shakes her head. "Hasn't felt right."

Before this conversation, there's no question I classified myself as a whore. Now… is there such a thing as a mega-whore?

Shelly has had zero sex. None. I, on the other hand, have lost track of how many women I have bedded. Hell, it's only the beginning of May and I have gone home with more than a dozen women this year.

"Not sure what to say, Shell. But don't let Mom's need for grandchildren pressure you into something you don't want." I toss a quick thumb over my shoulder. "If you don't want to be with him, cut it off. When the right guy comes along, you'll know it. You'll feel it. And if you don't want kids, there is nothing wrong with that. That's your choice to make. Happy, romantic relationships don't always equal marriage and children."

"Do you want kids?"

Do I? At some point, when things were good between me and Rochelle, I considered the idea. But Rochelle was past the safe age of bearing children and I dismissed it. Would I give it more thought now? Couldn't be sure. With the right person, anything is possible. But I don't dream of picket fences and children's laughter. Not like some people do.

I shrug. "Not sure. Haven't put much thought into it."

"I don't think I do." She shoves another fry in her mouth.

Reaching across the table, I take her hand. We hold each other's gaze a beat. "Then do what makes you happy, little sis."

We finish lunch and pay. Shelly waves bye to Tom and we go separate ways in the lot after a hug and promise to see each other Sunday. On the way home, I replay our lunch together. My confession and Shelly's. And the fact our mother is practically guilting us to fulfill her own desires. Something I will chat about with Mom soon. Need to nip that in the bud.

Difficult enough to find a partner you love and trust. Going balls to the wall with commitment plus family is a whole other realm. One I am not ready for.

Sean texted when I got home from lunch with Shelly and asked everyone to come in early for a staff meeting. No details, just a *be here an hour early*. So, here I am. In the office. Waiting to hear what is going on.

Peyton shuffles past the office. I jump up from the chair, jog out, and call her name. She stops and assaults me with a smile. *Damn.*

"Hey," she says.

"Hey, yourself. Sorry you had to come in early."

Her shoulders bounce up a beat as she gives me a lopsided smile. "No worries. It happens every now and again."

We take a seat at the same table after greeting a few others. Ani and Sean walk in soon thereafter and the room goes quiet. Too quiet. My knee bounces beneath the table and I mentally yell at myself to stop.

"Thanks, everyone, for coming in early," Ani announces, with Sean at her side. "Wanted to touch base with everyone. Maybe start having staff meetings similar to this once a quarter, so we're all abreast of how things are going." Unscrewing the cap, Ani drinks from a bottled water then continues. "Foot traffic and sales have been on the rise since last quarter. And we're looking into ways to keep the momentum going."

Shit. I was supposed to search ideas for the slower nights and send them to Ani. A task I started but never finished. That is priority number one as of now.

"That being said," Ani continues. "Sean and I will be looking at staff changes." Several sets of eyes go wide.

"Sorry, let me clarify. We will be adding more staff. So, if you know anyone in need of a job who would be a great addition to the family, pass along the news."

For the next fifteen minutes, Ani carries on with sales numbers and I tune her out. I see the sales numbers for Roar on a nightly basis. Business has been on the rise. Not sure if the themed nights are a hit or if the new apartment complex blocks away has brought more foot traffic. Either way, the influx in business is a good thing.

Out of the corner of my eye, I spy how attentive Peyton is of Ani. How she hangs on her every word. Glued to sales totals from the fourth and first quarters. Giving a nod when Ani mentions the uptick in patron count. Or a subtle smile when Ani looks her way.

Peyton seems more invested than a typical bartender. While most of the staff zones out, she zeros in. This minor detail makes me question Peyton and Ani's relationship, and what her attentiveness means.

What am I missing here?

SIXTEEN

PEYTON

"LET'S end this quarter with a bang," Ani cheers as she wraps up the meeting. Then she claps her hands and everyone parts like the perfect comb over.

Those who aren't working tonight share hugs or good-byes before heading out the back. The rest of us shuffle off to our designated areas to prep for another busy night. Just as I remove fruit from storage to slice and add to the condiment trays, Ani sidles up to me.

"Before you get bogged down, let's chat."

I nod, set the fruit down, and wipe my hands clean. Ani leads me around the bar and toward the hall. As we pass Micah and Sean, I don't miss the way Micah follows us with his eyes. *Great*, something else I will need to handle. Micah's curiosity.

In the office, Ani closes and locks the door. She ambles to the couch, lowers herself onto the worn leather and gestures for me to do the same. Without hesitation, I join her.

"Been a little bit since we last chatted. How are you?"

I sink into the cool leather more, rotate to face her, and tuck a foot under my bottom. "Oh, you know. Much the same."

"And Micah?"

My head teeters left, then right. "That has improved. Surprisingly."

Ani rubs her hands together in front of her mouth. "Do tell."

I wouldn't say Ani and I go way back. But we have known each other coming up on seven years. We met three years after my father died. At the time, my mother still suffered severe depression and was having trouble making ends meet. I still lived at home when Dad passed and refused to let my mother live alone. So, I stayed, stepped up and got another job when one wouldn't cut it.

That is how Ani and I met.

During the day, I scanned groceries at the local super-market. The job was dull and monotonous, but it paid a decent wage and provided benefits. I met plenty of inter-esting and odd people, drummed up conversations about random items they purchased and smiled until my cheeks burned.

Ani came through my checkout line with a barrage of alcohol. Red and white wine, tequila, whiskey, vodka. You name it, she placed it on the belt. Along with soda and fruity concoctions. Beep after beep, I stared down at each bottle and assumed this woman was throwing one hell of a party. I'd asked, *"Where's the party. I'd love to tag along."*

It had been a joke. Something to make my customer laugh. A way to spark conversation. But Ani jumped on board and invited me to her place. At the time, she and Sean were engaged. The wedding a couple months out. They'd met late in life. Both established in running their own business. Both ambitious. They also fell instantly and madly in love.

In their lavish home, we partied and laughed and I made them the grossest mixed drinks ever. We laughed harder. Ani said she and Sean were thinking of buying a bar and that I should work for her. She'd train me, of course. The job sounded fun at the time, but I was worried about leaving Mom home alone.

So, I got a second job at a fast-food place on my days off from the supermarket. Ani and I still kept in touch. Text messages. Random girly days at the salon. The occasional trip to the beach.

As time moved on, Mom got better. She also met Harold. Once I knew she was happy, I moved on too. Moved out of my childhood home and rented an apartment with Reese. It felt amazing to finally be on my own. To be my own woman.

Time after time, Ani begged me to come work for her. Told me all the lavish details when she and Sean bought the club in Tampa five years ago. It wasn't in the best part of town, but it wasn't horrendous either. And the neighborhood was cleaning up. The club was always busy and they saw larger profits each year.

When she begged me again, just over a year ago, I caved. I had never seen her so giddy.

My first night working, the first time I laid eyes on Micah since high school, I spilled our shared history with Ani. From day one, she has known it all.

"He apologized."

Her jaw drops as she smacks the air between us. "Shut up. Are you serious right now?"

"Wouldn't joke about it."

"How did that come about?" I recount the story as she sits back and stares at me in awe. "Who knew? Don't get me wrong, I was hopeful things would get better soon."

"Me, too. I've about had it with his constant antagonizing bullshit."

She reaches across the space and pats my forearm a minute. "You know I love catching up, but we should talk business too. For at least one minute."

I roll my eyes. "Always such a party pooper," I tease.

"Never," she gasps. "I'll address that later. Did you come up with any ideas for Mondays and Tuesdays?"

"Yes." I inch closer and share a list of ideas that may drum up more business for the slower nights.

Ani leans an arm against the back of the couch. A hand at her chin and forefinger over her lip. Her attention focuses solely on me while I talk animatedly. Ani is my friend first and boss second. Which may be one of the reasons she values my opinion more. Years ago, she met *me.* Got to know and bonded with me before business was added in the mix. When she asks my opinion, it isn't only a business transaction. She *wants* and values my input.

Ideas fly from my lips. Charity bingo nights. Karaoke. Bar Olympics. Trivia nights. Plenty of bars do these things. Some nearby, others across the Bay. But we have the space to accommodate more bodies. Yes, we may need to invest in more tables, chairs and equipment. But the profit some of those nights would bring to Roar is endless.

Most bars offer food. Roar does not. But I toss out the idea of offering small options. Food that doesn't require a kitchen. Either that or connect with local businesses and have them serve or cater food. They pay a fee to set up and split their profits between them, Roar and the charity if we chose to offer bingo.

Of course, drinks would be offered. Maybe special drinks for different nights at a different price point. Again, splitting profit with charity.

When I finish, Ani claps her hands and presses them to her lips. "I love this, Peyton. Thank you. When I'm back at my computer, I'll mull over what days will work best for each. Make some calls and create a marketing plan." She reaches forward and takes both my hands in hers. "Still on board with—"

A knock at the door cuts her off and I nod in answer. "Yes," I say as the door handle clicks, but doesn't open.

Ani rises from the couch. Her heels clap against the concrete as she nears the door. Lock disengaged, she twists the knob and opens the door. From my seat on the couch, I spot half of Micah past Ani's petite stature.

Once, twice, thrice, his eyes dart between me and Ani. Brows pinched and eyes narrowed. Countless questions written on the lines of his face. Questions he will surely ask once Ani leaves. Questions I need to avoid answering until Ani gives me the go-ahead.

Hello, awkward party of one. Especially since Micah and I are trying to heal our past.

"Hey, Ani. Just wanted to let Peyton know I did most of her prep, but there's some left before open." Dark-blue eyes glimmer at me across the room.

With a shake of her wrist, Ani glances down at her diamond-encrusted rose gold watch that cost more than my monthly rent. "Shit, Peyton. Sorry. Didn't mean to keep you so long."

I have never been envious or bitter toward Ani and Sean and their obvious wealth. Simple things make me smile. Not to say I haven't wondered what it would be like to live a lavish lifestyle. Would my purchase habits change? I'd like to believe the change would be subtle. That I would maintain my same style, just purchase better quality items.

I rise from my spot on the couch and walk to the door. I rest a hand on Ani's shoulder and turn my attention to Micah. "No worries. I'll head out."

Squeezing between Ani and Micah, I head down the hall and out to the bar. A moment later, Micah strolls out with Ani on his heels. She looks my way and winks.

Micah doesn't miss the interaction. His brow twitches before he joins Sean and Ani. They chat another minute before Ani shoulders her purse and hooks herself on Sean's arm.

She guides him over to the bar and they both say goodbye before leaving through the back door.

Micah's eyes burn my profile, but I don't spare a glance in his direction. Now is not the time to answer all his questions. Ani and I agreed not to share what's coming until she and Sean are ready.

I finish prepping the bar. Cut the last of the fruit, fill condiment bins and stash the extras in the fridge beneath the bar. All the while, Micah leans his hip against the counter and watches me like a predator.

Neither of us says a word. A battle of wills. But my will is stronger. And he will cave long before me.

"Whatever," he grumbles and pushes off the counter. He stomps across the club and checks in with everyone working tonight before unlocking the doors.

The doors open and the masses flood the bar within minutes. Worries of Micah giving me the death stare for the next seven hours vanish. One after another, I focus on the crowd. On pouring shots of whiskey and tequila. Filling mugs from the keg taps. Mixing fruity froufrou drinks and blending daiquiris. Spreading smiles and jokes and laughter.

At some point, I sense Micah behind the bar. I keep my eyes on the task at hand, but catch him out of the corner of my eye. He slings drinks on pace with me.

Muscles stretch his black button-down taut while he works. Forearms and biceps flex as he shakes and pours martinis. Jaw more defined by the light layer of stubble and his occasional smile. And every once in a while, he dances to the music while working.

I hate and love how I notice him now.

Before our first night at Teddy's, I was aware of Micah. Knew where he was—to avoid him. Didn't seek him out, but stayed attune to his whereabouts. Of when he walked the floor or stepped behind the bar.

Now, I am much more cognizant.

Years ago, I saw Micah with rose-colored glasses. Dreamed of a boy my mind construed as appealing. Soft hair, long muscular legs, strong arms, and stare-at-them-all-day eyes.

Although he still acts immature, Micah is very much a man. A man my eyes refuse to shift away from. A man I notice now more than I care to admit aloud.

The way his slacks hug his long, thick, muscular legs and rest low on his hips. How his broad chest tugs at his shirt when he stretches or reaches certain directions. The flex of his forearms that makes me bite my lower lip. Far too often, my eyes trail up the exposed skin of his neck. From the hollow of his throat, up over his Adam's apple, to the sharp line of his jaw. From there, his lips garner my attention. Pink and plump and soft looking.

Fingers snap in front of my face. I blink and look to my right.

"Sorry, what?"

Two striking blue irises search my face. "I called your name three times."

"You did?" Someone needs to slap me from my damn daydreams.

"Yeah." He steps closer. Close enough for me to smell his sweet, woodsy amber cologne. Close enough for me to identify the gold flecks in his eyes like stars in the night sky. "Everything okay?" His eyes dart between mine, on the hunt for answers.

I don't trust my voice or my words right now. So, eyes locked on his, I nod. In my periphery, his hand twitches at his side. Balls into a loose fist, then flattens out. Inches forward, then lands back at his side.

He licks, then captures his lower lip before setting it free. "You sure?" He inches closer. So very close. My breasts centimeters from grazing his chest.

Heat slicks my skin. My pulse hammers in my ears as my breath comes in short, shallow bursts. He licks his lips again and my eyes drop to witness the action. I swallow and mentally whimper. My tongue eager to taste him.

"Yep," I choke out, then clear my throat. "Everything's fine." My voice cracks on the last word like a pubescent boy. *Great.* 'Cause that will convince him.

"If Ani gave you a hard time earlier" —he jerks his thumb toward the office— "I'll speak with her."

I shake my head. "Not necessary. We were just catching up."

His brows pinch. "Catching up?"

"Mmhm. Girl talk."

Micah steps back and goose bumps prickle my skin. He squints but relaxes his eyes just as quick. Then he throws me a smile. Not the one that makes me want a second helping. But the one painted in hard lines and artifice and bullshit. Before I say another word, he shifts his gaze elsewhere and walks off.

Tempting as it is to rake my eyes over Micah's broad shoulders and ample ass, now is not the time. Instead, I focus on the actual retreat. On the tension in his shoulders. The hand rubbing at the back of his neck. The rush in his stride and flat expression on his face when I glimpse his profile once more.

He weaves between the tables and heads for the outskirts of the room. At the wall, he glances back to the bar and sees me staring after him. He crosses his arms and widens his stance. His body stiffens. Lips form a flat, tight line. Then he simply shakes his head.

One, two, three breaths. His eyes hold mine captive. My thoughts a prisoner to him. Until he breaks contact, mouths what looks like *whatever,* and gets lost in the crowd.

Just as things were on the upswing with Micah, I ripped it to shreds. "Whatever," I mumble to myself. Soon, it all changes anyway. Best to keep things as they have been. With Micah at a distance.

SEVENTEEN

MICAH

Fourteen days have passed since the meeting at Roar. Fourteen days since I knocked on the office door and waited for Ani to unlock it. Fourteen long-as-hell days since I asked Peyton what she and Ani were discussing in the office. And nearly just as long since she gave me some bullshit answer.

An answer I have done my best to ignore and move past. An answer my gut tells me isn't all lies. But it isn't all truth either.

Peyton and I, since the night before the meeting, aren't the same people. As individuals or within feet of each other.

For more than a year, Peyton was at my throat. A lioness out for blood. Claws extended and ready to attack. She did her best to ignore my advances, but I never backed down. Never cowered under her snarl.

Now, she teases me. Eggs me on with her smart mouth

and mischievous smile. Has switched from calling me Micky—*thank god*—to starlight. Which isn't any better, but sounds less creepy.

And I have taken the liberty of calling her hellcat—a name I reserved for when I was alone with my fist and thoughts—more openly.

But fourteen days ago, some other force in the universe shifted. Made Peyton look at and talk with me in a way unlike our previous interactions. Yes, she still has that feisty edge I live for. But now, it has softer edges. And not knowing if Ani is the reason behind the change irks me.

At the end of the bar, Peyton delivers two beers and two fingers of whiskey in a tumbler. A man with dark hair and a protruding belly hands her a bill, flashes a toothy smile, then walks off with the drinks. The moment he disappears, she spins and catches my eyes on her.

In one, two, three strides, Peyton stands less than five feet away. "You looking at my ass, starlight?"

The corner of my mouth curves up and I waggle my brows. "What's it to you, hellcat?"

She steps closer. So close her breasts brush the starched cotton of my button-down. "Maybe I don't want your eyes on my ass."

"No?" She slowly shakes her head. "Then where *do* you want them?"

A millimeter at a time, her lips form a wicked smile. "Get more creative."

I press us impossibly closer. Her breasts flatten against

my pecs. One of my legs between hers. Lips a breath apart. *Fuck*. In one move, my lips would crush hers. But damn if the foreplay doesn't turn me on.

"Creative, huh?"

She hums and the vibrations ripple through my chest, my abdomen, my balls. "Yes, creative." Her breath hot and damp on my lips.

Jesus fuck.

I lick my lips—almost lick hers—then unwillingly inch back. "I'll work on that."

She turns to the register, rings up the drinks, cashes the tab out and puts the excess in the tip jar. "Good. Creativity is the spice of life." She winks, then sashays down the bar alley to the next waiting customer.

Screwed. One word and the definition of my current existence. But I wouldn't want it any other way.

The rest of the night goes much the same. We work and tease and laugh. She provokes and bats her lashes with a wicked smile on her lips. Bets me she mixes and serves better drinks. Draws attention from the crowd as she challenges me to a face-off. My hesitation widens her smile and she pushes harder.

"What's the matter?" She leans in, her breath hot on my ear. Her sweet scent in my nose. "Afraid to lose?"

I lean away, lock on to her radiant violet irises and shake my head. "What do I get when I win?"

"Ooh, confident." Her eyes drop to my lips and I stop breathing. "Who says you'll win?"

"Can't deny facts." I lick my lips and her eyes follow

the movement. Her breathing hiccups once. But once is more than enough.

"We'll see." She spins to face the crowd. "Ladies and gentlemen," she shouts with hands in the air. "Can I have your attention?" Everyone within earshot faces the bar and falls quiet. "Boss man and I are having a little show-down." The crowd hoots and hollers and whistles. "He says his drinks are better than mine," she yells. Men boo at this and she laughs. "So, I challenged him to a duel of sorts. Who wants to be the judge?"

Cheers erupt from the crowd and three people slap a twenty on the bar top.

I sidle up to her, my hand brushing hers. "Three people, three different drinks."

"Agreed."

Over the next few minutes, we decide on rules for the challenge. One—the customer selects their preferred drink. But it cannot be premade or from the tap. Two—they don't watch us make or serve the drinks. They will be blindfolded. Three—they will blind taste test the drinks and choose the winner before removing the blindfold and meeting the maker. Four—best two out of three wins.

The three people shuffle up to the bar and take a seat as the crowd steps back. Becky and Jake—two of the servers—step up between them. After the rules are explained, makeshift blindfolds made from Roar tank tops are put in place.

Contestant one requests a mojito. Peyton and I dive for shakers and get to work.

I pinch a cluster of mint leaves from the bin, toss them in the shaker and muddle them with a pestle. Then I measure rum and lime juice before pouring it in. I glance over and spot Peyton adding fresh lime and crushing it with the mint. *Fuck.* Should have used fresh. No going back now.

Simple syrup and ice go in next. I cap the shaker and make a show of blending the ingredients. Several shakes later, I swap the cap for the strainer and pour the drink in a glass, adding a splash of soda water. I place the drink on the bar and Becky helps the first contestant find the glass.

As I rinse the shaker, I peer over at Peyton. She pours her drink, unstrained into a glass, adds soda water and garnishes it with sugar crystals and a mint leaf. Good thing these people aren't basing the winner off of appearances, because mine is nowhere near as fancy as Peyton's liquid art.

The man sips mine. Swishes it around in his mouth. Lets it sit on his tongue a moment. Then swallows. He asks for water, takes a sip, then moves to Peyton's drink. Follows the same taste test routine. And then, silence. After seconds that mirror hours, he raises an arm for the drink he preferred.

Peyton. "Damn it," I mutter under my breath.

The crowd roars as the man removes his blindfold. While we move on to the next contestant, the man throws Peyton a wink and sips his mojitos.

Contestant two orders Sex on the Beach. I bite my cheek to restrain the dirty joke on the tip of my tongue.

We both grab high ball glasses and get to work. This go-around Peyton measures with a jigger. And I don't measure at all. I have made Sex on the Beach thousands of times over the years. Enough to know how much to add without measuring. Enough trial and error to know women suck it down and request another.

Cranberry and orange juice, vodka and peach schnapps, a small scoop of ice and an orange slice and cherry to garnish. Peyton and I add straws and stir at the same time and deposit the drinks in front of the woman. Jake guides her to the glasses and she tastes each one.

Without hesitation, her hand flies up and declares me the winner. Like a child, I stick my tongue out at Peyton and she mocks me in return.

We step over to the last contestant. A lumberjack of a man—inches taller than me, thick beard and more muscle than necessary. His appearance intimidates me. Thankfully, this is all about the drinks.

"White Russian," he announces after Becky taps his shoulder.

A simple drink. Also a drink that is easy to fuck up if not measured correctly. Of course, the drink with fewer ingredients makes me sweat the most.

While Peyton grabs the vodka and coffee liqueur, I fetch the cream from the fridge. I measure out the vodka while she measures the liqueur. Then we swap. I let her add the cream to hers first, then pour it in mine as she hands over her drink.

Cream swirls like storm clouds as it blends with the

alcohol. The man stirs the drink, then lifts it to his lips and tastes. Every person within ten feet of the showdown remains deathly quiet. He sets the glass down and repeats the process with mine. His poker face as hard and unforgiving as stone. Then he tastes them both again.

Dampness coats my skin and stains the armpits of my shirt. My palms clench and unclench as if the muscles glitch. My foot bounces and knee taps the cabinet beneath the bar.

Why the hell does the outcome have me on the edge of a cliff?

I peek over at Peyton and see her biting her lower lip. Watch her pick at the bottom hem of her shirt. When she notices me checking her out, she throws me a half smile.

Her apprehension is cute as fuck.

The bar erupts in cheers and I shift my eyes back to lumberjack man. Who has a hand in the air. The hand that says I just fucking won.

"Hell yes!" I shout as Peyton pushes her lower lip out to pout. And fuck if I don't want to suck on her lip.

"What's my punishment?" she asks as we clean up and business returns to normal.

My bicep grazes hers as we clean glasses and I freeze. Heat starts as a low simmer at my elbow and burns hotter as it nears my chest. A peek down at her still hands tells me she feels it, too.

"Have to think on it," I rasp out. "I'll let you know before we leave." Once everything from the *Micah makes the best drinks* contest is cleaned up, I dry my hands.

"Going to do paperwork," I tell her, then walk on uneven legs to the office.

Behind the closed door, I adjust myself and groan as I sit. The worn, stiff chair does me no favors as I shift to find a more comfortable position. Damn, I was on edge. Her pouty lips and punishment inquiry… my dick grew ridiculously painful beneath the zipper.

I close my eyes and her face pops up behind my lids. The occasional flyaway lock of blonde hair on her cheek. How her violet irises glow when she gets excited and the gray flecks enhance the darker rim. Her not too thin, not too thick button nose. And her perfect fucking lips. So pink and fleshy and suckable.

My eyes fly open as I curse and adjust myself. Again.

I wiggle the mouse to wake the computer and open the invoice spreadsheet. Dragging the wire basket across the desk, I get to work plugging numbers and updating inventory. Spreadsheets… a surefire way to kill arousal.

Peyton enters the office as I pick up the last invoice. "Last call," she informs me.

My eyes dart to the upper right of the screen and note the time. Almost two in the morning. "Well, shit."

She laughs. "Time flies when you're having fun."

I wave an invoice in the air. "Were you a math nerd?" Only numbers people get excited over this kind of stuff. Not that I failed math, but when they added letters with the numbers to equations, I questioned everything.

"Wouldn't say *nerd*. But me and numbers are good friends."

She spins and starts for the hall. "Peyton."

"Yeah?" She eyes me over her shoulder.

"Hang out with me tomorrow."

"Sorry, what?" She backtracks and faces me again.

"Call it your punishment. Hang out with me." A wince stretches her lips. "My friends will be there. And my sister."

"Uh…" Her eyes dart around the room a moment then land on mine. "That sounds…"

"Fun?"

"Actually, I was going to say awkward."

I raise my right hand, then lay it over my heart. "Swear it won't be."

"Says the man who knows everyone attending."

"Cora remembers you. And by proxy, Shelly."

"No, they remember high school Peyton. The loner girl who preferred dark spaces and hidden alcoves."

"Don't you still?" I tease.

"Shut the hell up." I laugh. "Micah, we've hung out a couple times. Yes, things are less shitty between us now." I wipe away a nonexistent tear and she flips me the middle finger. *You wish.* "But I don't think we've reached the 'let's hang out with other people together' phase of our friendship yet."

"At least you admit our friendship." She rolls her eyes. "C'mon. Please?" I exaggerate my plea and aim for my best sad-puppy expression.

A groan rumbles in her chest and spills from her lips. "You are so annoying."

"Before the contest, you agreed to winner's choice," I remind her with a smirk.

"True. But I didn't think it would be you forcing me to hang out with you and a group of people I don't know." I give her a look that says, *really?* She narrows her eyes as she tries—and fails—to give me her most menacing expression. "What?"

"Don't you pretty much do that every night we work?"

Once again, she presents me with her middle finger. "It's different and you know it."

"Please, Peyton," I say, softer this time. "Promise not to make it weird."

Peyton hangs her head. She stares at the floor and taps her thigh with her fingers. When she lifts her head, the look in her eyes stops my heart. Veiny damp eyes stare back. Her chin wobbles as she clamps down on her lower lip.

The chair legs scrape the concrete floor as I bolt up and dash over to her. I halt in front of her, desperate to frame her face in my hands and soothe her. But I don't know if she will shirk my touch. Only one way to find out.

One at a time, and with slow precision, I bring my hands to her face. She doesn't shy away from my touch and that small action has my heart galloping in wide-open pastures.

"Hey." I tip her head little by little until our eyes meet. "It'll be okay."

"You can't know that."

"I'll make sure of it," I vow.

"I-I just can't..." She swallows and gathers her thoughts. One deep breath, then another. "I just can't go through that again." She holds my gaze. "How people were all those years ago."

"You won't. I promise." Fuck, I want to kiss her. Seal my words with our joined lips.

She nods. "Okay. But if shit goes south" —she gestures between us— "this is done."

"Then nothing will go wrong." She takes another deep breath and I reluctantly release her. "Give me your number and I'll text you the address and time."

This snaps her back to reality. "You want my phone number?"

"Yes," I drawl out. "To text you the info. And in case you get lost, you have my number."

That sounded like a legit reason to ask Peyton for her number. Right? Not that I couldn't get it from the employee contact list. But I'm not that much of a dick.

"Fine," she huffs out. I hand her my phone and she texts herself from my phone. When she hands it back to me, I read the screen.

Micah: Starlight 😜

"Couldn't resist?"

"Nope." She starts for the door again. "Need to go finish up. See you tomorrow."

Sunday. "Tomorrow," I parrot.

"You did what?" Shelly shouts in my ear. I yank the phone away and rub my ear.

"Shell," I drag out her name with a groan. "It's too early to yell."

"I don't care," she yells louder. Thank fuck the phone is still a good six inches from my face. "When you text your sister that you invited Peyton Alexander to our Sunday night get-together, what did you think would happen?"

"Maybe that you'd text me back with shouty capitals. You know I work until three in the morning. Cut me some slack."

She laughs some twisted, maniacal sound. "You want *me* to cut *you* some slack?"

"Please." I bring the phone closer, hopeful she got all the yelling out of her system.

"Micah…" she huffs and I picture her eyes rolling. "What possessed you to invite her?"

A question worth asking since Peyton and I don't have stellar history. But we decided to be adults. I extended my long overdue apology for labeling and shunning her during high school. For intentionally getting under her skin at work. For every single pain she endured with the ripple effect of my words.

More than anything, I hold immense gratitude for

Peyton.

Peyton didn't have to accept my apology. But she did. She didn't have to agree to Teddy's the first or second time. But she did. She rose above and acted more mature than most. We aren't children anymore, but plenty of people our age refuse to grow up. Thankfully, that doesn't apply to us.

"Shell, please don't make this weird."

"It is weird. You don't agree?"

"I don't," I say with an air of confidence. "Was I an asshole to her more often than not? Yes. But we talked it out. Laid everything on the table. I apologized, Shell. And she has slowly let me in. We're friends." Although, I hope to one day be more than friends with Peyton. After wrapping my arms around her, after inhaling her sweet scent up close, I want so much more.

For now, though, I plan to keep that secret locked up tight.

"I just… how?"

"It's not something I question. She's willing to give me another chance. Willing to be friends. And if it doesn't work out, then it ends." I refuse to fuck up with Peyton again. Refuse to not have her in my world.

"It's still weird."

"Only if you make it that way." I take a deep breath, then rest my forearm over my eyes. "Both of us are trying. Can you do the same? Maybe let Cora and Gavin know too. They're the only other people in our circle that know her."

The line goes quiet. Too quiet. I lift my arm and pull the phone away to see if the call dropped. Nope. Just my sister in her head. And for someone who preaches love and fate and all that cosmic mumbo jumbo, she fights my friendship with Peyton hard.

But I give her a moment. To gather her thoughts and formulate her words. To swallow down reality and move forward with a smile on her cute face.

"Fine," she huffs out. "I'll talk to Cora and Gavin. But I make no promises on how they'll behave."

"You're my favorite sister."

"I'm your only sister, dumbass."

"Which is why you're my favorite." She growls on the other end. "Love you, Shell."

"Guess I love you, too."

The call disconnects and I toss my phone on the comforter. I roll over, bury my face in the pillow and groan.

When I asked Peyton to hang out tonight, I didn't realize I would have so much prep work. To tame my sister and spread the word to the other two people who knew Peyton. To ask them to be cordial and *normal*. But I should have expected it.

Bringing new people into our circle is a big deal. And not something we do often. But the invitation has already been delivered and accepted. Now, I need to do my part. I need to make sure tonight feels like every other Sunday. Just friends hanging out and enjoying life.

'Cause that is all Peyton is… my friend.

EIGHTEEN

PEYTON

I FLING a shirt across the room and Reese laughs. "Not helping," I say as I poke my head out of the closet.

Reese lays across my bed, feet dangling off the side, and holds up the most recent flying article between his thumb and forefinger. Then proceeds to twirl it like a lasso. Definitely not helping.

"I have never seen you so nervous about hanging out with a *friend*?"

I storm out of the closet, stomp across the lush carpet and stop in front of him. Hands on my hips, I pin him with what feels like my *shut up* glare. And what does he do? He laughs harder.

I snatch the shirt from his hand. "And I've never seen you be such a jerk. But here we are."

"Ouch." He sits up and presses a hand to his heart. "You wound me."

"No." I smack his bicep and a hiss leaves his lips. "But now I have."

He rubs the red palm print on his arm and inspects it far too long. "That really hurt."

"Then I hope you never get into any physical altercations." I riffle through the shirts on the bed in the hopes one will stand up and say *pick me*. But shirts don't stand up. Nor do they speak. "Will you please help me?" I give Reese my best pouty lips and sad eyes.

"Peyton…" He rests a hand on my shoulder. "We aren't teenagers anymore. This is not a date. Quit thinking you need to look perfect. He said it's a group of friends hanging out. Right?" My eyes on his, I nod. "Just be comfortable. Throw on your favorite jeans and graphic tee. Pick a hoodie to take, just in case."

"Ugh." I fall face-first into the mountain of shirts. Inhale the lavender detergent and dryer sheet scent as I take a deep breath. The smell does little to calm me. "Why did I agree to this?" My voice garbled by the cotton.

A warm hand rubs up and down my back. Slow and steady and rhythmic.

Reese has always had the touch. A way to soothe me without effort. If he felt like less of a sibling, our relationship could have been much different. But I love Reese how he is and who he is in my life. He has been my foundation for years. The friend who walked home with me in middle school. Who shared corny jokes and never held anything back. The friend who took my hand in high school, came to my defense and never let me down. Who let me cry in his arms while he stroked my hair and reassured me everything would work out.

Even now, while he razzes me, it isn't meant to be serious. More like an icebreaker. A joke to lessen the anxiety wreaking havoc in my veins.

"Because you're a glutton for punishment," he muses. I lift my head and give my best death stare. "Joking." He lifts his hands in defense. Then his expression turns more serious. "Honestly, you always try to see the best in people. Even those who have wronged you." He shrugs and toys with the shirt in his hands. "You talking and hanging out with Micah, that's you giving him another shot. A chance to make amends."

I hate when Reese is right. When he turns somewhat philosophical on me. Makes me see the truth behind my actions. They aren't bad truths. But speaking them aloud can be jarring.

I wiggle into a sitting position and lift my eyes to his. "Guess you make a valid point." He opens his mouth and I slap my palm over his lips. "Don't you dare."

"Wha—?" he mumbles against my skin.

"Say I told you so." I pull my hand away.

"I wasn't—"

"And don't lie." My finger jabs his direction, inches from his face.

Reese's booming laughter echoes off the walls. "Fine, I was. Can't help myself."

My palms slap against his chest, then shove him back. "Always such a pain in my ass."

"You love me." He winks.

I sit back on my haunches and stare at the mess on my bed. "And if you love me, you'll just tell me what to wear. Isn't that what besties are for?"

"Like a fifth of the time." He sticks his tongue out and makes a face at me. "But sure, I'll help." Searching the hurricane of cotton on my bed, he plucks a shirt from the pile. "Wear this with your black boyfriend jeans and all-black Chucks."

The shirt lands on my head and shields my eyes. "Hey." Reese just laughs. The bed shifts as I tug the shirt off. I jump up and follow him to the door. "Thank you." His eyes soften. "I know this isn't a date, but I've never felt this nervous about hanging out with people. And you always make me feel better. So, thank you."

Reese lifts a hand, clutches my hair and gives a slight tug. "You're welcome. That's what friends are for." He flashes his sweet smile. The one that only appears on rare occasions. "If he hurts you, though…"

"He'll answer to you," I finish.

"Damn straight."

Reese all but shoved me out the front door and latched the security chain so I would leave.

Once I was dressed, he suggested I leave my hair

down and put on minimal makeup. That was how I spent most of my days not at the club anyway. But when it actually came time to leave, I had second thoughts. Argued all the reasons I should stay home, slip on pajamas and eat pizza while watching Netflix. Reese wasn't having it.

Nervous as I am, him shoving me out the door was a good thing. Sometimes, I need that push. And he knows when to deliver.

The music quiets in the car as the Australian male Siri voice chimes in and tells me to turn left in a quarter mile. Something about that voice makes cell phone navigation much more pleasant. I turn onto the street and the voice takes over the speakers again, telling me my destination is a hundred feet on the left.

But I don't need to guess which house it is. Nope. Because there is only one house on the street with an overflowing driveway, cars in the yard and cars on the street.

Spectacular.

Two houses down, I park my SUV on the curb. Micah's gray pickup is in the driveway, which can only mean he has been here quite some time. I tap my phone screen and check the time. Only ten minutes after he told me to arrive. Would have been here sooner if I hadn't stopped up the street for bottled water.

One last deep breath. I grab my hoodie off the passenger seat, exit the car, and shove the fob in my pocket. Unlocking my phone, I type out a quick text to Reese.

Peyton: Why am I here? There's like 10 cars.
Reese: Exaggerate much 🙄

Since I can't smack him, I send him a picture of all the cars.

Reese: Sorry 😔 **Stay an hour at least.**
Peyton: Fine 😒

Phone tucked in my back pocket, I trudge for the house. A black Bel Air sits next to an off-roading Jeep in the driveway. "Black Dog" by Led Zeppelin belts out as I step closer to the door. Just as I lift my hand to knock, a dog barks from inside the house.

I step back and glance at the window. A husky has his snout shoved between the blinds as he rattles the slats. He barks again before someone shushes him.

The door swings open and I feel like I stepped back several decades. A petite brunette smiles at me as she wrangles the dog. Her hair swept up in a ponytail. A bandanna knotted in a headband atop her head. Denim hugs her legs and a graphic tee depicting hot rods is tied above her navel.

Not only is she pretty, she also makes me feel welcome when I know only one person here.

"Hi." She extends her free hand and I shake it. "Please, come in. I'm Autumn. And this" —she points to the husky currently licking a little girl's face— "is Spartan and Clementine."

"Peyton," I say and step inside. "Thank you."

"Hope you're hungry." Her red-painted lips curve up farther. "Sometimes we get carried away at the store."

My stomach grumbles at the mention of food, but I'm thankful she doesn't hear. Don't think I can eat right away. "Smells wonderful. Thanks for having me."

"The more, the merrier. Follow me." She starts for another door. "Everyone's out back." My feet stick to the floor and I swallow. Autumn peers over her shoulder, then comes back to my side. She wraps a tattooed arm around my shoulders. "No need to be nervous. Everyone here is family. If anyone fucks with you, they'll answer to me."

I may have only just met this woman, but I like her already. "Appreciate it."

"If you want, when we get outside, I'll introduce you to everyone."

I sag under her arm. "That'd be great."

The door opens and Spartan bolts out with Clementine on his heels. "Sparty, wait." She chases after him and disappears into the yard.

"Simple Man" by Lynyrd Skynyrd starts playing through a speaker off to the side. Two steps down, we land on a paver patio. Hickory and oak drift in the air from a smoker. Tables span the side of the house with paper goods, drinks, and food filling every inch.

Autumn takes my hand without hesitation and tugs me toward the smoker. And several men. None of them Micah. But I feel his eyes on me.

Here we go.

"Jonas," she calls out and a man spins to face us. Roughly the same height as me, he has messy brown hair that's long on top, but buzzed short everywhere else. He sports a Black Sabbath shirt, loose jeans and bare feet. And the way he smiles at Autumn makes me feel as if I'm interrupting their privacy.

"Yes, scarlet." I look to Autumn and she mouths *nickname*.

"This is Peyton. Peyton, this is my boyfriend, Jonas."

He steps closer and extends a hand. "Nice to meet you, Peyton." We shake and it feels more welcoming than awkward. "Burgers, brats, and chicken should be done soon. Help yourself to whatever." He gestures to the buffet.

Tonight will be an abundance of handshakes and *thank yous*. But I don't mind. From the overall vibe, everyone here seems nice.

Next to the grill with Jonas, I meet Reznor, Rex, and Trevor. Reznor and Rex work at the same tattoo shop as Autumn. Both decorated in tattoos and have a few visible piercings. Reznor seems the quieter of the two, only talking when he has something to say. Trevor is introduced as Jonas's best friend. They have known each other since girls were gross, as Jonas puts it.

"Alright, let's go meet some other faces," Autumn suggests.

Maybe it's the fact I meet new people and have random conversations weekly that has kept me from freaking out so far. The panic I felt before arriving has cooled and now simmers in the background. Autumn, being a gracious hostess, might have something to do with it. Whatever the reason, I'm grateful the urge to puke has tapered off.

The next cluster of people are more of Autumn's tattoo family. Penny—who has bubblegum-pink hair and pops chewing gum more often than not—jumps up and hugs me.

"Pen, don't scare the girl. Jesus," Autumn scolds.

Penny steps back and smiles. "Sorry." She glances at Autumn. "If the guys didn't scare her, no one will." *Pop.*

"Let's not test it."

Then, Autumn introduces Tatyana and Ashton—Reznor's girlfriend and son—and Iliana. We exchange greetings and chat a moment. Penny pops her gum twenty times in less than ten minutes. She speaks with animated hands and doesn't care what anyone thinks. I love her automatically.

Autumn wraps up our conversation with them and prepares to shift us to the last group outside. Where Micah sits with three other people and talks. Where he has kept an eye on me since the moment I stepped outside.

I may not have looked directly at Micah, but I have known exactly where he is from the moment Autumn led me out back. Felt his eyes roam my untamed hair, my face, my body. Heard the occasional falter in his words as he spoke with friends. Caught him staring out of the corner of my eye as I interacted in his world.

"Hey, guys," Autumn says as we approach. "Cora, Gavin, Shelly, this is Peyton."

Familiar names. My eyes dart between their faces as I shove my hands in my back pockets.

The woman next to Micah bears the same eyes and blonde locks, and I assume this is his sister, Shelly. Makeup paints her eyes and face with perfect lines and strokes. And she wears pink as if she would own no other color, but it doesn't look bad on her. Micah mentioned her the night he apologized to me at Teddy's, but she seems otherwise familiar.

Across from Micah and Shelly is a woman and man who I presume to be Cora and Gavin. Both have black hair—hers cut to her shoulders and his almost just as long, but only on the top of his head. Gavin has his arm around Cora in a way that says they are a couple. A swift glance at her left hand tells me they're married. And god, do they make a beautiful couple.

Shelly pops up from her seat and steps up to me. I expect another handshake and generic greeting. Instead, she surprises me. Her arms wrap around me and squeeze tight. "If he hurts you, I'll kick his ass," she whispers, then steps back and holds me at arm's length. Her eyes don't leave mine until I nod. "You may not remember me. We went to different high schools, but I saw you near the track when I'd stop by to watch Micah run." I stiffen. "We were a year behind you." Shelly points to Cora and Gavin.

Cora rises from the lounger and offers her hand. "Nice

to formally meet you, Peyton." Gavin follows suit and shakes my hand.

Just as I open my mouth to return the sentiment, Autumn hollers after Spartan—who just stole food off the table—then excuses herself.

Awkward, party of one?

"Shell, scoot over," Micah says. For a split second, I silently beg her to move closer to Micah and leave me the open end of the seat. But my plea goes unanswered as Shelly slides farther from Micah. He pats the cushion. "Come sit."

I shuffle between Shelly's legs and the unlit fire bowl to sit on the lounger. When my butt hits the seat, I lay my hoodie over my lap and tuck my hands underneath, where I fumble with the threads without prying eyes.

"How's your Sunday been?" Micah asks.

All eyes land on me, and I remind myself to inhale every other second. Cora and Gavin look at me with kindness as they curl into each other. Shelly practically bounces next to me. Everyone appears genuinely interested in my answer.

I can do this. Have nonwork conversations with Micah and get to know these people.

"Somewhat boring. Reese and I hung out."

Micah's whole frame goes rigid at the mention of Reese. Is that jealousy I detect? Interesting. May have to keep that tidbit in my arsenal.

"Reese Triggs?" Cora jumps in.

I peer up at her and smile. "Yeah. You know him?"

"Just remember him from high school. Nice guy."

"The best," I say, with dreamy eyes.

"You two still attached at the hip?"

"When we're home. We both work odd hours, but try to have at least one day off together."

The lounger shifts beside me and I turn to see if Micah is getting up. He isn't. Instead, he inches forward, leans closer with his eyes on me, rests his elbows on his knees and clasps his hands. "You live with him?" The growl behind his words doesn't go unnoticed by anyone.

I bite my cheek to resist smiling. His jealousy flashes like a neon sign in a porn shop window. It's amusing and annoying at the same time.

"Yep." I pop the *p*. "For years. Did I not mention that?" Not that I *need* to mention anything to Micah. We are just friends. My inner circle—not that I have much of one—and romantic life aren't his business.

"Can't say I remember you telling me," he says with too much bite for my liking.

"Well, he does. He also happens to be my best friend. If that's a problem for you…" I lift my brows in question.

"It's fine," he mumbles.

Beside me, Shelly shakes with silent laughter. And for a beat, I wonder if she and Cora tag-teamed to rile up her brother on purpose. If that's the case, we will be friends in no time.

Ready to jump on the 'terrorize Micah' train, I open my mouth to add gasoline to the fire. But Jonas cuts me off as he yells the burgers, brats, and chicken are ready.

The vultures flock to the buffet, but Micah and I stay seated a moment longer.

His vibe has gone from antsy to excited to irritated in minutes. Not sure what he expected when he invited me here, but I won't sit around and be the reason he pouts. He either needs to accept who I am and how I live or leave me be. I refuse to change who I am for another person. Especially Micah Reed.

I bump his shoulder. "You good?"

He rotates his head, but doesn't face me fully. Licks his lips. Eyes on the fire bowl a moment before his gaze meets mine. In those bold blue depths, I see more than expected. Curiosity and confusion. Regret and fear. But most of all, desire.

The ground wobbles. My heart beats faster, harder. My breath all but forgotten.

It's no secret I thought Micah lusted after me. Hell, as much as I despised him, his eyes continued to visit my dreams. By now, I had memorized the constellation the gold flecks formed in his eyes.

But that was all fantasy. All in my head. Right?

Apparently not.

"Sorry for my reaction. It was juvenile," he admits.

"Yes, it was. I forgive you." The blue in his irises brightens. "Don't do it again." His brows pinch above his nose. "Act jealous."

"Peyton, I—"

I hold up a hand and stop him. "I will let you finish as long as you don't say you're not jealous." My arm presses against his as I lean closer. Our lips inches apart. "Do not lie to me," I whisper.

The chatter and music around us fades away. All I see are his twinkling blue eyes, guiding me like the North Star. All I feel is the heat of his body and breath on my skin, on my lips. If either of us pressed forward, our lips would meet. Soft and hot and ready.

"Peyton, I was jealous. Am jealous," he confesses, only loud enough for my ears. His pupils dilate. Breath comes in bursts. He licks his lips and I *feel* his tongue ghost the edge of my lower lip.

I close my eyes but don't dare move. "Why?" The single word loaded with several questions. Why are you jealous? Why me? Why does it matter?

Micah remains tight-lipped until I open my eyes. And when I do, I swallow at the intensity staring back. The swirl of fire and hunger in his eyes.

"Thought it was rather obvious," he declares, voice gruff.

"Humor me," I whisper.

The corner of his mouth kicks up. "Peyton, how can I not be jealous of any man who sleeps under the same roof as you?"

"I live in an apartment. Sure there's more."

"Smart-ass." I smile. "Seriously, though. If I haven't made it obvious enough, I kind of have a thing for you."

"Kind of have a thing?"

He rolls his eyes and shakes his head until our noses bump. "No, not kind of. I *have* a thing for you."

The attraction between me and Micah has been plain as day for weeks. Not sure if his feelings go beyond then, but that's the first time I really paid attention. Neither of us can deny the spark. The ever-expanding ache between us.

But we have history.

Yes, I accepted Micah's apology. Forgiving him, on the other hand, may take more time. It's easy to let the words leave my lips. *I forgive you.* Feeling them, though, is a completely different wall to scale.

"Micah…" I inch back from him. Drag in a deep breath and hold it for five, four, three, two. "I… I don't know how to respond to that."

In my periphery, I follow his hand as it moves from his space to mine. And then he rests it on my thigh. Not too high, but somewhere in the middle, at the edge of the hoodie. Warmth radiates through the denim and heats my skin. I forget, for the umpteenth time, how to breathe.

"Don't need to. Just wanted you to know." He gives my thigh a slight squeeze, then rises from the lounger. I already miss the scent of his cologne in my nose. "C'mon." He holds out his hand. "Let's grab some food."

I take his hand and we shuffle over to the table. We fill our plates with too much food and each grab a bottle of beer. Once we resume our seats, conversations shift to lighter topics. Autumn regales us with stories of outlandish tattoos. Jonas shares his mechanic wet dreams about working on a 1965 Shelby Mustang. We all hem and haw, but don't appreciate it the same as he does.

Gavin and Cora talk about upcoming photo shoots—she photographing a wedding and he's modeling a new line of exercise gear.

I listen as they all carry on. In comparison, my life seems boring. Yes, I meet people from all walks of life in Roar. But I interact with them for maybe a few minutes. It's pure coincidence if I pour all their drinks for the night.

Sometimes, though, boring isn't so bad.

When everyone cleans their plates, Reznor, Tatyana, and Ashton say their goodbyes. With a little one to tend to, they still have plenty to do once they get home. Penny, Rex, Trevor, and Iliana leave next. As each person leaves, I get hugs instead of handshakes.

I take my phone from my pocket and check the time. Almost nine.

Micah taps my foot with his. When I look up, he tips his head toward my phone. "Hot date?"

With a shake of my head, I tell him, "No. Just don't want to be out too late. I'm at the ALF tomorrow."

"Finish your drink first?" He poses it as a question. Leaves me the opportunity to choose.

I lift the beer and swirl the contents. Two, maybe three, sips left. "Yeah."

For the next fifteen minutes, the ladies chat with me. Ask what it is like working at Roar. If I deal with a bunch of pervs. I joke and tell them the only perv in Roar is Micah. Everyone but Shelly laughs. She merely slaps him.

When my bottle empties, I toss it in the trash, gather my hoodie and start my goodbyes. Shelly gives me a more exuberant hug than the one I received upon arrival. She also reminds me she will kick her brother's ass if he hurts me. Cora and Gavin hug me next. Their embrace warm and friendly. Autumn and Jonas are next in line. After hugs are exchanged, Autumn says she hopes to see me again.

As weirded out as I was before I arrived tonight, leaving feels more nerve-racking. Like I am leaving behind family. Such a strange sensation, burning in my chest.

Micah trades hugs with everyone after me. "I'll walk you out."

"You don't have to."

"I know. But I'm heading out too. Plus, it's late and I hear there are some crazy old men in this neighborhood."

I laugh with a shake of my head. "Whatever. Let's go."

The front door clicks behind us as we step onto the porch. And suddenly, every sense amplifies.

I shiver as Micah's cologne gets caught on the breeze and drifts up my nose. Cicadas sing alongside the occasional whoosh of a car driving on the cross street a hundred feet away. I jump when the motion light kicks on and beams down on the driveway. Then heat flushes my skin when Micah rests his palm on my lower back.

Breathe, Peyton.

Thirty-seven steps later, we reach my car. I reach into my pocket and press the fob to unlock the door. But I don't open it. Instead, I stand there, frozen, staring at Micah like I'm broken.

"Thanks for inviting me," I finally squawk out then clear my throat. "I had a nice time."

Micah takes a step closer. The toe of his shoe inches from mine. "Glad you came. I had a great time, too."

Before the words good night leave my lips, he steps forward and snakes his arms around my waist. And then I feel him toe to top. Pressure and heat and… desire. I drag my fingers up his arms, lace them behind his head and close my eyes as I breathe him in.

His lips hover near my ear. Breath ebbing and flowing and heating my skin. If he kissed me right now, I wouldn't stop him. Don't think I could. Not with how good he feels flush against my front.

A hand trails up my spine and halts at the base of my skull as his fingers comb through my loose strands. "I love this. Wish you wore your hair down more often. But know why you don't."

My head swirls with want versus need. An internal battle of whether I should take a step back or press my lips to the spot beneath his ear. In the end, my rational side waves a flag in attention and I ease back.

"Thanks again," I whisper, inches from his lips. "Talk to you later."

He licks his lips and nods. Which is the perfect time for me to go. Before I launch myself at him and kiss the hell out of his soft lips. Then question my sanity.

I open the car door and slip inside. "Let me know you got home safe." He closes the door then taps the roof and walks to his truck with steady steps.

My eyes drift low in the side mirror and zero in on his ass. His jeans hang low and loose, but the definition of his glutes more than noticeable. When he reaches his truck, he unlocks the door but doesn't open it. No, he peeks over his shoulder at me. Well, my car.

The motion light on Jonas and Autumn's house kicks on and creates a halo around his frame. His face unreadable. But his body language begs for more. Tells me way more than his unspoken words.

My heart pounds, pounds, pounds in my chest until he gets in his truck, cranks the ignition and drives off. My knuckles burn and whiten as I fist the steering wheel and watch his taillights in the rearview. Then he turns and disappears into the night.

I gasp and relieve the fire in my lungs. Take a few deep, methodical breaths and cool the burn in my chest. Once my heart slows, I put the car in gear and drive home with one question swirling like a cyclone in my head.

What the hell is happening between me and Micah Reed?

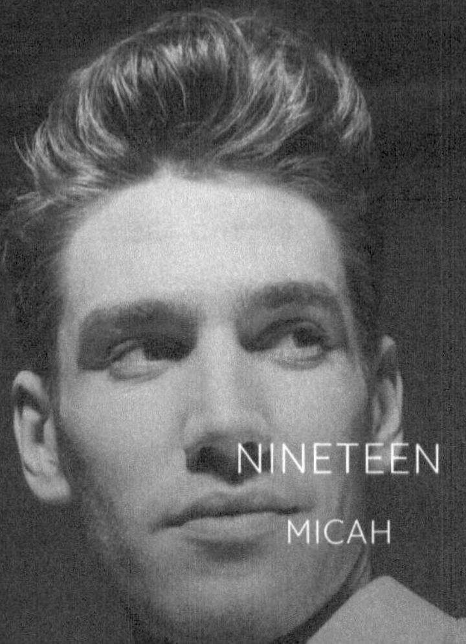

NINETEEN

MICAH

PEYTON SITS PARKED on the street as I turn and she disappears from view. Why hasn't she left yet? Did I freak her out? I half expected her to bolt the second she got behind the wheel. But her headlights hadn't even come on before I turned the corner.

I jolt when my phone rings through the truck's audio. Shelly's name flashes on the screen and I tap the answer button on the steering wheel. Had I forgotten something?

"Hey, Shell."

"Don't hurt her."

Jesus. Hadn't been gone ten minutes and am already on her shit list. Suppose that's how it is between siblings. Always keeping each other in check. Or trying to, at least.

"I won't."

"I'm serious, Micah." Micah, not big brother. Serious is an understatement. "I saw you."

She saw me?

"What does that mean, Shelly? You saw me."

A huff of irritation rustles through the phone line and I picture her rolling her eyes. She doesn't say anything as my knuckles stretch and pale against the steering wheel. My thumb hovers over the disconnect button, but I pull it back. Shelly may annoy me at times, but she would have to commit genocide for me to ignore her.

"Outside." She blows out a breath as I sort through my thoughts, but come up with nothing of substance.

"Be more specific. We were all outside tonight."

"Why is this so difficult?"

The question is meant to be rhetorical, but I answer anyway. "Because you won't spit out what you want to say."

"Argh," she groans. "Fine. You want me to just come out with it?"

"Would make this call a little less one sided."

"Outside. At her car. I saw you… holding her."

I pinch the bridge of my nose and thank the traffic gods for a red light. Irritation spreads like the molten searing of a branding iron. Scalding at the epicenter, but distributing the sting in an effort to temper the pain.

"Were you spying on me?" I bark into the truck cab.

"No," she counters with a fevered pitch. "Not intentionally. I was a couple minutes behind you. When I stepped out the door and saw your truck, I was confused. So, I looked for you—from the porch—and saw you at Peyton's car."

Can't remember the last time I felt stabby toward

Shelly. Compared to friends who had siblings, Shelly and I had a great relationship. Sure, we didn't always see eye to eye, but no one does. When she admitted to seeing us, I assumed she followed us outside all ninja-like. Seeing us by accident… I can't be mad at her.

"Sorry I snapped at you."

"You're forgiven, big brother. Still doesn't change things. Don't hurt her."

Bless my sister and her need to look out for others. Any other time, I would deem the trait admirable. Mom and

Dad did their damnedest to raise us as respectable and responsible. *"Lead by example."* Those three words spoken by Mom or Dad at least once a week during our childhood. With the exception to high school and my whore habits post-Rochelle, I have done my best to uphold said qualities. To be an example.

But we all get tested from time to time.

"I love how protective you are, Shell. And I have no intention of hurting Peyton."

On the other end of the line, a beep echoes, followed by a soft thump and electronic dings. After a beat, she speaks up and sounds farther from the phone speaker.

"You may not intentionally. But your life has been a hot mess for a short while. Don't let that bleed into her life."

Hot mess doesn't remotely describe the path my life has taken since Rochelle fucked me over. Literally.

The day I walked in on Rochelle and the young stallion she mounted, in the bed we shared no less, I lost my shit. I have never been physically violent toward women, but furniture and picture frames and inanimate objects were fair game. I'd flung them across the room. My fists so tight, blood spilled from the crescents in my palms. Holes littered the hallway drywall—a smarter alternative than jail after beating the guy's ass.

The worst part of it all… she wasn't sorry. Rochelle had zero regrets bringing another man—who looked barely old enough to be a man—to the bed we shared and fucking him. Not a single ounce of remorse. How had I become so blasé about who she was and her predatory ways?

Because I was a fool.

We hadn't been living together full time—thank fuck. But once I kicked her to the curb, threw all her shit outside, along with the mattress, I made a pact with myself. To never let a woman so close to my heart again. To never let a woman take the reins and steer me down an unknown path.

Not bedding the same woman night after night helped solidify my pact. But these last few weeks, Peyton has me second-guessing said agreement.

"Swear I won't hurt her. Not intentionally."

"Good to hear." The relief in her voice filled the truck cabin. "Will I see you at Mom and Dad's party?"

Ah, yes. The parents' thirty-fifth wedding anniversary. Our parents don't always insist on our appearance, but if we missed this occasion, we wouldn't hear the end of it.

"Wouldn't miss it."

"Cool." A car horn honks in the background. "Well, I'm on my way home. Talk to you later."

"'Kay. Love you, Shell."

"Love you, too, big brother. Night."

The call disconnects as I turn into my driveway. I cut the lights and engine, then stare at the tan-painted single-car garage door. Let my eyes lose focus as I watch tree limb shadows dance over the house. House, not home. The only way it would ever feel like a home is if I wasn't alone.

In my mind's eye, I pictured what having a home would be like. How two people blended their lives together and became one. Similar to Gavin and Cora. On so many levels, I envy my best friend. Not that his and Cora's journey was an easy one. Life ripped them apart. Obstacles stood in their way. But they persevered. Because they wanted each other more than anything else.

I would kill for that type of love. Love that bulldozes walls and eviscerates loneliness. Love that pulls you in, wraps its arms around you, and never lets go. That crushes all insecurities and makes you feel safe in your vulnerability. That is the love I want.

But after the bullshit with Rochelle, letting another woman near my heart scares the shit out of me.

Without realizing it, Peyton has unintentionally wiggled her way in. Staked a claim on my heart. And fuck... here I am, handing it over. No resistance. No second-guessing. Just willingly plucking the scarred organ from my chest and presenting it to her, in the hopes she will know how to handle it.

Fuck.

I exit the truck, check the mailbox—then remember the mail doesn't run today when I see the box empty—before I amble inside. I flip the kitchen light on, empty my pockets, and grab a beer from the fridge. I pop the cap, chuck it in the trash and take a long pull from the bottle. After flipping the light off, I snatch my phone from the counter and wander down the hall to my bedroom, bottle at my lips.

Plopping down on the mattress, I don't bother with the light. It isn't long before I polish off the beer, strip my clothes, set the phone on the charger, and slip under the covers.

Alone in bed, the silence is deafening. I close my eyes and images of Peyton flash behind my lids like an old movie reel. In the last two weeks, I had seen her smile more often than not. And her smile is magnificent. Like sunshine after the rain. Blinding, yet you can't seem to look away. Marry that smile with her radiant violet eyes and golden hair, she rendered me speechless more often than not.

When had Peyton become such a fixture in my head? In every waking—and sleeping—thought I had?

For more than a year, we were at each other's throats. The constant back and forth. Her yelling at me and vice versa. She did it out of disgust and a hatred for her high school bully. I did it because I loved to work her up, to ruffle her mane. Can't speak for Peyton, but for me, taunting her is the best version of foreplay. A lead-up to where we are now.

Unfortunately, I have no clue where we go from here.

Do I really want another relationship? Dates and intimacy and late nights filled with laughter. Shared time and small tokens of appreciation. A voice buried deep in my psyche screams, *"Yes, idiot. We want all those things."* But another voice—one closer to the battlefield, one more recent—speaks up and reminds me of what I went through last time I traveled down that road. *"You'll just end up here again. Hurt and alone."*

My eyes snap open and stare up at the ceiling I am all too familiar with. "No," I whisper into the darkness. "Peyton and Rochelle are nothing alike." Peyton would never hurt someone she cared about. Not after all the bullshit she has dealt with.

Question is, does Peyton care about me? On any level?

Without a second thought, I blindly reach for my phone on the nightstand. I squint at the screen and open up the messaging app. Before I stop myself, I tap on the text history with Peyton and type out a message. Seeing as she works at the ALF tomorrow, she probably won't answer. But this can't wait.

Micah: Is this too much?

I stare at the blue bubble on the screen. The word

delivered beneath it. Then I lock my phone, toss it on the bed and press the heels of my palms to my eyes. "I'm a goddamn fool."

The words are barely out of my mouth when the phone vibrates the bed. I pat the blanket until I locate the phone and see a text alert. From Peyton.

Peyton: Is what too much?

How do I translate my thoughts into simple terms? My brain knows the words, but my fingers forget how to type them. My lips forget how to say them. But I do my best to spell it out.

Micah: Me. Us. Hugging earlier.

I hit send and close my eyes. The text is ridiculous. It explains nothing and probably confuses her further. Why does my brain turn to mush whenever Peyton Alexander is in the mix?

Peyton: The hug threw me off. But I won't lie and say I didn't like it.

Peyton Alexander just admitted to liking my arms around her. My body pressed to hers. My lips near her skin.

Micah: I liked it too. More than expected.

Peyton: Oh yeah. How much more?

Is she flirting? Or does my bewildered brain have me misconstruing her message? It's late and she is probably in bed, half asleep.

Micah: Enough that I still feel your heat on my skin.

Fuck. I slip a hand beneath the blanket and grip my hardening cock. Eyes on the screen, I take a deep breath as the dots dance inside the little gray bubble.

Peyton: Where do you feel it?

Fucking hell. Is this seriously happening? In five simple words, Peyton has me virtually on my knees, begging for relief. Without hesitation, I would worship her like no other.

Micah: You really want to know?
Peyton: Humor me.

I laugh into the darkness. Those two words. We toss them back and forth to lighten the moment. But those two words weigh heavily each time they are said.

Micah: Fisted in my hand.

And just like that, my innocent inquiry has flipped to

sexting. Well, suggestive sexting. Will my response freak her out?

Peyton: And how does that feel?

This woman will be the death of me. Via text messages or her smart mouth. Either will do, though.

Micah: Nowhere near enough.
Peyton: Sometimes, not enough makes the end result that much sweeter.
Micah: What end result would that be?

I will not put words in her mouth. Other things, perhaps, but not words. With our history, Peyton needs her voice. Needs to use it to guide me. To guide us. I won't mislead her, but I also want the same in return.

Peyton: My crystal ball says that still remains to be seen.
Micah: Hmm. Think your crystal ball may need to be cleaned.
Peyton: Really?
Micah: Yep. I offer up my ball cleaning services to you.

Oh lord. I really need to think before I type and hit send. And I'm not drunk. Maybe a little buzzed, but not drunk.

Peyton: I bet you do.
Micah: Sorry. Was that too much?
Peyton: I'm a big girl, starlight. I handle balls just fine.

And now my vision fills with images of Peyton and the ways she could *handle my balls*. I am so fucking screwed.

Micah: You really are a hellcat.
Peyton: You wouldn't want me any other way.

There are several ways I wouldn't mind having Peyton Alexander. But it is too early to put those out in the open. Even with both of us braver behind our screens.

Micah: True. Question… why do you call me starlight?

Her new nickname for me is quirky and cute, but it also feels childish. God, I hope it isn't something so inane.

Peyton: Really want to know?
Micah: Humor me.

Seconds drag on for minutes as the dancing gray bubble pops up and disappears again and again. Either she is typing a novel or she deletes her words and starts over. The wait is gruesome.

Peyton: Because of your eyes.

Not a novel. And definitely not what I expected.

My eyes? What about my eyes made her come up with starlight? I picture Shelly's twin irises. The rich blue with lighter hints. But nothing makes me think of starlight.

Micah: What about my eyes?
Peyton: Hidden in the blue, you have these little gold sparks. Like stars.

Like stars. I read those two words over and over. Sift them through the confines of my mind. Interpret the fact she has studied my eyes hard enough to notice small gold flecks. *Like stars*. That every time she uses the nickname, it has more meaning than other pet names people share. That she sees deeper than surface level. *Like stars*.

Micah: I never noticed.

The screen dims after no response for a couple minutes. I tap the screen and it brightens. Then I note how late it is. Seeing as she has to be up earlier in the morning, it wouldn't surprise me if she fell asleep.

Micah: Night, hellcat. Sweet dreams.

I lay my phone back on the charger and stare up at the ceiling. After texting Peyton, staring at the slight texture above the bed seems less interesting. Worth less of my time. So, I close my eyes and let my imagination wander.

Images of Peyton from earlier in the evening pop up from my memory. Of her relaxed attire and loose strands. Of her easygoing smile and breath an inch from my lips. How at ease she was around my friends, my family. And how perfect she felt flush against my chest, my hips. Most of all, I recall the way her brilliant eyes studied mine.

Like stars.

TWENTY

PEYTON

Small waves crash along the shore. Salt licks my skin. Cocoa butter and the distinct smell of seaweed float through the air. Seagrasses ruffle in the wind between the parking lot and white sand. The sun bright and high in the cloudless blue sky.

I peek up from my romance thriller as Ani exits the water and treks back to our spot in the sand. For a woman in her late forties, Ani is smoking hot. I have never been sexually attracted to women, but will openly admit when they steal my attention. Ani works hard for everything in her life—physically, emotionally, and financially—and it shows.

Our friendship is one of the greatest gifts, and I thank my lucky stars she entered my checkout line years ago.

Ani has given me so much. More than I ever expected. She provided me with opportunities I wouldn't have easily come by without her. But she is also a great friend.

Without a doubt, one of my best friends—after Reese, of course.

Over the years, my tally of female friends has remained small. One—I don't have time for petty nonsense. Drama happens, but I don't need women who provoke and promote drama in my circle. Two—I enjoy the more laid-back nature of guy friends. Plus, guy friends give better hugs when you need them.

But Ani is the exception in my circle. Her drive and no-bullshit attitude make her admirable. She busts her ass for what she wants and ignores everyone who tells her she can't have something or accomplish her goals. As a woman who wants more from life, I hold Ani in high esteem. With her guidance, I have the opportunity to become a better version of myself too.

Women empowering women tops crushing them beneath your heel any day of the week.

Ani flops down on the lounger next to me, slides her sunglasses into place, and sips her water. "The water feels amazing today. We need more beach dates."

I bookmark my page and set the book in my bag. "Agreed." I stare out at the water and how the sun shimmers along the surface like stars. In a blink, my thoughts drift to Micah and his starry-night-sky eyes.

Two weeks have passed since I hung out with him and his friends. Since he wrapped me in his arms and touched me more like a lover than a friend or coworker. Since he texted me from his bed and our conversation went from concerned to heated to confessional.

And since that night, Micah Reed has texted me daily.

Random and not-so random messages. Texts asking how my day was at Gulfside. A barrage of questions in an obvious attempt to learn every fine detail of who I am.

"Favorite style of music?"

"Favorite movie snack?"

"Last show you binge watched."

"Place you want to visit, but haven't."

A different question hit my messages every day. Even days when we would see each other at work. Some I answered within minutes. Others I left unanswered for hours. Not because I didn't have an answer, but because there is something thrilling about delayed gratification.

"You ready for tonight?"

Tonight… I have been ready and waiting for this day for ages. The day I become more than just a woman behind the bar. The day I take the next step.

"Yes. Already adjusted my schedule at Gulfside."

"I love that you'll still be there one day. They're lucky to have you."

When Ani called me last weekend and said things were moving forward at Roar, I spoke with human resources at Gulfside. And Ms. Jenkins. HR accepted the change without complication. They understood the younger staff wouldn't stick to the same routine. But they were excited when we stayed. Ms. Jenkins, on the other hand, was a bit peeved. Not that I would only be at Gulfside one day a week, but that I'd still show up.

The woman loved me as much as Nana did. Wanted to

see me thrive in the world. Wanted me to not be "one of those people that works more than lives." I promised her this change would help me do that. But I still need Gulf-side. Need the solace it provides when life is hectic. Need the conversations and interactions with Ms. Jenkins that parallel to those I shared with Nana. Moments I miss more than anything.

"The feeling is mutual." I take a deep breath and lose focus as I stare out at the water. Then twist to face Ani. "How's this going down?"

Her legs sweep over the edge of the lounger as she looks my way. A hand pushes her sunglasses into her hair. Eyes survey my face. "Are you nervous?"

Am I nervous? I scrutinize my own feelings. The expanding flutter beneath my diaphragm. The one that sparked to life when Ani called last weekend. But it was the same sensation when I agreed to work for her. Delight. Exhilaration. Having the chance to be more.

But I also can't ignore the lump in my throat. The one I woke with this morning when realization kicked in. When I stared at the text notification on my phone.

"Morning, hellcat."

It wasn't necessarily the text that had my body in slight hysterics. Micah started texting me that same message following the night I hung out with him and his friends. And I love seeing it each morning.

Today, though, his message sent a wave of panic. Has me second-guessing what happens next. Not about the overall change at Roar, but how Micah will react with the announcement. Will he be pissed? Or will he praise me? For some stupid, girlish reason, his reaction matters. Suppose that's what happens when you get closer with someone.

"Yes," I answer honestly. "What if this pisses people off?"

"And by people, you mean Micah." Ani poses it more as a statement than question.

I huff out the irritation I have with myself. Irritation over the fact that I am worried what a guy thinks. "Not just him." Half-truth. "But also Gina and the others who have been there longer."

Ani reaches for my hand and clasps it between hers. "This is happening because I want it to. It isn't just about you. The move is also smart for business. Sean and I always mull over business decisions before putting them into action. Hard and heavy. This decision wasn't made because we're friends or on a whim. I believe in you and what you have to offer. And that's why I'm doing this."

My breath comes easier. "Thank you. Didn't know I needed to hear that."

"You're welcome." She drops my hand, then shifts to lie back on her lounger. "How do you think he'll take it?"

She doesn't have to say Micah's name for me to know who she's talking about. "Wish I knew. Things have changed between us. But I don't know him well enough to answer."

"Well, don't let it worry you. He's a grown man. If he can't handle it, that's his problem. Not yours."

Every rational part of me knows Ani is right. That if Micah gets upset with tonight's announcement, it is on him. But part of me still feels as if I am betraying him. Betraying the friendship — or whatever the hell -ship — we formed. Things between us get better with each passing day. I don't want all that to go down the shitter.

I only hope he takes the news with a managerial mindset and does not let it bruise his ego.

You can do this, Peyton.

I stare at the back of Roar from the comfort of my car. The aged brick more red than brown today. A fresh coat of paint over the club name adds an extra pop. Large string lights near the roofline already lit, although the sun doesn't set for another two hours.

Parked two spaces to my right is Ani and Sean's Tesla. Another space down is Micah's truck. Both vehicles empty of passengers. Seeing both adds a new layer of nausea.

Get out of the car. Go inside.

"Ugh." I grip my hands at ten and two on the steering wheel and rest my forehead at twelve. "Why is this eating at me?" What I wouldn't give for a couple saltines right now.

Leaning back, I press my head into the rest and drop my hands. I take a few steadying breaths. *In through the nose. Out through the mouth.* When my pulse settles and the compulsion to vomit wanes, I step out of the car, shoulder my purse and head for the employee entrance.

On any other day, if I were to walk in Roar two hours before open, it would be quiet. A radio may be on, quiet in the background. But otherwise, the space would be still. Peaceful. The calm before the storm.

But today is a new day. And new days come with music at normal levels and the chatter of several close people. I stroll past the office, skipping the time clock or stashing my purse. When I enter the main area of the club, the space seems smaller. Claustrophobic. Restrictive. The walls inching closer to the tables.

All eyes shift my way as I step out from the hall. Smiles and waves and greetings I don't hear beyond the white noise in my ears. I pinch the front of my shirt, pull it off my chest, then push it back rapidly, over and over.

Is it hot in here?

Ani pats Sean on the shoulder, then strolls over to me. "Peyton?" I hold her gaze. "You okay?"

I nod. "Just need some water."

She shuffles me over to a stool and forces me to sit. "I'll grab you some. Sit tight."

Ani waltzes over to the bar as Micah takes her place at my side. Brows drawn together, he bends at the knees so we are eye to eye. For one, two, three breaths, he doesn't speak. Then he reaches for my hand. His warm touch a partial balm to my anxiety.

"You look like you've seen a ghost." He lifts a hand

and lightly brushes my cheek with his knuckles. "If you need to go, they'll understand."

My eyes dart between his and memorize each gold fleck against their inky sky backdrop. Certain I may not see them this close again, I etch them into my mind to recall when I am alone.

"I'm fine," I choke out as Ani approaches with water. "Just have a lot on my mind."

Ani sets the glass on the table and winks before going back to Sean. She whispers in his ear—a signal the meeting is about to start. My stomach churns and I sip the water in the hopes it will settle.

"Want to talk—" Micah starts, but is cut off when Ani speaks up. He shifts to stand beside me. Hand on the back of my chair. Thumb absently drawing small circles between my spine and shoulder blade.

"Thank you all for coming in early or on your day off." Ani and Sean flash bright white smiles to everyone. "We called this meeting to update you on new changes with Roar." A mix of excitement and concern mar some of the faces in our group. Others remain impassive.

I grip the edges of the seat until pain shoots up my forearm. The next words out of Ani's mouth will be the ones I have waited to hear for far too long. Words that will change *everything*. I relish and fear the change. But I won't let anyone snuff out what I worked hard to achieve.

Not even Micah.

"First announcement… Roar has a new manager on

staff." Micah freezes beside me and Gina, two tables over, looks ready to puke. *Right there with ya, girl.* "Everyone, please join me in congratulating Peyton on her promotion."

Applause and cheers erupt and echo throughout the room. But one clap stands out more than the rest. The one less than a foot from me. Slow and exaggerated and far from congratulatory. Each time his hands smack together, I twitch in my seat. Jump at the vibration of anger each strike sends my way.

This is exactly what I expected would happen. That Micah would go off the emotional deep end. Instead of smiles and hugs and overall happiness for what I achieved and earned, I had a feeling the opposite would happen. My assumptions weren't wrong.

Without hurry, I peek to the right. Prepare myself for the sight that will undoubtedly make the pain beneath my rib cage worse. But no amount of preparation will ease the anger and hurt I see on Micah's face.

His nostrils flare. Eyes cold and distant as he meets mine. A measured headshake full of disbelief. And then he breaks contact. Not just his eyes, but also the hand he'd had on the back of my chair. With each harsh breath I take, he takes a step away.

Asshole.

Fuck him. If me achieving success pisses him off, he can crawl in a hole and weep like a toddler. Alone. I will not lower myself so he feels better about himself. Fuck. That.

I sit up straighter, pick up my water, and sip it as Ani continues.

"Gina, we'll be switching you to Tuesday through Friday. Micah, your days will remain the same. Starting next week, Peyton will work Monday through Thursday. We will also add three new bartenders, two servers and another doorman." Light chatter kicks up, then dies down when Ani continues. "They will be arriving for introductions in a half hour. I wanted to give the original Roar team this moment before they joined us."

Micah leans forward, his breath hot on my ear. "Can we talk later?" he growls.

I purse my lips and meet his gaze as he rights himself. "Sure." My mouth stretches into a tight, forced smile before I face Ani again.

Over the next fifteen minutes, Ani shares the changes coming to Monday through Thursday. All the ideas I tossed out at her plus drink specials for each night. She drones on about contacts who are eager to partake in charity bingo night and companies who want to host trivia night for their employees. With each new idea that leaves her lips, Micah grows more frustrated and tense.

More than a month ago, Ani asked Micah for ideas to boost the slower nights. Asked for his input because of his role in the company. She'd also asked Gina, who suggested board game night, speed dating, and painting parties. Some of which Ani plans to incorporate once or twice a month. But Micah never responded. Never gave a single suggestion.

Maybe it had something to do with me and the distraction I provided. Or maybe his head was elsewhere. Distracted with other things I was unaware of. Either way, he didn't hold up his end of the bargain. And now, he has to deal with what Ani and Sean decided. Without him.

The new employees arrive and introductions are made. Josiah, Caleb, and Mable will join Adam and Kaylynn behind the bar. Charity and Dylan will be new additions to the tables with Becky and Jake. And Julio will work with Dan and Ted. The new cliques chat among themselves and get to know each other. All of the new additions will be working with us tonight, so management will get more time with them.

Before long, Ani announces everyone needs to start prepping for open. She shoots me a worried look, but I wave her off. Micah may be upset, but that is his burden to carry. Not mine. As the meeting carried on, this sank in more and more. That I should not be wrung tight because Micah cannot handle life and the positive things happening in mine. If he can't step off his pedestal one minute and allow others to shine with him, I don't need him in my life. Period.

So, I let it go. Enjoy the bliss of promotion and all the possibilities in my future. And later, I will celebrate with a drink and the people who cheer me on. Life is too short. I don't have the time or patience for someone not in my corner.

Fuck Micah Reed and his piss-poor attitude.

TWENTY-ONE

MICAH

No way this happened overnight. No way Peyton did not see this coming before today. Yet, she never said a goddamn word. Not once. None of our conversations hinted this colossal change was coming.

Manager.

Peyton just got promoted to manager after working at Roar for one year. One fucking year.

How hard had I slung bottles before Sean and Ani considered me management material? The first time Sean broached the subject had been three and a half years in. *"We need to see more professionalism,"* he'd said. *"You have what it takes, but need you to step it up. Show us you want it."* Those days, Sean and Ani spent more time at Roar than not.

But they rarely set foot inside nowadays. Not unless they were meeting with me or Gina or an event happened during the day. Yes, they kept tabs on their business. But they were less involved with the actual day-to-day functionality. They left that up to management and staff, only stopping by if things were amiss.

So how did Ani know Peyton was management material? Without working side by side with her a single night, Ani had no idea how Peyton worked inside these walls. And I hadn't received any calls, texts or emails asking my opinion on Peyton's work ethic. Only the occasional generic inquiry when Ani stopped by to grab bank deposits or paperwork for the accountant.

The only reasonable explanation is Peyton and Ani's friendship. But I had to know. I need answers from the source. Peyton.

As the meeting came to a close, Peyton stood from her stool and took a step toward the bar. The color had returned to her cheeks. Her skin less clammy and gray. Eyes more alert and chin held higher.

Before she stepped out of reach, I took her elbow. She jerked to a stop as her eyes flashed to mine. Lips are a brutal flat line. A crease between her brows. If she had claws, I'd be shredded to bits by now.

"Can we talk?" My voice low as my eyes dart toward the hall, to the office.

She drops her gaze to my hand, then brings it back to my face. The ferocity in her stare makes me drop my hand and take a step back.

"Please," I add in a softer tone.

Am I angry? Absolutely. But not for the reasons Peyton presumes.

"Fine. But make it quick. I need to do prep."

Behind the bar, Adam and Kaylynn get to work with Josiah, Caleb, and Mable. Without being asked, they went into instructor mode. Showing their new coworkers how Roar operates. By the time Peyton and I finish our talk, the bar prep will be done with time to spare.

Without another word, I storm toward the office. The *tip-tap, tip-tap* of Peyton's heeled boots clacks loud in my wake. I step into the office and move off to the side. Once she steps in, I slam the door and lock it.

"What the hell, Micah?" Her tone is fire and rage and trembles slightly.

Feet away, I huff out a laugh. "You're angry at me? Seriously? Seems a bit backward."

Her nostrils flare as her chest expands and contracts in rapid succession. The muscles of her jaw flex and tighten. Fists balled at her sides. "How so?"

"Shit like this doesn't just happen overnight, Peyton." I wave a hand in the air. "This type of change gets planned. Weeks and months ahead of time."

"Your point?"

I take a step in her direction. "You think I'm mad at you? Mad about the promotion?"

She waves a hand in the air, up and down the length of my body. "Body language speaks volumes. As soon as it was announced, you retreated from me."

I had pulled away from her. Stopped touching her. Stepped out of her bubble. Only because I felt betrayed. Betrayed by my bosses. And betrayed by Peyton, a woman I thought I had a connection with. I needed to hear everything without distraction. Needed to absorb the words being spoken. And I couldn't do that with Peyton so close.

I take another step in her direction. "I'm not mad at *you*. More like the situation."

"Not a fan of me being on the same level," she bites out.

A smaller step. Her body close enough for me to touch. "That's not it either," I say with a shake of my head.

"Then what is it, Micah?" She cocks a brow. "Humor me."

The corner of my mouth twitches, then relaxes. "Do you know how long I've worked here? How long it took me to step into a management role?" She doesn't answer or react. "Longer than you. I busted my ass for three-plus years before it was even a possibility. And even then, it came with stipulations."

Peyton's shoulders lift, then drop. Her lips puckered and eyes unyielding.

"Not to sound petulant, but it feels like I had to bust my ass for something that landed in your lap."

Her spine stiffens, the action inching her closer. "You think I haven't paid my dues, Micah? You think Ani just handed me this? Goes to show, you don't know shit." She spins to face the door. "This conversation is done."

Before she takes a step, I grip her elbow and twirl her back around. "No. Uh-uh. Not done yet."

Peyton steps into me. The tip of her nose a millimeter from mine. "What else is there to say?"

My hand drops from her elbow and lands on her hip. Her lips part just enough for me to notice. I rest my other hand on the opposite hip. Her breasts brush my chest as her breath coats my lips. Her violet irises sparkle and don't deviate from my pinned stare.

"Why did you hide the news? All the texts and times we've talked, you never mentioned it. Why?"

She exhales and I briefly close my eyes. *God, I want to taste her lips, her skin.*

"Nothing was set in stone. Ani and I talked about it here and there, but she never gave a timeline. Until last weekend. As in four days ago."

I fist her hips, but not enough to bruise them. "Still could've told me." The words practically inaudible.

"Micah…" My name rolls off her tongue and lights a fire beneath my sternum. "I wasn't trying to hurt—"

My lips crash to hers. Hot and aggressive and hungry. For one, two, three beats of my pulse, she doesn't kiss me back. I start to back away as defeat and mortification form a dark cloud overhead.

Until she fists my shirt and hauls me closer. Fuses our lips together again and licks the seam of mine. I part my lips and she dives in. We lick and taste and wage war with our tongues. Peyton tastes of sweet cream and something distinctly her.

A groan builds in my chest, rises up my throat and spills from my lips. I snake my arms around her waist and draw her impossibly closer. Her hands trail up my chest, my neck, my face until her fingers fist my hair.

An inferno blazes around us as I walk her backward. Her back hits the wall, the bulge behind my zipper pressing hard against the junction of her thighs. I run a hand down the side of her leg, then hoist it up to hook my hip.

My hips circle once, twice, and she moans against my lips. Sucks them between hers. Dives back in and siphons my tongue like a succubus. Devours me whole. My dick on the cusp of tearing my slacks.

Bam, bam, bam.

"Peyton? Everything okay?" Ani jiggles the door handle.

Our lips break apart on a gasp and I inch back. But only enough for her to speak.

Chest heaving, she looks up and licks her lips. "Fine," she pants out. "Be out in a minute."

Ani jiggles the handle again. "I heard yelling. Don't piss me off, Micah."

I huff out a laugh. "Everything's fine." I lock on to my new favorite color. Violet. "Wouldn't be in my best interest to piss you off."

Another shake of the handle. Relentless. "If you're not out in five minutes, we'll be having a different conversation soon. An unpleasant one." Not a second later, her heels clack against the concrete and grow quieter with each step.

Without hesitation, I kiss Peyton again. This time, the kiss is less rushed. More tender. Engrossing. And all too soon, with much reluctance, I break the kiss and take a step back.

"We should get back out there," I say, and drop a chaste kiss on her lips.

"Yeah. Okay." She steps into me, hands framing my face, and returns the kiss. "Let's go." Another kiss.

Fuck. If I don't put five to ten feet between us, we will never leave this room. Not that I *want* to, but we need to. We have a job to do and a boss outside this room that will bite my head off if neither of us make an appearance soon.

Peyton steps over to the small mirror beside the door, flattens some of the kinks in her hair and adds a swipe of gloss to her lips from a tube in her pocket. Her eyes meet mine in the mirror as the brightest smile stretches her lips wide. She spins around, then steps into my space. Without a word, she runs her palms up my chest, my neck, then combs her fingers through my hair. And fuck me, I don't want her to stop.

Her hands drop to my collar and straighten the folds. Eyes locked on my lips as she swallows. When her hands fall, her eyes lift to mine again. "Time to work, starlight." She drops one last kiss on my lips before turning on her heel, unlocking the door, and strutting out of the office.

My tongue sweeps over my lips, her coconut gloss sweet on my tastebuds. Tonight may be the most challenging yet, but the test is worth the prize.

This has to be the slowest Wednesday in humankind. Slow-est.

Monday to Thursday has never brought in crowds like the weekend, but I don't remember them being this slow in months. With kids out of school, the start of summer usually has mothers stopping by for half-priced cocktails. For whatever reason, tonight is dead.

The new staff left more than an hour ago. They sliced enough citrus to fill the condiment bins for the next three nights. Fifteen minutes ago, I told Kaylynn she could head out for the night as well. Seeing as Roar is only open another hour, Ani wouldn't be too pleased if unnecessary staff stood around with nothing to do.

"Cosmo, please," a brunette says as she parks herself on a barstool.

"Coming up." I get to work on her drink and make light conversation with her. Generic topics such as the weather and asking if she has kids.

I pour the drink, place it on a napkin in front of her, and slide my hands back to my side of the bar. She plucks a bill from her purse and goes to hand it to me. When I reach for it, she takes hold of my hand and keeps it prisoner.

"If you're not busy after—"

"Micah," Peyton barks from the other end of the bar. I glance her way and smile. "How's the rash?"

Dear god, woman.

I sincerely hope Peyton has no concerns about me picking up other women. Not when I kissed the hell out of her three hours ago. But the way she marks her territory without it being obvious to outsiders has me biting my cheek.

"Better since the cream."

The woman quickly removes her hand. "Never mind." She hops off the stool. "Have a good night." And then she waltzes over to a table of women, whispers something to them and they all look my way with wide eyes.

I wipe down the bar top and head toward Peyton. She restocks the disposables—one less thing to do tomorrow before open.

"Did you enjoy that?" I ask when I reach her.

She bats her lashes excessively. "Whatever do you mean?"

"Cute."

"What's cute?"

I love how she plays coy. Goes toe to toe with me or lips off. But this new possessive side… I think I love this side the most. The spunk and bite and territorialism. The unspoken claim only I hear when she fends off other women. Her silent, *"He. Is. Mine."*

Fuck. The ownership makes my dick swell.

One year ago—hell, two months ago—I would never have imagined this raw hunger I harbor for Peyton. Or vice versa. But damn, do I love the energy vibrating through my body. The extra bounce in my step. The constant compulsion to smile. The rapid beat of my heart and expansion of my lungs.

Never imagined I would feel like this again. That I

would want more than friendship or meaningless sex with a woman. That I would want to caress and taste a woman more than once.

But Peyton… she changes everything.

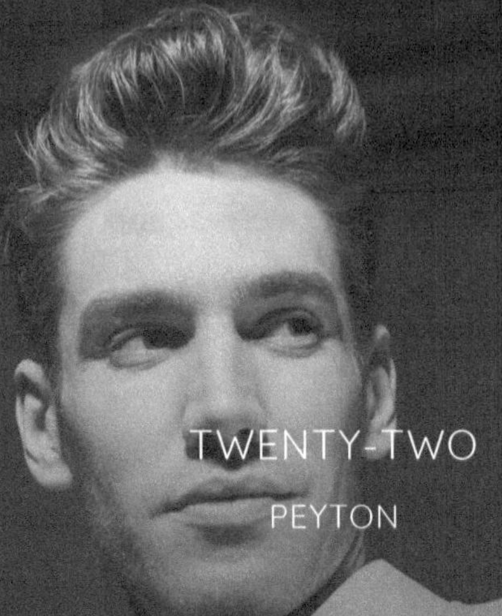

TWENTY-TWO

PEYTON

"Hang out with me tonight."

"At Teddy's?" I ask, unsure what his definition of hanging out entails.

Micah shakes his head. "We can get food, but that's not what I mean."

I seriously hope after one kiss—a really fucking great kiss—Micah doesn't think I will sleep with him. No doubt the man holds me captive with his looks alone. But I am not like one of the floozies he has taken home time and time again.

Never once have I given up the goods easily. I make men work for more. Make them woo me and prove their loyalty. One and done is not my style. Never has been, never will be. And Micah Reed will not change this.

"What *do* you mean?"

A small step brings him close enough to touch. His eyes drop to my shoulder as he reaches up and toys with the end of my ponytail. "Come back to my place." I wince. "Or yours. The place doesn't matter. I'll order pizza and we can watch a movie."

From point A to B in no time. For a short time, he had me fooled. Had me believing he could be more than a douchebag. The occasional brush of his skin on my arm. Confessions in softer tones. The way his eyes searched mine—deeper, harder. Guess I read the signs wrong. Read him wrong.

"Um." I stall a moment to find the right words to let him down. "Not sure what you thought would happen tonight after that." I point toward the office. "But I don't hook up."

Bright, wide eyes fly up and take me captive. "Peyton, that's not what I meant. Wasn't my intention to suggest—"

"Then tell me your exact intention."

He takes another step closer. A knee comes between mine and knocks them apart. Heat licks my skin—could be his, but I know it comes from within. With each erratic breath I take, he inches closer. Close enough to taste, but I fight the urge. Remind myself we are at work. And kissing Micah behind the bar is not a good idea.

"Pizza, a movie and you sitting on the couch. Believe it or not, I can behave. May take a bit of effort, but it's possible."

No sex. Possibly no making out. Sounds like a solid plan. Although kissing Micah again, away from prying eyes, is definitely on the to-do list. Not that I plan to share this news. For now.

Dinner and a movie and couch time with the man I just kissed. The first man I kissed in more than a year. And damn, what a kiss it was. One for the record books.

If I agree, will either of us keep our hands—and lips—to ourselves? Better yet, which of us will cave first?

"Okay, I'll hang out. But the moment you start sneaking bases, I'm out."

Micah tips his head back and laughs. The rumble loud and deep and unrestrained. Has he ever laughed like this around me? Not to my recollection. But I love the way it shakes his frame. The way his throat reddens and his Adam's apple bobs.

"Noted." He fetches the broom and starts sweeping behind the bar. "Let me know where you want pizza from? I'll order when we leave and pick it up on the way."

"You got it, starlight."

Over the next half hour, we do all the end-of-night tasks. Jake leaves once he wipes down the tables and stools, then cashes out. After Micah takes the tills to the office, we do one last sweep of the club and shut everything down.

On the way to our cars, I tell him where to order my ham, pineapple, garlic and onion pizza from. He makes a face but doesn't insert his opinion. Smart man.

"Mine or yours?" he asks.

My mouth goes dry. I work to hide my sudden need to excessively swallow. "Yours," I choke out.

The hint of a smile twitches at the corner of his mouth. "I'll text you my address, in case we get separated. See you in a bit." Then, as if second nature, he presses a chaste kiss to my lips before going to his truck.

His truck starts up, but he doesn't leave the lot until I drive off. For most of the drive from Tampa to Clearwater, we ride in line with each other or side by side. I feel like a fool with this painful smile stretching my face most of the ride. But no one sees or judges it. So, I leave it in place as the wind whips my hair and the radio plays loud rock tunes.

When I hit the first red light after crossing the Bay, I plug Micah's address into the map app and connect it to the car audio. After I turn off the main road, I scope out the area. This stretch of town is slightly unfamiliar. The map tells me to take the next right.

My brows pinch in the middle. *I cross this exact street almost daily. A couple miles down the road.*

A left turn, then another right. "Your destination is on the right," the navigation announces.

I park on the street and stare out the window at a quaint house. The streetlight one house down illuminates the yard more than the dual lamps on either side of the garage. From the front, the khaki and rich green house appears small. But the extended roofline past the tall wood fence indicates otherwise.

A tall oak, with a trunk too round to hug, occupies a hefty section of the yard to the left of his driveway. Thick branches with lush foliage extend over the house, driveway, and street. On the right of the driveway, white flowers highlight two mature crepe myrtles.

A short distance from the left of the garage, three small steps lead up to a screened-in porch. Soft white light brightens the lanai enough to see a wood bench swing at the end, pair of Adirondack chairs and small table.

As I lean forward and squint to see the flowering shrubs along the porch front, headlights flash in my rearview mirror. I lift a hand to shield the light and drop it as Micah's truck turns into the driveway.

I open the car door and Micah jogs over before I step out. "The street isn't busy, but it's probably best to park behind me."

"'Kay."

In the thirty seconds it takes me to start the car and park in his driveway, my body sprints into panic mode. Sweaty pits, clammy hands, stomach in knots. The whole shebang.

Before I exit the car, I remind myself Micah and I have already hung out. Eaten after work a couple times. I joined him and his friends at a get-together. Hell, I kissed the man like no other only hours ago.

So why the sudden freak-out?

Because we have never been truly alone.

Dining out came with the steady flow of patrons and restaurant staff. Hanging out with his friends… well, that explains itself. And earlier tonight, when we couldn't keep our mouths off each other, people stood less than twenty feet from us—the office walls and door our only form of privacy.

But inside the four walls of Micah's home, it would

only be me and him. No one to stop at our table to interrupt conversations. No one to jiggle door handles and inhibit us from touching. Or kissing.

Micah strolls over and opens my door, two pizza boxes balanced in his other hand. "C'mon." He jerks his head toward the house. "Let's get inside and eat."

He shuts the door and I press the fob's lock button. I follow his sure steps on slate pavers. Slow down as we approach the screened porch. Stop breathing as he opens the front door and gestures me inside. He flips a switch beside the door and warm light filters through the space.

"Make yourself at home." He sets the pizzas down on the coffee table and starts unbuttoning his shirt. "Be back in a sec." He disappears down a short hallway.

I step farther into the room, the scent of Micah's cologne and lemon float in the air as my eyes scan every square inch. The house isn't small but feels big for one person. Has Micah always lived alone?

Light oak planks the open floor plan. The exterior wall to the right has more windows than concrete or drywall. During the day, I picture the living and dining area bright and warm and serene.

An earthy-brown couch with a chaise faces the front wall of the house. A natural-edge, wood coffee table with wide iron legs sits within reach, a television mounted feet from the front door. Warm light spills from a lamp between the television and wall of windows, and a second lamp near the corner of the couch.

Across the room, near the windows, is a dining table—

the same natural edge as the coffee table — with two chairs on either side. Large round bulbs hang at uneven lengths from thick black cords. In the dark, I bet they glow like stars. Like Micah's eyes. Beyond the table, a large, sepia-tone world map is pinned to a corkboard. A collage of photographs surrounds the map and I step closer to view them.

I reach out and stroke a finger over a younger version of Micah. One I remember from years back. When life was simple and not so simple. In the photo, he has an arm around Shelly and who I assume is their mother. All three of them smiling without a care in the world.

"That was in the Smoky Mountains."

I jump and slap a hand over my chest. "What are you, part secret agent?" He laughs with a shake of his head. "Don't sneak up like that."

"Didn't mean to." Another chuckle leaves his lips. He presses his front to my back as his arms snake around my waist. "Just saw you here and didn't want to disturb you." Warm, soft lips press against the skin beneath my ear. "I like seeing you in my space."

I wiggle out of his arms and twist to face him. "And how many other women have you delivered that exact line to?" The question is meant to be a joke, considering all the women that have left Roar on Micah's arm.

But guilt swirls like a waterspout beneath my diaphragm as his face pales. *Shit.*

"The women I left the club with… they never set foot in this house." His eyes close as he inhales deep. On the exhale, his eyes reopen. "The last woman to step foot in this house brought another man." Dark, starry irises swallow me whole. "You being here… let's just say it's a big step."

Wow. Just wow.

Way to make an ass of yourself, Peyton.

"I didn't—" I fumble over my words. Unsure how to pedal back and fix my mistake. "Sorry."

A hand brushes mine before our fingers intertwine. "Let's eat." He nods toward the couch.

We plop down on the sofa and I open the pizza boxes as Micah scans a list of movies on the television. When I look up, he selects *Pulp Fiction*, presses pause and sets the remote on the table.

"Want a drink?" He rises from the couch and ambles toward the small, yet spacious kitchen. Whoever designed the kitchen knew how to make the most out of the limited space.

I follow Micah with my eyes. Take in his relaxed demeanor and attire. Drop my gaze down his backside and swallow. Something about gray sweats and a snug cotton tee…

He fetches a pitcher from the fridge and sets it on the small island while getting glasses. The island sits askew in the open space, three barstools on the side facing the living and dining area. The overall vibe of the kitchen is a blend of dark wood cabinets, stainless steel appliances, and light granite counters. A large window over the sink faces the backyard. For someone who doesn't cook, his kitchen is dreamy. I would cook in it.

Wait. What?

Why does being here—in Micah's space, his home—feel so natural? So comfortable? Why does it conjure thoughts of us wrapped up in each other? Laughter and flour handprints and water fights with the sink sprayer.

"Water, please," I croak out and turn to face the television.

Snap out of it, Peyton.

When half of my pizza—and all of Micah's—vanishes, I set the box on the table and pat my belly. Micah scoots over until our arms bump, and then he rests a hand on my thigh. The contact is simple and non-suggestive. Yet it warms me more than the summer evening.

I rest my head on his shoulder and do my best to focus on the movie. Which works out... until Micah kisses my hair. Then does it again. And again.

His hand on my thigh takes on a new weight. Feels heavier and hotter.

Before I overthink what happens next, I lift my head and rotate to lock on this softer side of Micah. I hold his gaze for three breaths before dropping my eyes to his lips. I lean closer, slowly eradicate the space between us, and kiss him.

A low frequency hum purrs in my bloodstream when our lips collide. The kiss is soft and chaste at first. A slow buildup to the fiery kiss we shared earlier, but equally soul stirring.

Our tongues stroke with languid movements. Hands and fingers explore uncharted terrain but don't cross the line. A hand slips under the back of my top and guides me back to lie on the couch. One of his legs wedges between mine. His weight above me is welcome and constant and perfect. The planes and lines and musculature of his frame mold to mine as the kiss picks up tempo.

My hands trail up his chest, his neck, and fist his hair. He moans and rocks his hips forward, grinding his thick erection against the junction of my thighs. Lust clouds every rational thought, and I do it again. He breaks the kiss with a gasp. Teeth nip along my jaw, my ear, the column of my neck, the base of my throat. Then he licks leisurely up, tasting me, until our lips crash together.

We kiss like horny teenagers. His erection rock hard between my thighs. My panties drenched and clit throbbing. But neither of us leads the moment beyond heavy kissing and light petting. Micah staying true to his word—that nothing further would happen tonight—makes my heart happy and body frustrated.

As if my thoughts were broadcasted aloud, he breaks the kiss and gasps. "You'll be the death of me."

Before I get a word in, he shifts us both so we lie on our sides and face the television. His front to my back. His hips lined up with mine, I'm acutely aware his erection hasn't calmed whatsoever. And I love that he doesn't hide his body's reaction.

He reaches for a throw pillow and tucks it beneath our heads. His hand on my hip dips as his fingers trail the faint line of exposed skin between my shirt and pants. Fingers skirt beneath the shirt hem and splay over my belly. Although his hand doesn't move, the tips of his fingers paint small circles near my navel. I feel every whirl and loop and stroke, at the point of origin and throughout my body.

I close my eyes. Forget about the movie. Forget about everything except the tingles rippling over my skin from his touch. How can something so simple feel so damn good?

Then he licks up my neck from the curve of my shoulder and I moan. Press my ass against him. Lose myself in the intoxication of it all when his free hand clutches my throat. Squeezes enough that I see his starry irises behind closed lids.

"You have it wrong," I choke out.

He licks and nips his way to my ear. Sucks my lobe between his teeth. "What's that?"

I lift a hand over his at my throat and hold it there. "You'll be the death of me first."

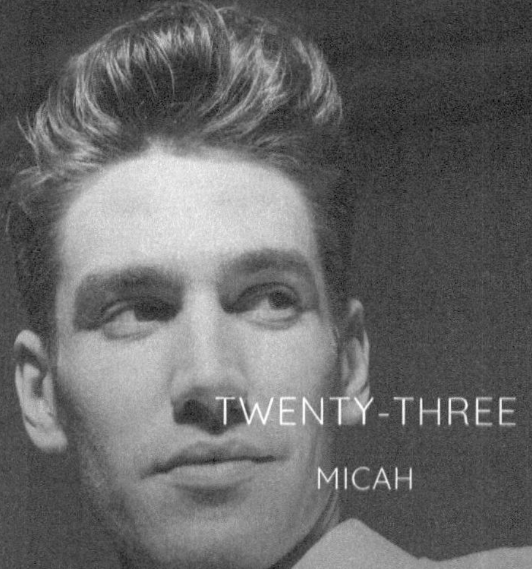

TWENTY-THREE

MICAH

Bzzt. Bzzt.

Peyton twitches in my arms, then relaxes. Her chest rises and falls in a steady, rhythmic tempo. I nestle more into her neck and curl my arm tighter around her midsection. Hold her closer as I drift back to sleep.

Bzzt. Bzzt.

I shake half awake. Peyton groans, twists in my arms, snuggles closer to my chest and burrows her face near the base of my throat. My leg drapes hers as our lower limbs tangle. I draw her impossibly closer. Kiss her hair. Cradle her against the length of my torso. Her warm breath at the hollow of my throat soothes and settles me back to sleep.

Bzzt. Bzzt.

Peyton grumbles against my chest and I tighten my hold on her.

Bzzt. Bzzt.

"Who is that?" I complain, my words like sandpaper.

Peyton shifts in my arms and I open my eyes. I look down at her as she peers up. Inch down to press my lips to hers. Her phone buzzes on the coffee table again. For the umpteenth time.

She stretches an arm behind her and slaps the table until it lands on her phone. When the screen lights, she bolts upright. "Oh, shit."

If I wasn't awake a minute ago, I am now. "What's wrong?" I scrub a hand down my face and blink several times to shake off the sleep.

"It's after eight." I stare at her and patiently wait for the reason why this is a bad thing. That was the best sleep I have gotten in weeks. No sense in complaining. "In the morning. As in, I stayed the night at your house."

"This is a bad thing?"

Unlocking her phone, she opens her text messages and starts typing. "No. Yes. No."

My hand draws lazy circles on her lower back. "Take a minute to wake up. I'm sure everything is fine."

She drops the phone in her lap, then gives me her profile. Stares at the ceiling as her weight presses into my side. "It is. But Reese is freaking out because I didn't come home or let him know I was staying out."

I wiggle to the cushion edge and rise from the couch. Head toward the kitchen for water before I say something irrational about their close relationship. The water staves off an inkling of my jealousy. So, I drink more.

Last thing I need to do after sleeping with Peyton in my arms all night is to piss her off. My unjustifiable green monster needs to sit the fuck down and chill the fuck out. I have no right to be jealous over a friendship she's had for decades.

Peyton saunters into the kitchen, steps up behind me, and wraps her arms around my waist. Her arms crisscross over my chest as she presses her palms flat to my pecs. God, I love the feel of her body against mine. No awkwardness or mismatched placement. She fits every angle and curve as if meant to be there.

"He's not mad because I stayed out," she whispers along the curve of my neck. "Just wanted to make sure I wasn't lying in a hospital. We usually text or leave notes when staying out late. He was worried. That's all."

My rational brain processes this and shakes a finger. *Don't be a dick. They are just friends.*

I rotate my head and drop an innocent kiss on her lips. "Glad you have someone who worries. Sorry."

"No need to be sorry." Her arms form parallel lines on my stomach and constrict. "All this between us…" Warm lips trail up my neck and my eyes roll shut. Fuck, every touch Peyton gives feels amazing. "Is new. For me and you."

I twist in her grip and wind my arms around her. Drop my lips to hers, but don't deepen the kiss. When we break apart, I tuck loose tendrils of her hair behind her ear. Study her freshly woken features —hair in a messy topknot, pillow crease lines on her cheek, brows a bit shifty, eyes bright but not yet alert.

If I woke up next to her each morning, it would be a great life.

I kiss the tip of her nose. "Gonna go brush my teeth." Her eyes widen as a hand covers her mouth. As if she just thought about her own morning breath. "Probably have extra toothbrushes in the bathroom." She lifts a brow. "From the dentist goody bags." I kiss her forehead, wrap her hand in mine, and lead her to the bathroom.

After we get the bathroom to ourselves a moment, I dig out a spare toothbrush. We hover near the sink, squeeze paste from the tube, and brush simultaneously. And it's so bizarre. How scrubbing our teeth together is the most normal my life has felt in a long time.

"Confession," I say as we enter the main space of the house. "Although I fail at cooking most foods, breakfast is not one of them. So, you're in luck." She laughs as I guide her to the barstools. "Have a seat, hellcat. I'll whip us up something. Promise it'll be edible."

Peyton parks herself at the breakfast bar, props her elbows on the counter, and rests her chin in her hands. Her violet eyes sparkle as they follow my every move. And damn, I love how good it feels to have her eyes rake over my backside. To survey my body without shame. Heat my skin and drive me wild.

From the fridge, I collect eggs, milk, cheese, and butter. Sausage links from the freezer and the loaf of bread on the island. I set a pan on the stove, crank the heat to medium-low and add some oil. Next, I crack eggs in the bowl, add milk and whip them together. All the while, Peyton watches me in mesmerized silence.

Domesticity has never been something I pictured in my life. Mom and Dad have it down to a science. A natural flow whenever they are together. Synergy. Anyone in their presence sees it, feels it. Obviously it exists, but I never considered I'd have the same simplicity in my own life. Not even with Rochelle.

But as Peyton's eyes follow me around the kitchen, watch me season and mix and flip, my mind considers new possibilities.

I drop bread in the toaster, then add shredded cheese to scrambled eggs as the sausage finishes. After I grab plates from the cabinet, I fish a butter knife from the drawer. The toaster clicks and the bread pops up. I butter, then cut the slices in half and add them to the plates. Followed by the eggs and sausage.

"Your breakfast, m'lady." I deposit a plate in front of Peyton and hand her a fork. "Coffee, milk or juice?"

"Coffee, please."

I brew us both a cup from the Keurig, then join her at the breakfast bar. We eat in relative silence. Her knee bops mine a few times until she leaves it there. Until our plates empty, we find some way to keep physical contact. Knee or foot or elbow. The contact has my chest fluttery and limbs tingly.

"Really should head home," Peyton says as she sips the last of her coffee.

She slides down from the stool, ambles to the couch,

and puts her shoes on. Usually going separate ways from a woman gives me relief. But as Peyton collects her purse and phone, an ache builds beneath my sternum.

"Would it upset you if I said I don't want you to leave?"

A soft smile tugs at the corners of her mouth. "Quite the opposite. But I need to shower, put on fresh clothes, and do errands before work."

I follow her to the door, but neither of us moves to open it. "Know it wasn't intentional, but I'm glad you stayed." Inching closer, I plant my hands on either side of her and box her in. "Haven't slept like that in a long time."

Her palms flatten on my pecs. "Oh, yeah. And how's that?"

My head lowers, lips an inch from hers. "Solid. Restful." I drop my lips to hers and taste the coffee on her lips. "All because you were in my arms."

Pink paints her cheeks as she swallows. Her reaction sends a rush throughout my body. "Me, too," she admits with an unfamiliar level of softness.

I dip down and take her mouth again. She fists my shirt and I drop my hands to her hips, heaving our bodies closer together. Her lips part and our tongues duel. Hands trail up my chest and dive into my hair, clenching the strands and tugging. A growl rises in my chest and spills into her as she deepens the kiss. Mouth fucks me near my front door.

Then she breaks the kiss, pins me in place with her

vibrant irises, and inches back. "Really should go." Her breathy words lack oomph.

I drop a kiss on her lips. Then another. "Okay. I'll walk you out." After a quick adjustment, I unlock the door, take Peyton's hand, and lead her out the door.

The car beeps when she presses the fob, but she doesn't get in immediately. We exchange a few more chaste kisses before she opens the door and slips behind the wheel. The engine starts up and she rolls down the window.

"Best unintentional sleepover," she says, leaning out the window. I bend and kiss her one last time. "See you tonight."

"Tonight." I tap the roof of her SUV. She rolls up the window and backs out of the driveway. Within seconds, her car vanishes from sight.

I trudge my way to the front door and stumble inside. Flopping down on the couch, I rest my head on the pillow we shared not long ago. Inhale her lingering coconut and mint scent on the throw pillow. And bask in the simplicity and tranquility I felt—still feel—with Peyton in my space. In my arms. In my world.

Lost fucking cause. Might as well etch it on my skin now.

I straight up pouted when Peyton arrived at Roar

fifteen minutes prior to open. With all the extra prep done yesterday and Kaylynn showing Mable and Caleb more tonight, Peyton didn't need to rush. Which means I got zero alone time with her beforehand.

And now, I stomp around the club with a permanent frown and childish demeanor.

"Someone's not having a good day," Peyton teases when I step behind the bar.

I bump our shoulders together. "Hmm. Wonder why?"

The corner of her mouth kicks up in a playful half smile. "Maybe someone needs a nap or caffeine." Her tone pouty and mocking. Makes me want to bite her lip.

"Or…" I drawl the two-letter word out as an idea sparks. "Maybe I need to take someone in the office." Her violet eyes go wide. "To show you how the invoices need to be cataloged, of course."

Her frame sags a hair, but her eyes don't leave mine. Unspoken questions on whether or not sneaking off to the office is a good idea. The fact I won't see Peyton every night at Roar is the perfect reason. Although, we are most definitely seeing each other outside these walls again. Often.

I approach Kaylynn as she explains the non-serving aspects of the job to Mable and Caleb. Both listen with rapt attention. "Hey." Kaylynn shifts her gaze and pauses her instruction. "You all good out here if I teach Peyton management tasks in the office?"

Kaylynn scans the club. Still early, the place doesn't

have much activity. The Thursday crowd usually picks up in an hour. "Yeah, boss. I'll come get you if it's busy."

Peyton hesitates until I round the corner of the hall. Her heels clap on the floor in quick succession as she catches up. Not a breath after the office door closes, and the lock flips, I smash her against the wall. Kiss her hard and rough. Grind my stiffening cock to the junction of her thighs. Moan as her taste hits my tongue.

We kiss like brutal beasts ready to shred the other's clothes. Fingers fist my hair and yank hard. I bend at the knees and rub my pulsating cock over the seam of her pants. A sweet whimper exits her lips and I swallow it down.

All we have done is kiss and dry fuck. If she gets this turned on and desperate with our clothes on, she will no doubt ravage me when we are skin to skin.

Presumptuous of me to assume Peyton and I will have sex, I know. Although I plan to take my time with Peyton, not jump the gun and ruin the foundation we are building, our relationship will go next level. And beyond.

I break the kiss, take a step back, and smash my palm to my dick. "Fuck, hellcat."

She bends at the waist, drops her hands to her knees and gasps. "Back at ya, starlight."

It takes a hot minute, but once our breathing levels out, I guide us to the desk. "We really should do some work. Can't drag you in here constantly and leave you still not knowing what to do." I chuckle.

Peyton drags a chair from the guest side of the desk

and parks it next to the one reserved for the manager on duty. For the next hour, I slip on my leader mask and focus on the task at hand. Peyton hangs on every word as I go over payroll, inventory, invoices, and scheduling. Watches my every move as I key figures into the spreadsheets. Asks questions to clarify how often we do full inventory and handle the cash each night. In my unbiased opinion, Peyton learns and catches on quickly. Which is great for two reasons.

One—I don't have to repeat myself. Not that I wouldn't have if necessary. And two—I get more alone time with her while I show her the ropes. It's a win-win.

TWENTY-FOUR

PEYTON

Everything has fallen into place. Work. Life. Both feel more on track than any other time in the past. For once, I am headed in the right direction.

Can't remember the last time life flowed so smoothly. Had this level of comfort. Streamlined without effort. Maybe with Chad?

Chad Lark—the first guy I dated, post high school. Guys in high school weren't worth my time, effort, or energy. But Chad was different. Mature and kind and gentle—although he knew how and when to be rough and harsh. In our two years together, we were inseparable. A team. He was the marrying type and I would have said yes.

Unfortunately, Chad never got to ask.

One morning, Chad didn't wake up. The coroner said a natural defect caused the chambers of his heart to not contract as normally. He died peacefully in his sleep. He was twenty-two. We had started planning for the future. Hinted at taking the next step. Neither of us aware that his heart had a sooner expiration date.

They say you never forget your first love. The sentiment is true. I will never forget Chad.

Sadly, I have dealt with enough heartache to last multiple lifetimes. One can only hope I have met my quota.

Life is on an upswing. Work is taking steps along a positive path. I busted my ass—contrary to what Micah believes—to get here. Learned so much about the business and have done my fair share of hands-on. Ani groomed me little by little over the span of our friendship. Long before the announcement of my promotion, she pegged me as her go-to person. Someone she trusted. Someone she wanted to help run her business. I was more than thrilled to be chosen by her. Ani will always be more than my boss. She's the sister I never had growing up.

Outside of work… well, that seems to be pretty damn good too.

In a matter of months, I went from loathing Micah Reed to fantasizing over our next kiss. The way his lips devour, the way he puts every ounce of passion into each kiss… my body quivers. Trembles and whimpers, imagining the idea of more. Of his bare chest against my breasts. Of his hands and fingers tracing lines and peaks and valleys as he maps my body. Of his lips on my breasts, my abdomen, and between my thighs.

"Hey." Micah sidles up to me behind the bar. "Everything alright? You're flush." Starry eyes survey every exposed inch of my skin.

I pour a glass of water and drink it. "Fine. Just got warm."

When the glass empties, Micah inches closer and brings a hand to my cheek. "Sure you're alright?" I knock his hand away and he has a light bulb moment. Leaning closer, his lips and hot breath brush my ear. "Were you thinking about me just now? About us?"

I breathe in short, quick bursts. My breasts rise and fall and graze his pecs. Heat blooms from my chest, paints my skin, my neck, my cheeks. Fingers trail up the side of my thigh, stop at my hip bone and squeeze.

Part of me worries what our interaction looks like from an outsider's perspective. Are we the center of attention? Can people not look away? Not that Roar has brought in a crowd tonight.

The other part of me doesn't give a damn and aches to drag him closer. Smash my lips to his. Kiss him like he is my last meal. Ignore the audience and take what I want.

"Yes," I answer, breathy. No sense in skirting around the truth.

"What were you thinking about?" His tongue licks the shell of my ear. My eyes roll shut as my bones turn to putty. "Tell me, Peyton."

Jesus fuck. Now is not the time for this conversation. Roar—among employees and patrons—is not the place to have this conversation. But with each passing second, my will to steer this talk in another direction becomes more difficult.

I hook fingers in his front pockets. Eager to pull him to me, but keep him rooted in place. "Was thinking about last night." I lick my lips. "Kissing you."

"Kissing me then?" He nips my earlobe. "Or kissing me now?"

"Both," I admit, softly. "How I want your hands on my skin."

His chest vibrates as a growl tears up his throat. A hand fists my hip. "Come over again tonight."

It isn't a question. More like a directive. I hate the way I love his subdued demand.

"We aren't having sex," I whisper, in the hopes no one hears this not-safe-for-work conversation.

The hand on my hips tightens and releases. "There're other ways to enjoy each other without sex. Figured you'd know that, hellcat." He inches away. "Come over."

The lights and '80s music flood back in as cool air smacks my face. My eyes scan the club, behind the bar, but no one pays us any attention. At least not now.

"Yeah, okay."

A bright, toothy smile lights up Micah's face. I love this smile. "Perfect." He smacks my ass. "Now, get back to work."

The rest of the night goes as slow as last night. Week-days during the summer can be hit or miss for places like Roar. Hence why Ani wanted fresh ideas. New attractants to draw in the same crowd and maybe new people. With

Ani, her market research, and how she wants things perfect from the get-go, the new changes will be great for business.

As the night wears on, the crowd thins and Micah lets the staff leave early, one by one. With thirty minutes until the door locks, Kaylynn and I start stocking and cleanup while Micah serves.

Sweeping the floor behind the bar, I peer down at the opposite end as a blonde woman steps up. In a blazing-red dress that leaves nothing to the imagination, she smiles at Micah and leans toward him. A shiver rolls down my spine as he returns the smile. Although it's forced, I recognize the familiarity between them.

He says something and grabs a shaker, ready to mix her a drink. But she shakes her head. With each stroke of the broom, I inch my way down the bar and closer to them. Micah's face reddens as he works his jaw, then says something else. Their conversation too quiet for me to hear yet. So, I sweep down the line faster.

"I just want to talk," she complains as I pretend not to hear.

Still far enough away, Micah might not realize I hear the exchange.

"Before we hooked up, I told you there'd be nothing else. What's there to talk about?"

Not that I didn't know Micah was a manwhore. But hearing him verbally duke it out with some desperate floozy is insane. Another reason to resist temptation and not have sex with Micah yet.

"I really don't want to do this here," she shoots back with a huff.

"No one's stopping you from leaving." Micah waves a hand in the air.

I step closer after sweeping the same square footage for too long. Micah has to know I am within earshot now.

"Why are you being such an asshole?" she shouts.

Now is when I opt to turn around. Time for me to get acquainted with my managerial role. We don't get a ton of bullshit in Roar, but every now and again, we have to deal with the belligerent and physically violent.

"Ma'am." Her eyes snap to mine and she stiffens. "Not sure what the problem is, but you need to calm down or leave. Your choice."

She crosses her arms and forces up her breasts. "I'm not leaving until I talk with him."

"And I already said, not happening," Micah states as I sidle up to him and form a stronghold.

"Fine," she huffs out. "Don't want to go somewhere private? We'll do it right here." My brow pinches at the middle, and Micah rolls his eyes. "I'm pregnant, asshole. And you're going to be a daddy."

To be continued...

The conclusion of the Insomniac Duet, A Love So Bright, will be here May.03.2022. Preorder A Love So Bright from your favorite retailer and have it available to binge on release day!

More By Persephone Autumn

The Click Duet

High school sweethearts torn apart. When fate gives them a second chance, one doesn't trust they won't be hurt again. Through the Lens (Click Duet #1) and Time Exposure (Click Duet #2) is an angsty, second chance, friends to lovers romance with all the feels.

The Inked Duet

A man with a broken heart and a woman scared to put herself out there. Love is never easy. Sometimes love rips you apart. Fine Line (Inked Duet #1) and Love Buzz (Inked Duet #2) is a second chance at love, single parent romance with a pinch of angst and dash of suspense.

Transcendental

A musician in search of his muse and a woman grieving the loss of her husband. Two weeks at an exclusive retreat and their connection rivals all others. Until she leaves early without notice. But he refuses to give up until he finds her again.

Distorted Devotion

Swept off her feet by love, life takes a dark, unexpected turn. Now the love of her life may be the cause of her death. Check out this gripping, romantic suspense.

Undying Devotion

A long-term couple with a secret life. Their friends envy the bond they share, but remain oblivious to their lifestyle and how deep the bond lies. A turn of events has her wanting to spill every secret.

Beloved Devotion

She asks the love of her life to marry her. When her girlfriend hesitates, then says yes, she is determined to learn why. As the pieces start to fall in place, she discovers she doesn't know her fiancée at all.

Depths Awakened

A small town romance which captivates you from the start. Two broken souls have sworn off love. Vowed to never lose anyone else. But their undeniable attraction brings them together and refuses to let go.

Ink Veins

Persephone Autumn's debut poetry collection, Ink Veins, explores topics of depression, love, and self-discovery with a raw, unfiltered voice.

Broken Metronome

When the music of the heart dies…

Broken Metronome is an angsty poetry collection full of heartache and the possibility of what may have been.

Thank You

Thank you so much for reading **Restless Night,** book one in the **Insomniac Duet**. If you wouldn't mind taking a moment to leave a review on the retailer site where you made your purchase, Goodreads and/or BookBub, it would mean the world to me.

Reviews help other readers find and enjoy the book as well.

Much love,
    Persephone

Insomniac Duet Playlist

Here are some of the songs from the **Insomniac Duet** playlist. You can listen to the entire playlist on Spotify!

overwhelmed | Royal & the Serpent
forget me too | Machine Gun Kelly (f. Halsey)
kiss kiss | machine Gun Kelly
Dancing With A Stranger - Acoustic | Sam Smith,
Normani
Karma | MOD SUN
Wonder - Acoustic | Shawn Mendes
Nightlight | Illenium, Annika Wells
Crazy | TELLE
Her | Majid Jordan
Movement | Hozier

Acknowledgments

Sometimes acknowledgments are so fucking hard. You never want to forget anyone. You also don't want to sound repetitive. Whatever 🐧

To my family and friends… 2021 was a shitty year in so many ways, but was amazing in others. We made it through another fire. Here's to hoping this year will be better. IT WILL BE BETTER!

To Ellie McLove and Rosa Sharon… I couldn't imagine having a better team of kick ass women working on my books and making them better. I will never learn commas or when to use lie, lay, laid, or lain… and I'm so glad you know the right way.

To Kat Savage… thank you for making me pretty book covers and not getting annoyed with me when I reach out on a whim. When random thoughts strike and I email or text, I always feel like the annoying step-child. But you say you still love me… so thank you 😊 I'll try to be less annoying this year.

To all the authors I've connected with… gratitude isn't a big enough word to describe what I feel having each of you in my life. This author life is tough a lot of the time. We have to stick together and help each other out. So many thank yous!

To the readers and bloggers who read my words… sending you all virtual hugs. Every time I read one of your amazing reviews or see your posts about my books, I cry. Spilling pieces of yourself on paper isn't easy, but your kindness makes it so worth it each time I start a new book. A million thank yous to each of you!

And if this is your first Persephone Autumn book… thank you for taking a chance on my words. I hope you loved Micah and Peyton, and the future books to come.

Persephone Autumn lives in Florida with her wife, crazy dog, and two lover-boy cats. A proud mom with a cuckoo grandpup. An ethnic food enthusiast who has fun discovering ways to veganize her favorite non-vegan foods. If given the opportunity, she would intentionally get lost in nature.

For years, Persephone did some form of writing; mostly journaling or poetry. After pairing her poetry with images and posting them online, she began the journey of writing her first novel.

She mainly writes romance, but on occasion dips her toes in other works. Look for her poetry publications and a psychological horror under P. Autumn.

www.ingramcontent.com/pod-product-compliance
Lightning Source LLC
Chambersburg PA
CBHW050817190726
48286CB00007B/1895